YA
MIL

Mills, Emma

Foolish hearts

foolish
hearts

Henry Holt and Company
New York

foolish

hearts

emma mills

Henry Holt and Company, *Publishers since 1866*
Henry Holt® is a registered trademark of Macmillan Publishing Group, LLC
Copyright © 2017 by Emma Mills. All rights reserved.
175 Fifth Avenue, New York, NY 10010
fiercereads.com

Library of Congress Cataloging-in-Publication Data

Names: Mills, Emma, 1989– author.
Title: Foolish hearts / Emma Mills.
Description: First edition. | New York : Henry Holt and Company, 2017 |
Summary: Claudia agrees to coach actors in her high school's production of
A Midsummer Night's Dream, leading to new friendships—and maybe even new love.
Identifiers: LCCN 2016058474 (print) | LCCN 2017028556 (ebook) |
ISBN 9781627799386 (Ebook) | ISBN 9781627799379 (hardcover)
Subjects: | CYAC: Friendship—Fiction. | Dating (Social customs)—Fiction. |
Theater—Fiction. | High schools—Fiction. | Schools—Fiction. | Shakespeare,
William, 1564-1616. Midsummer night's dream—Fiction.
Classification: LCC PZ7.1.M6 (ebook) | LCC PZ7.1.M6 Foo 2017 (print) |
DDC [Fic]—dc23
LC record available at https://lccn.loc.gov/2016058474

Our books may be purchased in bulk for promotional, educational, or business
use. Please contact your local bookseller or the Macmillan Corporate and
Premium Sales Department at (800) 221-7945 ext. 5442 or by e-mail at
MacmillanSpecialMarkets@macmillan.com.

First edition, 2017 / Designed by Liz Dresner

Printed in the United States of America

1 3 5 7 9 10 8 6 4 2

For Bridget, who helped make it all possible

one

It's at Amber Brunati's annual Pink Party that everything begins to unravel.

The invitation—on thick pink paper, naturally, with gold and turquoise swirls—had declared it to be *the last great luncheon of the summer.* As if my summer had been packed to bursting with a whole host of other themed luncheons instead of babysitting jobs and shifts at Pinky's Sub Shop. It also implied that there had been a number of mediocre luncheons this summer, as this was meant to be the last of the *great* ones.

I stare around Amber's backyard at clustered tables covered in pink gingham cloths and at the girls around said tables. We're all wearing pink except for Iris Huang, who had the nerve to arrive in lavender (Amber's angry whispers carried clear across the lawn), and Kaitlyn Winthrop, who is technically wearing magenta. This seems to incense Amber even more, because while we all know that Iris's dress is a big official *eff you* to the entire Pink Party construct, Kaitlyn doesn't seem to realize that she's committed a faux pas.

"Someone get that girl a color wheel," Amber hisses angrily to

Madison Lutz, sitting to my left. "Someone get her a fucking Pantone booklet because magenta is not pink. We all know magenta is not pink, right?" She looks to me. "Right?"

"Abso-tootin-lutely!" I declare loudly, because I am a moron.

It's quiet for a split second, and then a laugh escapes from Madison.

Amber doesn't laugh, but her lips twitch in amusement. "Yes. Good. Thank you, Claudia. Glad we're all on the same page."

In truth, we are rarely all on the same page. More often than not, they're all on one page, and I'm on a completely different one. It can't be helped most of the time. Society itself puts us on different pages. They drive Range Rovers and have celebrity deejays at their sweet sixteens. I had to scrape and scrounge and toast subs, and remake the subs that I toasted badly, just to buy a car. A car that isn't even 100 percent mine. My brother technically owns 40 percent of it and somehow manages to drive it 80 percent of the time.

But I don't say any of this to Amber for fear she might fling a tray of cookies at me. Instead I watch as Madison pats Amber's back. "You need to breathe, okay?" she says. "Eat a macaron. They have lavender in them, right? That's supposed to be calming."

"Lavender just makes me think of Iris, which makes me enraged," Amber says.

We all look across the yard to where Iris is seated with Paige Breckner. Together, she and Paige hold the titles of class president three years running (Iris), most popular girl in our grade (Paige), and cutest couple in our school (collectively).

Though "cutest" isn't quite right. I don't think anyone who knows her would use the word *cute* to describe anything relating to Iris Huang. Objectively, she has a roundness-of-face and smallness-of-stature that could traditionally be deemed cute. But she's also ruthless and unforgiving and, some would say, ill-mannered and incredibly unpleasant. Somehow, this doesn't seem to affect her political standing, but then again, that often seems to be the case in the real world as well.

But Paige and Iris have been the longest-enduring couple on record during our time at the Prospect-Landower School for Girls, and so they are automatically termed "cutest," because that's shorter than "longest-enduring couple on record during our time at the Prospect-Landower School for Girls."

I saw them once—I mean I've seen them lots of times—but once, after school, I saw them sitting on the low wall outside the lit building, sharing a pair of earbuds and listening to something on one of their phones. Their heads were bent together, and then all of a sudden Paige started dancing in her spot, mouthing along the words to whatever song it was.

Iris looked up at her, smiled, and then looked back at the phone. Paige started bopping harder, lip-synching more emphatically, pointing at Iris.

Iris ducked her head, blushed, focused on the screen until Paige got to her feet, took Iris's hands, and pulled her up, trying to get her to jump around. Iris looked flustered but . . . endeared, I guess. Fond in a way I had never seen her look.

When Iris finally relented and joined in dancing, the earbud jerked right out of her ear. She scrambled for it, accidentally yanking the other out of Paige's ear. They both ended up bent over laughing, leaning on each other for support.

It was sweet—that's why it stuck with me. A rare moment where Iris didn't seem completely steely but instead kind of awkward and fumbly and smitten.

So maybe "cutest" still means cutest, even where she's involved.

Right now, Paige is chatting with Sudha Prabhu, laughing behind one hand as Sudha gestures animatedly, while Iris looks for all the world like she's waiting in an airport terminal and her flight has just been canceled. In a sea of pink, she is unrelentingly purple.

At my table, Madison grins at Amber. "Deep breaths."

"I just want everything to be perfect," Amber says, eyes wide and strangely earnest as she looks around the table at each of us. "Is it? Do you like the food? Are you having fun?"

We all affirm the quality of the food and the fun we're having. I nod emphatically as I hork down a petit four.

"I know it's silly," Amber says, "but it's just, you know. Senior year and all. Everything we do is sort of the last time we get to do it. So it should be perfect, right?"

We double down on the reassurances, and finally Amber seems satisfied.

"Okay. Okay, good." She stands promptly, smooths down the front of her dress, takes a deep breath, and then heads off to the next table.

I adjust my own dress as the other girls start talking about school. I borrowed it from Zoe, so although it fits the color scheme, it's also a little too short and a little too tight. When I came downstairs in it, my mom said "Wowza," and my dad, brow wrinkled, asked, "What kind of party is this again?"

Truth be told, I'd risk Amber's wrath and wear the wrong color if it meant Zoe could be here with me, wearing this dress instead. She is my best friend, and there's only so much a text can convey. Some of this stuff you just have to witness to fully appreciate. And most of it, I'd probably have a lot more fun witnessing with her.

But Zoe goes to Springdale High School, and I go to PLSG, and this isn't really the kind of thing where you can bring a plus one. So I send her a quick text update and then listen in on Madison and Ainsley Stewart discussing some band they both watched on TV last night.

The rest of the luncheon goes well, much to Amber's relief. We eat fancy finger foods. We toast each other with fizzy pink punch. There are speeches filled with assurances that this is going to be the "best year ever" and a shit ton of light applause.

Paige stands at one point and thanks Amber for hosting.

If you're giving a presentation in class, Paige is the person who smiles at you when you catch her eye and nods encouragingly, like she's actually listening. We had gym together freshman year, and whenever she was captain, she insisted on everyone counting off instead of picking teams.

When she finishes her toast, she turns to Iris with a smile. "Do you want to add something, babe?"

They share a look—in the silence, Paige's expression shifts from hopeful to imploring—until finally Iris pushes her chair back and stands, holding up her glass of punch. She clears her throat.

"Careless tourism and destructive fishing practices are destroying our world's coral reefs," she says, and then takes a drink.

I can't tell if it's a joke. Like, admittedly you probably shouldn't joke about the destruction of our world's coral reefs. A few people chuckle uncomfortably anyway.

Iris sits abruptly. Paige is still standing, her glass raised.

The look on her face is stricken, but somehow she manages to recover a smile. "Thank you again, Amber," she says. "This is . . . a great way to end the summer."

And that's the last of the speeches. Conversation resumes around our little tables, and I excuse myself after a bit. Amber's mom points me in the direction of the bathroom, but once I get inside the house, I realize that her directions of "to the left and across from the music room" kind of hinge on knowing which room is the music room. Which I don't.

So I head to the left and open the first door I come upon, and to my disappointment, it isn't a bathroom but a bedroom.

I'm in luck though—there's a bathroom en suite. I dash in and take care of business, and then I spend way too long sampling the products in pretty bottles on the bathroom counter.

I'm admiring the scents that I've so expertly layered together (by squirting three random lotions on at the same time) when I hear sounds from the outer room: voices approaching and then the closing of the bedroom door. Sealing the voices inside.

"—believe you would act like that."

"I didn't want to make a speech. I thought that was obvious."

"*Coral reefs?* Seriously?"

"Tell me we shouldn't be more concerned about the state of the coral reefs."

Paige and Iris.

I'd always thought they were a good pair. People don't like Iris, generally, but they respect that she gets shit done. Conversely, everyone loves Paige. She's friendly and kind, neutral good through and through. She softens Iris. And I guess Iris gives her an edge. What's that saying—iron fist in a velvet glove? Iris is the former, and Paige is the latter.

"I'm not saying it's not true, I'm saying it's not *relevant to the situation.* This isn't a freaking Envirothon meeting!"

"Please. You know I don't like how those Envirothon kids conduct themselves."

"You couldn't think of one nice thing. About Amber, or the summer, or school, or anything. One nice thing. You could've said the punch is good."

"The punch tastes like Windex."

"*Iris.*"

"What?"

"At the very least, would it have been so hard to put on a pink dress?"

"I'm not gonna do something just because someone tells me to."

"You do tons of things because someone tells you to! You wear shoes in restaurants! You obey seat belt laws!"

"There's a big difference between doing something to prevent myself from flying through a car windshield and doing something to satisfy a meaningless color scheme at a meaningless party that neither of us actually care about."

"*I* care about it," Paige says, and something in her voice sounds frayed. "But that doesn't matter to you. What I want. You never even ask me. You just assume. You always—*always*—just assume."

Silence follows. And in this silence, I realize several things—first, that this is not just a little spat about a speech or a dress code. And second, that my temporal window for stepping out of the bathroom and announcing my presence has entirely closed. I'm in it for the long haul. I have to wait them out.

"I don't want to do this," Iris says finally.

A pause. "Do you understand though? About the dress? And the party? Do you get that it's important to me? And, like, how something that matters to me should be important to you, too?"

"It's stupid though," Iris says. "This whole thing is stupid. If it was something that actually *mattered*, I would—" She cuts off, starts again. "You know I would . . ." She doesn't finish.

"You would what?" A beat. "What would you do?"

"I don't know." Iris sounds sullen. "I would act like I cared more."

It's quiet. Behind me, a bead of water drips from the faucet into the sink.

And then there are footsteps in the outer room. I can't tell which of them has moved toward the other. Or if they've moved away.

When Paige speaks again, her voice is thick. "I love you, Iris," she says. "But you're the most selfish person I've ever met."

I press my ear to the door. I'm only human, after all, and this is possibly the best bit of drama I've unwittingly stumbled onto in the whole of my high school career.

"What are you saying?"

"I love you," she says again, and I'm fairly certain she's crying now. "But I want you to be different. I want, I wa—" Her voice hitches, like a sob. "I want you to be better than you are."

I dated a boy named Will Sorenson for almost a whole semester in tenth grade. January to April. We were going to go to his junior prom together that year, but he broke up with me just two weeks shy.

We were in his basement, and he was playing an online role-playing game called Battle Quest. His character—a humanoid dragon named Alphoneus Centurion—was approaching a snow-covered vista with a monster in his sights when Will glanced over at me and said, "So I don't know, I just think maybe we should break up, you know?"

Like we had been having a conversation this whole time that I had somehow missed. I pressed him to explain as Alphoneus Centurion launched a series of attacks against the monster.

"I just think that when you're with someone, you should . . . *feel* something. Right?"

"You don't feel anything with me?"

"I feel regular with you," he said. "But I don't feel . . . you know. Well, I mean, if you knew, then you'd understand, and you'd want me to feel that with someone else. And if you don't know, then that means you don't feel it either, and so we probably shouldn't be together anyway."

Alphoneus raised his ax. The monster was a goner.

Up until this moment, I thought that was the most crushing thing you could say to someone you're dumping. That you feel *regular* with them. It sort of managed to negate every sweet thing that we ever had together. Like it was all fake. One-sided, on my part. I was elated the first time he held my hand. I thought I might float off the sidewalk. And now looking back, I see that everything that was massive to me, everything that was meaningful—to him it was just *regular*.

But Paige Breckner just took the cake in the breakup department. *I want you to be better than you are.* If I were Iris, I would've disintegrated on the spot.

Iris does no such thing. She just speaks, after a long pause, her voice in stark contrast to Paige's. It's calm. Crisp. No hint of tears.

"Are you breaking up with me?" she says.

Paige doesn't reply.

"Are you. Breaking up with me?" Iris repeats, razor sharp.

"Yes," Paige says.

I realize I'm holding my breath. Waiting for—something. A reaction. A movement. A sound. Anything.

And then a sound comes. A loud one in fact—the very clear and deliberate peal of a bell.

For a split second, it doesn't make any sense. Paige breaks up with Iris and Iris responds by whipping out a handbell?

Then I realize. My phone.

I fumble with my bag. Purses are interdimensional sometimes, I swear—particularly when you're trying to get something out of one. I finally extricate the phone, but three more texts follow in the intervening time—three more pealing bells—that only serve to further sink me.

The silence that follows is deafening.

I look into my palm. I might as well see the texts that are my undoing.

I need an update, Zoe's first message reads.

Are you eating cahhhhviahhhr with Ahhhmber

And Mahhhhdison and Aaaaaainsley and Desk Lahhhmp

And all of your other fahhhhhbulous clahhhhssmates?

I almost laugh—it would be funny, normally, but now it's so terrible it goes from terrible back into funny.

Until there's the sound of footsteps that are most definitely approaching and a firm knock on the door directly in front of my face. Then it goes right back into terrible.

"Hello?" It's Paige.

I hold my breath. Maybe if I'm perfectly still, perfectly silent, they'll think that they'd heard wrong.

10

"We heard your phone," Paige says.

"How do you know it wasn't your phone?" I reply. Because. I am. A moron.

I squeeze my eyes shut. Take a deep breath. And then I open the door.

It's a Moment, between the three of us. There are just two hundred students at PLSG. Fifty girls a grade. And although I know Amber and Madison and Ainsley and Desk Lamp (there isn't really a Desk Lamp, but Zoe likes to make fun of the names, how "everyone sounds like an item from a furniture catalog, seriously") and all the others in a cursory manner, there aren't many of them that I have had genuine Moments with.

The thing about Moments is that just because a moment is one, doesn't mean it's a good one. They are not all Special, or Cherished, as picture frames and embellished scrapbook inserts would have you believe.

This is more of the Painfully Awkward variety. Me, clutching my phone in the bathroom doorway, looking quite like my ear had just been pressed against the door—because my ear *had* just been pressed against the door. Paige, her face red, cheeks wet, eyes puffy. And Iris Huang, resplendent and terrifying in lavender YSL, looking at me with a quiet, smoldering, single-minded rage.

Paige speaks first. "We didn't know anyone was in here," she says, and she's clearly putting effort into sounding something close to normal, though she doesn't bother to wipe the tears tracking down her cheeks.

"I didn't know anyone was out here. I didn't hear anything," I say, even though it's a lie compounded by another lie.

The silence is unbearable.

11

So I do what I do best, or what I do worst, I suppose—my greatest strength is also my greatest weakness. I break it.

"I had the faucet on," I say. "Really loud. And I pee pretty loud. I'm surprised you guys didn't hear me, it was like Niagara Falls in here. Just really . . . very loud in volume. A lot of . . . liquids . . . flowing in a . . . noisy fashion."

Paige blinks at me, clearly caught off guard, but Iris's eyes only narrow, the rage intensifying.

I have to get out of here.

"I'll just . . . leave you guys to it. . . . Not that I know what *it* is, not that I heard anything," I say, and make to leave, but Paige moves to the door first.

"No, I'm going," she says, and then quickly walks out.

Leaving me. And Iris. Alone.

Iris crosses immediately to me and holds a finger up to my face. She forces me backward, back into the bathroom, where I stumble over the rug and catch myself on the fancy towel rack.

"What did you hear?" she says.

"Nothing. I heard nothing."

"You're lying."

"I'm not."

"You are, you're terrible at it. If you go back out there and tell everyone—if you tell them—" She falters. And I would hardly believe it unless I saw it myself, but Iris's eyes swiftly fill with tears. Her lower lip quivers. It legitimately quivers.

Her voice is thick when she speaks: "I will *ruin* you."

And then she turns and leaves.

two

I go to work at Pinky's on Sunday. The day after Iris declared that she would ruin me.

When I rejoined the party yesterday, she was nowhere in sight. Paige had resumed her seat, but she was looking decidedly worse for wear and the rest of her table had clearly noticed. Sudha had one arm around her, their heads bent together in conversation, and Alicia Smith was kneeling at her side, holding up a pink patterned napkin so Paige could wipe her eyes.

Word would travel fast. I didn't need to tell anyone what I had heard. Furthermore, I didn't *want* to tell anyone. First, because it was no one's business, and second, because I didn't want the wrath of Iris Huang to befall me and my family.

I replay it in my mind as I pull a sub out of the toaster and deposit it on the counter in front of me (a little charred around the edges, but hopefully that would escape notice). No one had ever sworn my ruin before.

I would just steer clear of them both at school. I've managed to fly under the radar pretty effectively these last three years. It won't be hard to pull off a fourth.

Stealth mode, I think as I cut and wrap up the sandwich in patterned Pinky's paper.

Pinky's is "home of the nine-inch sub." *Fifty percent more than a Subway sub!* the sign declares.

"I don't think that's right," I said to my manager Aaron on my first day. "Because Subway subs are twelve inches? So really it's only seventy-five percent of a Subway sub?"

"They mean the six-inch," he replied.

"So maybe they should say that?"

"Home of the nine-inch sub, *fifty percent more than a six-inch Subway sub,*" Aaron contemplated, and then shook his head. "That's too much numerical information. It's too cerebral."

This was possibly the first time anyone had used the phrase "too cerebral" when describing Pinky's advertising. Because someone somewhere in the Pinky's marketing scheme had made the brilliant connection that sub sandwiches are vaguely phallic. And from that, all the penis-related Pinky sub campaigns were born.

Like the commercial where you see the guy standing from the back, and then a woman in front of him, and she says, "Nine inches?????" in this insane lusty voice, and then they pan to the side and show that he's holding a Pinky sub right at groin height? It's the worst. It is literally the worst. I'm a cog in the world's dumbest corporate sandwich machine.

But I needed a job. And Pinky's was hiring. So here I am.

Zoe comes over that evening when I get off work, and we ride our bikes to the Tropical Moose to get snow cones. The car is free—Alex is actually home for once—but I'm stiff from standing all day and I smell like Pinky's. I want to ride, to feel the late summer air rushing through my hair, to pedal fast and feel the burn of it in my legs.

I get a piña colada–flavored snow cone, Zoe gets a bubble gum one, and we manage to secure a table out front, the kind with the chairs that leave waffle patterns on the backs of your thighs. We're settled in when two little kids pass by clutching blue cones. A woman follows close behind but veers toward our table as they pass.

"You have beautiful hair," she says to Zoe, who smiles and nods in reply, her mouth full of slush. She pulls a face at me when the woman has passed.

Zoe does have beautiful hair. The rest of her is pretty magnificent as well—dark eyes with the longest lashes, flawless brown skin. One time a barista at Starbucks wrote *your smile is gorgeous* on Zoe's coffee cup. I took a picture of her holding the cup, smiling wide, and we put it on Tumblr, and to date it has over fifty thousand notes.

It makes sense to me, knowing Zoe as I do. Her outside matches her insides. I know goodness doesn't manifest itself as beauty—she's not pretty because she's smart, or funny, or kind—but it's fitting. She's my favorite person, and if one of us had to grow up ridiculously beautiful, I'm glad it's her. It just makes sense.

"I have calc and lit with Kris," Zoe says, continuing our previous conversation. "And AP Bio with Gabby, so that's something. What's your schedule like?"

I shrug. "What it's always like."

"Hey, how was the party? You never texted back."

Now there is no way Iris Huang could be privy to this conversation. Zoe doesn't even go to our school—she's at Springdale, the public school in our generic Chicago suburb. We live in one of the neighborhoods that's fare-and-a-half to get to if you take a cab from the city. PLSG is twenty minutes from Springdale, and most of the richest girls live even farther out. So the likelihood of Iris popping up and hearing me tell Zoe that I witnessed the Breakup of the Century (or at least of the Year to Come) is pretty slim. And usually I tell Zoe everything. But. Something in me just . . . doesn't want to risk it.

So I just shrug again and say, "The food was good. There was a lot of talk of this year being *our year*."

"Who did all the other years belong to?"

"Right? I asked Madison that. She looked at me like I was crazy."

"Too bad she can't buy a sense of humor."

"I'd sell her mine."

"You could buy another car with the money."

"Do you think I'm funny enough for car money?"

"For sure. You're minimum pre-owned Toyota Corolla funny."

I grin.

It's quiet as we finish our snow cones, but not a bad kind of quiet. With some people I feel the need to fill the space, but with Zoe, it's okay. It doesn't have to be constant. We can listen to the hum of crickets, the buzz of the tree frogs.

We ride back to my place when we're finished. I ask Zoe if she wants to come in, but she shakes her head.

"I should get back. It's officially a school night."

"Ugh."

"It was good while it lasted." Zoe smiles—her radiant Starbucks cup smile—and all at once I'm struck with something Amber said at the party—*senior year and all*. How everything we do is sort of the last time we get to do it. Tomorrow is the very last Back to School for us. Back to high school, anyway. Meaning that today—tonight, right now—is the end of the very last summer of the way things are. Next summer we might go off to college at different times. To different cities. Different time zones. I can't imagine it.

Or rather, I can. I just don't want to.

I don't say any of that. "Text me tomorrow," I say instead.

"Will do." Zoe gets back on her bike. "Night, Claude."

"Night."

I watch her pedal away.

three

My mom makes me stand on the front steps before I leave for school the next morning so she can take a picture. The annual first day of school stoop photo. Frames hang in the kitchen for each of us—a big print scroll across the top declaring *My School Days* with twelve little spaces underneath for pictures.

All of Alex's spaces were filled as of last year, and Julia's were finished long ago. Her frame doesn't even match ours.

Today is my last School Days picture. There is a 45 percent chance my mom will burst into tears before I leave the house. So I try to move the process along, shouldering my backpack, holding my lunch bag to my side, and raising one hand in a big thumbs-up. The traditional pose. The very last box to be filled.

"I just can't believe it," Mom says, tapping her phone screen half a dozen times, and the odds raise: 56 percent chance of tears now.

"We should get going," I say, moving to step off the porch. "Where's Dad?"

"Wait wait wait, let's get one of you and your brother." She turns. "Alex, get over here."

He's in the driveway, leaning against the car.

"I'm good actually," he says, not looking up from his phone.

"One picture."

He sighs, types one more thing, and then shoves his phone in his pocket and joins me on the porch.

"Closer together," Mom instructs. "Alex, put your arm around your sister—it's her last first day of school."

"Come on, Alex," I say, picking up his arm and slinging it around my shoulders. I poke his side, and he smiles for a second before twisting away. I hope my mom got the shot, because that's the only opportunity she's going to get this morning.

"No, one more with Daddy!" she says as my dad emerges from the front door, balancing a doughnut on top of a travel mug, but Alex is already heading back to the car.

"Who called the paparazzi?" Dad says.

"Excuse me, I am one photographer."

"Who called the paparazzo?" he amends, and then strikes a pose next to me. "Make sure to get my good side." And then, "We should take a selfie," he says when my mom lowers her phone again. "And send it to your sister!"

Sending selfies to Julia is something we do at least once a week, if not more. Since moving to Indianapolis with her husband, Julia has gotten a surplus of Wallace family selfies. I've always wondered how she feels about them. If it comes off as "We wish you were here!" like my parents intended, or if it's more like "We're all here and you're not!"

We take one regardless. I think Alex will just sulk in the background, but he tosses up a peace sign at the last moment.

"This has been great," Alex says, "but some of us have jobs."

"And some of us have school," I say.

"And some of us have jobs at school!" Dad declares.

I watch Alex drive away in my car. The main reason I wanted that car so badly was so that I could drive myself to school. But going in on it with Alex was the only way I could afford it. And Alex apparently needs the car more because his schedule is "flexible" and there's no point in it "sitting around all day" in my school's parking lot when he could be doing "like, stuff, I don't know, just stuff."

So Alex gets the car during the day, and I drive in with my dad. It is not remotely fair. But Alex maintains that he's way more experienced in the art of "not remotely fair," so this is, in some ways, retribution.

It isn't my fault that Prospect-Landower is a girls' school. It isn't my fault that our dad works there. And it wasn't my idea to go there in the first place. I wanted to go to Springdale with Zoe and all our friends.

"This is an incredible opportunity," my mom had said way back when, smoothing the hair off my face. "So many girls would be so happy for a chance to go to Prospect."

"Then one of them should go for me," I had mumbled, pressing a tearstained cheek into Mom's shoulder.

It's a privilege. I get that now. But it didn't seem like one back then.

My dad parks in the faculty lot, and we part ways at the lit building. PLSG isn't one big building but multiple small ones, like a tiny college. Brick buildings with black shutters and white trim. It's very picturesque. I guess playing up curb appeal is part of justifying the price tag.

I haven't checked like Zoe, messaging back and forth with

friends to confirm who I have what class with. It doesn't really matter much to me either way.

But I wish I had planned ahead—consulted some of the girls beforehand. Because then I would've been prepared to walk into British lit and see Paige Breckner and Iris Huang, seated at opposite ends of the room. Paige is in the back, buffered by Sudha and Alicia, and Iris is at the front, alone.

This might not be good, I think to myself, but there's nothing to be done about it.

"Just please come with me, I don't want to go by myself."

Caris Pearlman corners me after lit. A surprisingly uneventful class, actually. We went over the syllabus. We got a Chaucer excerpt to read for Wednesday. All in all, pretty anticlimactic compared to the scenarios I had imagined in my head.

The halls are clearing out now, a steady stream of girls heading toward the dining hall.

"I just need to give him something," Caris says, looking at me earnestly.

"But then maybe . . . I shouldn't, you know, be there. In that case."

Her cheeks flush. "Not like—that's why I want you to go with me. It seems so *illicit* otherwise."

I could see Caris Pearlman in Regency times, wearing an empire-waist gown, a long string of pearls around her neck, smiling behind a fan in some crowded London ballroom. She certainly fit the Regency romance sensibility. And I would know. My mom is an avid romance reader, and I snuck all kinds of books when I was younger—novels with women in satin dresses reclining on divans, or masked men in greatcoats on the cover, white shirts splayed open revealing bare chests. Always with titles like *The Duke and the Devil* or *Passion Is a British Rogue*.

Though I suppose Caris is the Before in the Regency romance scenario. Before the encounters with the British rogue and all that, driving the heroine *mad with lust* and whatnot.

Caris does not appear to be mad with lust in this moment. Instead, she is standing before me, clutching a cellophane-wrapped loaf of what she later informs me is zucchini bread, after I agree to accompany her, and we make our way to the Grove.

The Grove is a small stretch of woods that separates PLSG and the neighboring boys' school, Danforth Prep. It's back behind PLSG's library, and Danforth's athletic fields abut it. There was talk a few years ago about bulldozing the Grove and merging the two campuses, but there was enough outcry to stop that from happening. A lot of stuff about "maintaining the storied traditions of two treasured institutions." Thus these treasured institutions remain separate.

Though not so separate that any PLSG student or any Danforth Prep student couldn't just waltz through the woods to the opposite school. Or, as is the fashion sometimes, meet in the Grove itself and . . . I don't even know. Make out up against a tree. Smoke drugs.

("Smoke drugs?" Zoe said when I hypothesized this to her once. "Smoke. Drugs. Yeah, I bet that's it. I bet they get high on that reefer. They smoke that Mary Jane. Maybe they even *consume alcohol*. Can you imagine?"

"Okay, I get it. That was stupid."

"I'm not saying we need to corral your ass into this century, but we probably need to corral your ass into this century.")

Apparently, the Grove is also a spot where students occasionally meet to exchange first-day-of-school baked goods, as is the tradition between Caris and her boyfriend, Robbie.

Technically, we're not supposed to be back here at lunch. But of course that's never really stopped anyone.

I stand off to the side—glaringly superfluous now—as Caris and Robbie kiss and exchange snacks. If Iris and Paige are—were—the cutest couple at PLSG, Caris and Robbie are probably now the pair to beat for cutest in the PLSG–Danforth collective.

When Caris and Robbie start doing more kissing than talking (maybe she's more *mad with lust* than I thought), I wander off. There's no official path through the Grove, but one has been worn down over the years. A track cleared via repeated use.

I pull a sandwich out of my bag—it is lunchtime, after all—and start in on it as I meander through the trees. I hear voices up ahead, and I spot people as I round the bend leading down to Danforth's fields.

A group has gathered at the base of one of the tallest trees, just at the edge of the woods. A few girls from my class—Lena Ideker, Sudha, and Alicia, as well as a couple of juniors—are joined by several Danforth guys.

I recognize one of them in particular. I don't know Gideon Prewitt personally, but I know a good deal *of* him, because everyone knows of him. He's an undeniable presence in the social media scene of PLSG. Constantly referenced, constantly tagged, constantly popping up in pictures to press kisses against the cheeks of girls who are usually smiling so wide their eyes crinkle with it.

Right now Gideon is leaning into Lena Ideker's space. She's smiling coyly up at him, her back resting against the tree trunk behind them.

I could never look so cool. So unaffected.

I watch as he says something to her. She responds with a nod, says something in reply, and he throws his head back in a laugh. It rings out—a bright, loud burst of laughter—reaching even me where I stand.

"There you are!"

I turn as Caris and Robbie approach, holding their baked goods and each other's hands.

"Sorry. You seemed . . . involved," I say.

Caris's cheeks are flushed. Robbie's hair is much more mussed than it was when he first greeted us.

Caris ducks her head, but before she can speak, a call bursts out from the group nearby:

"ROBERT A. FISCHMAN," a deep voice bellows. We all turn. Gideon Prewitt is still standing with Lena under the tree, but he's looking our way, both of his arms raised in the air like a referee declaring *Goal!* "BIG FISH ROB. GET OVER HERE. BRING YOUR LOVELY GIRLFRIEND. BRING HER LOVELY FRIEND."

Robbie raises his eyebrows at us. Caris looks to me, smiles prettily, and I shrug.

So we go over.

Gideon Prewitt moves toward us when we reach the group. He shakes Robbie's hand enthusiastically.

"You've got some lip gloss on your cheek, pal," he says. "And on your neck. And—" He drops Robbie's hand and pulls the collar of Robbie's shirt aside, then wiggles his eyebrows at Caris. "Get it, girl."

Caris turns redder, her cuteness intensifying.

"How was your summer, Caris?" Gideon says. "Was it great?"

She nods rigorously. "Yeah, it was awesome." She grips Robbie's hand. "I mean, we mostly just hung out. But it was really fun."

"Well, then I don't need to ask Big Fish Rob how his summer was. Must've been the best if he was spending time with you." Gideon turns his gaze to me. "Who's your friend?"

"Oh, this is Claudia," Caris says.

"Third wheel extraordinaire," I murmur as I reach for the hand Gideon has extended toward me.

I don't think he's heard me, but his grin widens as he clasps my hand. "Nice to meet you. How was your summer?"

Are you personally responsible for the quality of everyone's summer? I want to ask, but I don't. "Very average," I say instead.

His eyes are bright. "Good. I guess? Is that good?" Before I can respond, he introduces me to the other guys in the group and then encompasses the girls in one sweeping gesture—"You must know these girls already, you must be blessed with their faces on a daily basis"—and then we hang out with them for a little while, until it's close enough to next period that I want to get back.

I nudge Caris, tapping at my wrist, and she nods.

Gideon flashes me a dazzling smile as we prepare to leave, while Caris gives Robbie a quick peck on the lips, and then another, and another.

"It was great meeting you," Gideon says to me.

"You too," I say, and I don't point out that today is not actually the first time we've met.

When Caris and I get back to the dining hall, lunch is almost over.

"Sorry," she says. "I'll share my cookies with you. Robbie's mom made them. They're my favorite."

"That's okay. I ate a sandwich in the woods." As you do.

She ignores me, fumbling with the Ziploc bag and then thrusting a large, lumpy-looking cookie at me. "Just take one. They're so good."

It appears I have no choice in the matter. "Thanks."

"No problem. Thank you. And thanks from Robbie." She gives me a winning smile and then heads off.

four

Brit lit, on the whole, doesn't turn out to be the powder keg I expected it to be. That week, we read excerpts from *The Canterbury Tales*. We do some critical discussion. Paige and Iris stay at their respective poles of the room, I stay in the center, and neither of them acknowledge me. By the end of the first week, I think that maybe this will be all right.

I am lulled into complacency. But then.

Then, the following week, Mrs. Dennings claps her hands and says, "We're gonna partner up."

Our first project of the year. A group project.

"We're going to need groups of two and one group of three."

I look immediately to Sam McKellar, sitting to my left, but she's already locked eyes with Polly Allman, sitting next to her.

Okay, fine. Me, Sam, and Polly then. Group of three, locked down.

But before I can catch Sam's eye, Polly has gestured to Kaitlyn, and they're all nodding to one another in silent agreement.

"We're the group of three!" Polly declares loudly, before I can beg them to reconsider.

So I'm the odd one out. I scan the room, trying not to look too frantic, but panic begins to well up as everyone else pairs off around me. That "I cannot be entirely left out" desperation, that "I cannot be the only loser without a partner" dread.

Mrs. Dennings must notice. "Who still needs a partner?"

Time to accept my fate. I raise my hand. And across the room, front row, opposite corner, Iris Huang raises hers.

Iris glances around and we lock eyes. Something flashes across her face, something akin to horror, but it quickly disappears, replaced with cool indifference.

"I'm happy to work alone," she says to Mrs. Dennings.

"No, I don't want anyone alone on this."

"I'd really prefer to."

Mrs. Dennings's lips twitch at the pushback, but she doesn't reprimand Iris. She just casts her eyes over the group as a whole. "If you'd like, I can always *assign* partners—"

The class lets out a collective groan of protest that not even Iris can withstand.

"Fine," Iris says. "Whatever. It's fine."

Brilliant.

I basically have to chase Iris down after class. I catch up with her at her locker, where she's furiously spinning the combination lock.

"Hey, we should probably exchange numbers or whatever, to plan for the paper."

Iris pulls down on the lock a little harder than strictly necessary.

"I will write the body of the paper," she says. "You will write the introduction and the conclusion."

"But that's not . . . equal at all. . . ."

"I'm sorry, I'm offering to do the majority of the work here and you're offended by that?"

"I'm not saying—"

"Intro. Conclusion." She picks a book out of the bottom of her locker and slams the door.

"What about the thesis statement? Like, we should decide that together, don't you think? You know, do some planning . . ."

"If it really matters that much to you, I'll write the first half, and you can write the second half. Sound good?"

"But I—"

"Good," Iris says, and walks away.

"She's a monster," I say that night.

"They're all monsters," Zoe replies, and on-screen, Zoe's avatar, Korbinian Brodmann, raises his bow.

"No, not—" I jump aside as Korbinian spins around me, shooting half a dozen arrows in quick succession and felling the first group of beasts surrounding us. "Not them," I say. "Iris. From school."

I switch from my saber to my broadsword and hack at a couple more.

"Geez, where's Alex?" Zoe says as we continue to get swarmed.

"Work. School. Who knows."

"He said he'd play. This tank doesn't know what the hell he's doing."

"Alex wouldn't tank anyway, he's trying to level up his mage."

Tanks play a critical role in online role-playing games like Battle Quest. They essentially function to distract monsters and bosses and allow fighters to get hits in. Alex is good at it—he's the best tank of the three of us—and he would've been better than the random person we recruited online.

We finish the rest of the dungeon off pretty quickly and score our loot. Not too bad for a routine sweep, though it would've been faster with Alex.

"Tell me about this girl again?" Zoe says.

"Iris. She's a nightmare. We're writing a paper together and she won't even talk to me."

"Why?"

"Because she's—" I stop, shake my head. "I don't know, she just doesn't like me."

"I find that hard to believe. Everyone likes you."

"You know we've been friends too long for you to lie like that," I say, setting my controller aside. We're in my room, Zoe on the bed with her MacBook and me at the desk on the old laptop I got from Julia. Technically it was from Julia's husband, Mark. It's terribly old, but it runs Battle Quest and it was free, and that's what counts.

I've been playing Battle Quest ever since Will Sorenson and I broke up. To say he got me into it in the first place wouldn't be quite right. I only ever really watched him play. It was after we broke up that I truly dove into it, and it was Julia and Mark who walked me through it. Showed me around the world of Aradana, leveled me up fast, ran me through my first dungeons.

I got Zoe and Alex into it, too, and now we're in a guild, single-minded in one mission: battling the Lord of Wizard.

The latest expansion is called Battle Quest: Lord of Wizard, but technically, the Lord of Wizard himself is only a character nominally. The story line is about a centuries-old pact between the Lord of Wizard and an ancient prince of Aradana who beseeched the Lord of Wizard to stop an encroaching civil war among the Aradanian people. The Lord of Wizard cast a powerful spell and brought the country peace on the condition that in a thousand years, he would return and claim one thing from the kingdom as his own. The prince, a somewhat short-term thinker, agreed.

A thousand years went by, and it wasn't until the expansion pack came out that it became clear that what the Lord of Wizard wanted from the kingdom was the throne.

The current prince refused, things escalated, and now the Lord of Wizard has sent troops to Aradana: an army of supernatural creatures—banshees, wendigos, the undead—and the citizens of Aradana have to fight back, slay the troops, the troop leaders, and finally the army's top general, and win the war.

That's all fine and good (to be honest, it's a lot like the war that was prevented in the original Battle Quest), but the real buzz about the expansion is that a series of side quests, performed in a precise order, accomplishing a very specific set of tasks and acquiring a very specific set of items, will allow you to unlock a secret story line that involves battling the Lord of Wizard personally.

We're determined to do it. People have been very tight-lipped about it online—some say it's because no one has ever reached that final battle, or because it's all just a rumor. But Julia and Mark are obsessed—they follow gamers, read message boards religiously, and have online friends who are dead serious about it—and they swear it's real.

Zoe and I play a little longer this evening, just doing random sweeps for monsters. We've been trying to unravel the rumored Lord of Wizard quests when the whole group is assembled, and Julia and Mark are probably still at work.

Alex shows up just as we're winding down.

He sticks his head in my door. "You guys wanna do dungeons?"

"We could've used you like an hour ago," Zoe says, one eyebrow raised.

"Sorry. Work. I can play now though?"

Zoe makes a face. "I should probably get going. I have homework, and Claude has to work on a paper with her new best friend, Iris."

"I thought you hated Iris," Alex says, looking at me.

"I don't hate anyone."

"Not even Voldemort?"

"I mean, yes, obviously. But I don't—"

"You don't hate the Joker?" Zoe says. "What about Darth Vader? Do you hate Darth Vader, or is it mostly, you know, like cool indifference?"

Alex leans against the doorframe. "Okay, Fuck Marry Kill: Voldemort, the Joker, and Darth Vader."

"Geez, you guys," I say as I go to shut down Battle Quest.

"Fuck the Joker," Zoe says.

"What?" Alex squawks.

She shrugs. "Ledger over Nicholson, though."

"Ew," I say, and Google pictures of the Joker, because I don't know what a Nicholson Joker looks like. Zoe knows more about movies than me. Movies, and art, and math, and science, and pretty much everything. Zoe's character isn't named Korbinian Brodmann for nothing—he's a nineteenth century neuroscientist who categorized different regions of the brain. My character, for contrast, is

32

named Viola Constantinople, which was literally the first name I thought of upon launching my character profile.

"Kill Darth Vader, and marry Voldemort," Zoe finishes.

"What the hell?" Alex says. "That's the exact wrong answer."

I don't want to participate, but I can't stop myself: "Why would you marry Voldemort? Why would you not kill Voldemort?"

"I think—"

"No, literally, who chooses to not kill Voldemort?" Alex says.

"I think I could change the course of his whole life," Zoe says simply.

"You don't think you could change Darth Vader?" I say.

"Nah, girl, Padmé tried."

"I feel like I would fuck Darth Vader, because he's got like powers and stuff, you know?" Alex says. "How would the Force factor in? How would we negotiate the suit and stuff? It's a guaranteed wild ride from start to finish."

"I hate everything about this conversation," I say, shutting down my computer.

"You love it. You love us," Zoe says, and she's right. I do.

five

Iris sends me exactly one half of a paper the day before it's due. I have to stay up half the night trying to finish it, but I do, and we get it in on time. Hopefully, this is the last joint effort she and I ever undertake.

It's a futile hope, though. I know when Mrs. Dennings holds us back after class, the week after the papers are due.

"I wanted to speak with you both privately before I hand papers back," she says quietly, though we're the only ones in the room and have taken seats in the desks closest to hers. "I've had you both before. I know you're very bright students." She picks up a paper off the stack on her desk. "But I was surprised by the quality of the work you handed in."

I see the grade printed at the top of the page, and it sets off a Klaxon in my brain. I can't afford to do badly in a class. Literally. I need a scholarship for college, so every little bit counts. Any little screwup could put that in jeopardy.

"What exactly are the issues?" Iris says curtly.

"I think the main thing is a real lack of cohesion," Mrs. Dennings says, not unkindly, and then outlines a number of other problems that make me regret Iris asking.

I stare down at my desk. I can see Iris in my peripheral vision, sitting up straight, her hands clasped in her lap.

When Mrs. Dennings finishes, Iris speaks: "Is there anything we can do to make it up? A revision? An extra credit assignment?"

Mrs. Dennings purses her lips for a moment. And then: "Yes, in fact. There is."

The halls are deserted when we get out of the lit room, lunch having started already. Iris pushes past me.

"Hey—" I start, and I'm not sure what I'm about to follow it up with, if the words *watch where you're going* or *don't take this out on me* or *this is your fault, too* will actually leave my lips, or if they'll shrivel up and die upon one look from Iris.

She doesn't give me the chance to find out, whirling around and beating me to it: "This is all your fault, you know."

Our next unit is Shakespeare. And conveniently, the drama department at Danforth Prep is doing *A Midsummer Night's Dream* as their fall production. In conjunction with PLSG.

So in addition to rewriting our paper, Iris and I have been "strongly urged" to audition for extra credit.

"At least we get a chance to make it up," I say. Overwhelming relief is my main feeling at the moment—maybe the semester's gotten off to a rocky start, but this one failure won't haunt my transcript forever.

"We shouldn't be in this position in the first place. We wouldn't be here if you hadn't fucked up."

"I didn't know what you were trying to say! Your thesis made no sense, and you didn't give me enough time to rework it."

"Like I'd let you rewrite something I wrote. Like I'd trust you with that."

It comes out before I can stop it: "I don't get why you don't like me. You don't even know me enough to not like me."

"I don't need to know you."

"Just because I—" *Overheard you getting brutally dumped.* I stop short.

"Because you what?" Iris says.

"Nothing."

She looks away. "This is your fault," she says again. "If you had finished earlier, we could've fixed it, *I* could've fixed it. But now we're being *High School Musical*-ed, and it's all your fault."

"We're what?"

"*High School Musical.* In the third one, they get in trouble, and the English teacher makes them work on the school play?"

She looks so angry, for a moment it's hard to comprehend that she's describing a Disney Channel franchise to me.

"You know the policy here, don't you?" she says. "If you audition, you have to work on the play. So no matter if we get parts or not"—*or not* will be the case for me—"we have to work on the show. One bad paper and our semester is fucked."

"It's not . . . fucked."

"Yeah, maybe if you don't have anything else going on in your life, but in case you haven't noticed, I actually *do* stuff around here."

"I do stuff," I say.

"What do you do?" Iris says. "I mean, besides take up space. What do you actually do?"

I open my mouth to speak but then shut it again. I have never met anyone with such a highly concentrated meanness in them.

"What?" Iris spits. I'm not intimidated—well, maybe I am, a little—but it's more of a bone-deep desire to avoid confrontation. I have a general life tenet that I feel can be applied to pretty much anything—*worth it* or *not worth it*. And fighting back is not worth it in this moment.

So I just shake my head. Iris's lip curls in disgust, and she turns and walks away.

six

Auditions for *A Midsummer Night's Dream* are held at Danforth Prep. It's a bigger school than PLSG, with a brand-new arts building, and I find myself there after school on Tuesday.

We're meant to assemble in the dining hall and sign in. I'm making my way through the hallway of the main building when I see Iris up ahead.

She's stopped outside the door to the cafeteria, staring at her phone. If she turns her head, she'll see me.

I duck behind a nearby statue that a plaque proclaims is Kenneth Danforth. Kenneth Danforth has a wide stance, and there's enough room behind him to nearly obscure me. I crouch down a little anyway—we're almost of a height, Kenneth and me—just for good measure.

I'm only there a moment when—

"What are we doing?" someone says in my ear, and I almost jump a foot.

I turn, and Gideon Prewitt is looking at me, eyes alight. "Are you hiding from somebody?"

It takes me a moment to recover, not just from the scare but from the full force of Gideon Prewitt's Gideon Prewitt-ness.

Madison Lutz had posted a picture of the two of them last weekend with the caption *The prince and me*. Gideon had his arms wrapped around her from behind, her hands clasping his forearm, their faces pressed together, smiling wide.

Baaaaaaabes, Amber Brunati had commented, followed by no less than six heart-eye emojis.

I swallow. "Yes," I say. "Death. That's why you scared me. I thought it was the grim reaper sneaking up on me."

A grin splits his face.

"Should I create a diversion?" he says. "I'm very good at that."

"It's fine," I say, and I can't help but sneak a look out into the hallway. Iris is nowhere to be seen. When I look back, Gideon's eyes narrow.

"You *are* hiding from someone. Who is it? What did they do? Or what did you do?"

"Nothing. It's nothing."

He evaluates me for a moment. "Ex-boyfriend?"

Ha. Will Sorenson graduated with Danforth's senior class last year and is thankfully nowhere within state lines. We both use the same server in Battle Quest, and even the chance of seeing him around Aradana is more than enough.

"No," I say, and glance around again but not for Iris. "Are you . . . are you meeting someone here or something?"

"Here behind this statue?" he says solemnly. "Yes."

"I just mean, why are you . . ." Talking to me. Of all people.

"Are you auditioning for the play?"

"Yeah."

"We've got to sign in. You want to go sign in?"

"Um. Sure, I guess. Yeah."

I follow Gideon to the dining hall. He holds the door open for me, and I approach the teacher sitting at a table inside with a sign-in sheet and a sheaf of forms. We have to rank what jobs in the crew we'd prefer if we're not cast, because Iris was right—we have to work on the production whether or not we get a role in the play. The audition alone guarantees our participation. Funny how they get you like that.

When I finish my form, Gideon is still bent over his, the tip of his tongue stuck between his teeth as he fills it out.

I hesitate for a moment, unsure if I'm supposed to say something to officially end this interaction.

But it was a one-off, I'm sure of that, so I don't say anything. I just turn and head off to a table near the back, having spotted Iris at an empty one in the middle of the room. I pull out a crumpled sheet of paper—my monologue—and try to smooth it out against the tabletop.

I mouth the first few lines. The words feel strange enough, but then I remember I'm supposed to put some kind of emotion into it, too. I try to make my face look impassioned.

And then Gideon plops down in the seat across from mine.

"What part are you trying for?" he says.

"I don't know." *None of them.* "What about you?"

"I'm going to be Oberon."

"You're pretty certain about that."

"I'm the best man for the job." He smiles, and his cheeks dimple. It makes something in my chest seize uncomfortably. A smile like that could be weaponized.

"It's funny we haven't met before," he says when my gaze darts back to my monologue sheet. "Did you transfer?"

"No."

"Do you go to many of the parties?"

I have to stop myself from snorting. "Not many, no." And then I can't help but say: "We actually have met before."

He blinks at me.

"At your birthday, freshman year."

It had been a source of great stress for me at the time. Gideon invited all the girls in our year at PLSG to his fifteenth birthday party at this deluxe arcade.

Most of the people in my class knew him—they had been in junior high together at Morningbrook Academy—but I had never met him before. I didn't even want to go to the party. But my mom said it would be a good opportunity to get to know the girls at school better. "And you never know," she said, raising and lowering her eyebrows suggestively. "Could be some cute boys there." Her eyes widened. "Ooh, or some good party favors!"

I did like the idea of good party favors, so I decided to go. But this led to a dilemma.

What kind of birthday present do you get for a kid you don't even know? Who, judging by the elaborate birthday party, probably already had everything he could possibly want?

I ended up giving him a gift card to Outback Steakhouse that my mom had gotten free at work. "It's his fifteenth birthday," Mom had said, presenting the card to me with a flourish. "Fifteen for fifteen, there you go, problem solved."

It didn't seem that simple. In fact, it seemed pretty embarrassing. But come party night, I left it on the gift table all the same.

41

I look at Gideon now, and I know that he has no earthly recollection of me giving him an Outback Steakhouse gift card for his fifteenth birthday. He doesn't even remember that I was there. He just blinks at me, friendly and uncomprehending.

"I think I'd remember meeting you," he says, leaning in a bit and flashing me that smile again.

He's either trying to flirt with me, or he's making fun of me. Really only the latter makes sense, so I just blink. "You actually did, though."

His face falls. "I don't remember. I'm sorry."

"There were like a hundred people there," I say, because he looks inexplicably upset, like a little kid who's dropped an ice cream cone. "It's not a big deal."

"Did you bring me a present? Maybe I'd remember from that."

"I, uh. It was a gift card."

"To where?"

"Outback Steakhouse."

"No way. I remember that."

"No you don't."

"I do, though. You know why? It's because I got a bunch of gift cards from the party, and Noah and I decided to spend them all in one awesome day. It was one of the last places we went. We had just eaten like fifty bucks worth of food at P.F. Chang's, but we still had the Outback Steakhouse card, so we went and ordered a Bloomin' Onion and ate the entire thing, and then we both threw up in the parking lot after. It was epic."

It does not sound epic. But I can't help but smile a little. "Well, I guess I made you a memory."

"You did!" he says brightly.

"Is it just me or are there more people here than last year?" Suddenly Sudha Prabhu is at my elbow, pulling out the chair next to mine. Alicia Smith circles the table and grabs the seat next to Gideon.

"Worried about the competition?" he says.

"Absolutely not," Sudha replies primly. "Hi, Claudia."

Alicia echoes it. "Hi, Claudia. I like your earrings."

"Thanks. I like your shirt," I say, because we are all wearing the same shirt. She doesn't smile, just pokes Gideon lightly on the cheek, right in the spot where his dimple then appears, as if summoned.

Sudha peers at the crumpled monologue sheet in front of me.

"Interesting choice," she says.

I frown. There were only three options for audition monologues tacked to the bulletin board outside the drama room. I'm not sure how it was possible to choose wrong, but apparently I had.

"Did you practice?" Sudha asks.

"Well, I didn't, like, actually . . . *rehearse*," I say. "But I read it, at least. That's something."

I had tried practicing in the mirror, but I felt ridiculous talking to myself and in the end just kind of gave the whole thing a whispered once-over.

Sudha gives me the saddest look, like she's somehow cognizant of my pathetic mirror practice. "Yes," she says. "It's something."

She'll go in there and crush her audition, of course. I'd expect no less. Sudha was Sandy in *Grease* last spring, and Emily in *Our Town* the semester before that. She has a lead role locked down, no matter what the production.

"You're gonna do great," Gideon says.

"Thanks, G." Sudha beams.

Gideon smiles back, but when Sudha and Alicia start chatting, he points at me and gives me a double thumbs-up, mouthing the words again like they were meant for me: *You're gonna do great.*

I smile a little and look back at my monologue.

seven

We get called a few at a time to queue up in the hall outside the band room.

Seated inside is the drama teacher at Danforth (Mr. Palmer, I'm informed) and the freshman lit teacher from PLSG, Ms. Ohlemacher. When it's my turn, Mr. Palmer, who's directing the show, tells me to start "whenever I'm ready," which is funny, because I'm quite certain all the practice in the world wouldn't make me truly ready.

I hate public speaking. I'm not sure what it is—there are literally only two people in here, and it's not like I don't talk in front of two people—my parents—literally every single day. But something about it being structured, and inorganic, makes my stomach twist and my palms sweat.

("Is it because people could be judging me?" I asked Alex once. "Like, because it's an opportunity for me to be judged?"

"I mean, if it helps, just know that I'm judging you all the time."

"Shut up."

He grinned. "I'm judging you right now.")

I hold the monologue sheet up, trying to stop it from rattling in my grasp as I read from it.

"Do you think you could do it without the paper?" Ms. Ohlemacher says gently when I'm finished.

"No."

"Well, let's have another try at it," Mr. Palmer says. "This time, I want you to really focus on how Titania must feel here. She's had a falling out with Oberon, and the world is going haywire as a result of it. She wants peace, but neither of them are willing to give in."

I try it again, try to think how Titania must feel, running into an on-again, off-again boyfriend like that.

My hands shake slightly less this time. A marginal improvement.

"Thank you, Claudia," Mr. Palmer says when I stumble to a finish.

Ms. Ohlemacher gives me a kind smile. "Yes, great, thank you."

I leave.

The next group has assembled outside. Gideon is toward the front, along with Alicia and another guy who I recognize from the first day of school in the Grove. Gideon pushes off the wall when I emerge.

"How'd it go?" he says, holding up one hand. I realize that I'm supposed to high-five it. "Did you nail it?"

"I don't know if I'd go that far."

"I'm sure you did awesome."

There's some misplaced faith. "Thanks," I say with a tight smile.

"Hey, this is Noah," Gideon says, gesturing to the guy behind him, who looks up from his phone. "Do you know Noah Edelman?"

"No."

"He's the greatest person I know."

Noah reaches out to shake my hand but looks Gideon's way. "You really got to stop billing me like that. People are gonna be disappointed."

"You could never disappoint," Gideon says, and even though he's smiling, I get the feeling he's not joking. "Noah's my best friend. We shared the Bloomin' Onion I told you about."

"Yeah, thanks for sponsoring that parking lot yak," Noah says with a smile.

"No problem," I say for want of anything better.

And now we're just standing awkwardly.

"So I should probably . . ." I gesture over my shoulder.

"Yeah, don't want to keep you," Gideon says. "Hopefully we both get cast, then we can hang out at rehearsals."

"Well, you've got Oberon locked down."

"Maybe you'll be my queen," he says, leaning in a little and wiggling his eyebrows.

"I mean, probably not. If there's like . . . a nonspeaking role for a tree or something, that'll probably be me."

"Hey." Gideon looks suddenly serious. "Don't sell yourself short."

I nod. "Yeah. See you guys." And I head away.

eight

"Are you going to wear a *doublet*? Hose? Better yet, are you going to wear one of those Shakespearean collars?"

"Collars?"

"Like the big accordion-looking neck thing."

"I don't know what you're talking about," I say, even though I know exactly what Julia means.

"Like the thing Shakespeare's wearing in literally every picture of Shakespeare ever."

We're both online that night, roaming the Aradanian countryside for monsters. I've got my phone pressed to my ear while we play. There's a text chat function in Battle Quest, but you can't talk aloud through the game itself. If there's a group of us playing, we usually just do some kind of conference calling online. But if it's just me and Julia, we get on the phone like we usually do—the same way she'd call me while she's grocery shopping or cooking dinner, or I'd call her while I'm waiting for a ride or something. We haven't lived under the same roof since I was in elementary school, or even in the same city since I started high school, but we manage to snag time together however we can, wherever we can. On the phone, or in Aradana, or both.

I shoot off a couple of arrows toward a nearby creature. It turns our way and we start attacking it in earnest. It's almost drained when Julia's avatar, Selensa Stormtreader, suddenly falls still.

"What are you doing?" I finish off the creature.

"Sorry, Mark just got home." I hear muffled conversation and then "He says hi."

"Tell him I don't say hi back. Tell him I respond with stony silence."

Julia relays the message, and I can hear Mark laugh.

Julia met him when she was a sophomore in college. I was in third grade at the time. He came home with Julia for Christmas that year. I don't really remember my first impression of him—I was more caught up with Disney's latest efforts and desperately wanting an American Girl doll. If I knew I was meeting my future brother-in-law, I probably would've paid more attention.

Though I do remember he brought Alex and me presents.

"He's just trying to win you over," Julia had said when Mark went off with my dad and Alex and I tore into our new loot.

"No, he's trying to win *you* over," my mom replied with a smile.

They got married three years ago. And now, "Oh good Lord," Julia mutters. "He wants to go look at strollers again."

Julia is pregnant, and Mark is unendingly excited. Julia—although she is the baby-carrying party involved—is somewhat less enthusiastic.

She texts me about it all the time:

He wants to pick out nursery colors.

He won't stop reading about breast pumps. I THINK AS THE PERSON BEING PUMPED I SHOULD BE THE MOST CONCERNED ABOUT THE PUMPING.

He's highlighting the baby name book.

We each get five vetoes, I've already used four. I'm gonna need to buy more vetoes.

I wouldn't understand Julia's reluctance if I didn't know her, but I do, and I know that she hates change. She gets anxious about the future. And I know that any apprehension on her side is just reflective of that.

I've seen her rub her belly when she thinks no one is looking. I've seen her gazing at baby shoes at Target.

It's part of her shtick, acting grumpy. A little negative. But I know she'll love that baby, I know how much she'll care for it.

Sweet little Cayenne or Ellipsis or Cherry Blossom or Aquafina.

I am barely exaggerating, Claude.

"I thought we were gonna do a dungeon," I say, making Viola Constantinople execute a complicated twirl on-screen because Selensa Stormtreader is still just standing there.

"Yeah, sorry," Julia says after more muffled conversation with Mark. "Gotta go. Have fun Shakespeare-ing."

"I'll try. Hey, if you're mean to me, I'm gonna send Mark a list of names from this play. You could have a little baby Oberon or Hippolyta."

"Oh geez. Don't you dare."

"Bet you wish you saved some of those vetoes."

"I'm hanging up now."

I grin. "I love you!"

It's quiet for a beat, and I think she really has hung up. Then, "Love you too. Bye."

On the screen, Selensa Stormtreader logs off.

nine

Zoe and I volunteer at Roosevelt-Hart on Thursday evenings.

It's a pediatric rehab facility, which is not—as Alex has inappropriately joked before—a place for toddlers on benders. It's actually a place for babies and kids who have been released from the hospital but aren't well enough to go home yet. Round-the-clock care, physical therapy, etc.

I pull up to Zoe's house, and she's sitting on the front steps, wearing her bright blue Roosevelt-Hart shirt. I'm wearing an identical one with *VOLUNTEER* across the back in big white letters.

We listen to Drunk Residential, our favorite band, in the car on the way there and sing along.

When we get to Roosevelt-Hart, we sign in at the front (the attractive desk guy smiles at both of us. I manage to get out a too-loud "hi" and an aborted wave, but Zoe chats amiably with him while I check in on the computer). Then we part ways—Zoe to the rec area, and me to the nursery.

Zoe likes to work with the kids closer to our age. But I

volunteered to be in the nursery. I like babies, and maybe part of me thought it would be an easier job.

It's quiet when I get in this evening. The lights are dimmed, and most of the little ones are sleeping. But I go up to the crib of a baby named Makenna, and she blinks big eyes back at me. A monitor at her bedside reports her heart rate, connected through a wire to a sensor attached to one of her big toes.

"Could I hold her?" I ask the nearest nurse. There's an impressive nurse-to-kid ratio here, so there's always one close by.

The nurse gets to her feet, reaches in for Makenna—we're not allowed to pick the babies up ourselves—and gestures to a rocking chair at the foot of her bed. I sit, and she places Makenna in my arms.

She's warm and cuddly and quiet, and I rock her until she falls asleep. Not a bad way to spend an evening.

We started volunteering here last year. As is usually the way, Zoe wanted to, and I followed along. She wants to go to medical school, and apparently volunteering in a "clinical setting" looks good on your résumé. Zoe is forever trying to get an early leg up on things.

I didn't know what kind of hospital Roosevelt-Hart was. That the majority of older kids were there because of brain and spinal cord injuries, and that the majority of babies and toddlers had had surgeries and needed breathing tubes, or suffered from failure to thrive, or were there because their parents couldn't care for them.

The first night we volunteered, it was dark when Zoe and I left the hospital. We walked across the wide parking lot, in and out of the paths of the parking lot lights.

It was quiet between us until I finally spoke, voicing the thought that had been running through my mind all evening.

"I don't think I can do this," I said, slowing to a stop in front of the car. Zoe crossed around to the passenger side, but neither of us got in. "I don't think I can come back here."

"Why not?"

I shook my head. I was trying not to cry, and my throat ached with it.

"It's just." Blink. Swallow. "Sad." Swallow again, around the massive lump. "It's so fucking sad, Zoe."

She looked at me for a moment, but her face betrayed nothing. Zoe could be so incredibly . . . placid sometimes. Unreadable. I didn't feel like she was judging me—I knew her well enough to know that she wouldn't—but I couldn't tell what she was thinking.

"Yeah, it is," she said finally, nodding. "But feeling bad won't help anyone. You or them. Pity's not gonna help."

"I know." A few tears slipped out, and I rushed to catch them, pushing up the side of my glasses, so half of Zoe was blurry when I looked back at her. "But I can't help it. It's not fair. Why do people have to go through that? Why do—*kids*—have to go through that? It sucks. Everything about it sucks."

"But there are places like this," she said. "And doctors and nurses and . . . and volunteers and stuff, to help take care of them and help them get better. That doesn't suck, does it?"

I shook my head.

"I think it's kind of awesome actually," she said, looking back at the building. It was a pretty new facility with a modern design, lots of windows. The lights from the lobby lit it up like a jewel box, glowing through the darkness. "It makes me feel good, to be a part of that."

"Maybe you're just stronger than me."

Her gaze returned to me, and she shook her head. "Bullshit."

"I don't know if I can do it."

"Bullshit," she said again.

We didn't say much more on the ride home. By the time we reached her house, I was more or less composed. We said good night, she went inside, and I drove home. We didn't talk about it again after that.

The following Thursday, I put my Roosevelt-Hart shirt on and drove to Zoe's to pick her up.

She didn't comment on it, but she was already waiting for me on the front porch, wearing her own blue shirt, so I knew she already knew I was coming. That I would go back, despite what I said.

She glances over at me tonight as I pull to a stop at a red light. "What?"

"What do you mean, what?"

"You're thinking really loudly."

"Yeah, I just . . ." I shake my head. "I was thinking about the play. They're posting the cast list tomorrow."

"Ooh, your dramatic debut."

"Ugh."

"It'll be fine. You'll do great."

I have no doubt she believes it. Zoe has always had faith in me, even when I wasn't sure if I deserved it.

The light turns green. I press the gas, and we go.

ten

The cast list is posted outside the PLSG music room the next morning. Apparently there are no nonspeaking tree roles in *A Midsummer Night's Dream*, so I find my name toward the bottom, in a list headed in big bold letters with the word *Crew*.

Only the girls' list is posted here. I wonder briefly if Gideon Prewitt secured the role of Oberon as my eyes catch on a few of the other names on the list.

Titania: Paige Breckner.

Hermia: Sudha Prabhu. No surprise there.

Helena: Lena Ideker. An interesting choice, to be sure. I didn't know Lena's interests skewed toward Shakespeare.

And toward the bottom, *First Fairy*: Iris Huang.

Huh. Who'd have thought. For all of Iris's ire, I guess she did a halfway decent audition. Better than me, at least, though that wouldn't have been tough.

We're all meant to meet in the auditorium at Danforth after school. I guess that's when I'll find out what exactly crew entails.

Painting scenery and stuff? Zoe texts me at lunch. *Operating the spotlight? Hey, maybe you'll open and close the curtain.*

I could handle that. Could build up some upper body strength at least.

You're gonna get so ripped, Zoe replies.

A *Midsummer Night's Dream* is really an ensemble show. There's no singular main character or narrator but a few different groups of characters, all of equal importance.

First there's the court—the Duke and his lady Hippolyta, as well as some royal hangers-on, who conveniently turn up at the beginning and the end of the show to set the scene, add commentary, and pass judgment.

Then there are the lovers—Hermia, Lysander, Helena, and Demetrius. Hermia and Lysander are madly in love, Demetrius is into Hermia despite it being an entire no-go on Hermia's side, and Helena is hopelessly into Demetrius, despite it being an entire no-go on Demetrius's side.

Next there are the Mechanicals—a rough-and-tumble group of people tasked with putting on a play for the Duke's impending wedding. And last there are the Fairies—the King, Oberon, and the Queen, Titania, and their respective crews.

Oberon and Titania are fighting, and the world is all out of whack because of it. Meanwhile, Hermia and Lysander run away to get married when Hermia's dad says she has to marry Demetrius. Demetrius follows them into the woods because he can't take no for an answer, and Helena follows him because neither can she.

This all leads to some capital-H Hijinks, and then when things are sorted, there's a play-within-a-play at the end that the Mechanicals put on, and it's all good fun.

I heard through the grapevine that Gideon Prewitt had indeed secured the role of Oberon. And although in theory Noah Edelman probably would've been a good candidate for Oberon's magical sidekick, Puck, Noah would be playing Nick Bottom, the head Mechanical who thinks he's an amazing actor and unwittingly gets turned into a donkey. Or a partial donkey, at least. Donkey from the neck up.

Everyone is gathering in the first few rows of the auditorium before the start of rehearsal. I spot Gideon and Noah down front with Sudha, Alicia, and Lena.

I take a seat as far back as I can get and still look involved, and I crack open my copy of the play while we wait for everyone to assemble. I haven't been sitting long when someone clears their throat behind me.

I glance around. Iris is now seated two rows back, glaring right at me.

What could I have possibly done? I'm literally just sitting here.

I face forward. But Iris clears her throat again, and when I turn back to her, she gestures toward the stage.

"Down front," she says pointedly.

I look ahead. Gideon has turned around in his seat and is waving at me. He smiles and then gestures like he wants me to join him.

There are people on either side of him, people that I'm not great friends with, and it would be so weird to just . . . *insert* myself in there.

I shake my head.

Gideon sticks out his bottom lip in a pout, and I crack a smile. But then his attention is drawn somewhere over my shoulder. I think for a moment that he's looking at Iris, but then Paige walks swiftly down the aisle next to us, raising a hand toward Gideon, who grins broadly, all pretense of pout gone. He says something to Noah, who gets up and moves to Alicia's other side, and Paige takes his vacated seat. The King and Queen of Fairies united. Gideon starts talking to Paige, and I am forgotten.

I glance back at Iris. Her face is arranged in an impressive scowl.

"What?" she snaps.

I face forward again.

Ms. Ohlemacher and Mr. Palmer make some opening remarks, have us all introduce ourselves, and then divide us into cast and crew.

Ms. Ohlemacher is in charge of the crew. There are about twenty of us who assemble backstage while the actors gather onstage.

We get our crew assignments based on what we said on the sign-in form at auditions. I had ranked costumes one, scenery two, and lighting three. After Ms. Ohlemacher rattles off a list of names for set building, she looks up from her clipboard and says, "For costumes we've got Claudia Wallace and Caris Pearlman." Caris grins back at me from a few rows ahead. "You'll be working with Delilah; she's designing for the show." She gestures to Delilah, who nods at Caris and then turns and looks at me with a short dip of her head, eyes serious.

Delilah Legere, or Del as everyone calls her, is actually one of the first people I met at PLSG. She sat in front of me in freshman English.

We aren't friends, but we're cool, I guess. I wouldn't say PLSG is cliquey, per se, but I wouldn't say it *isn't* cliquey either, and somehow, if I had to pick two girls in our class—in the whole school, even—who didn't somehow fit in with any of the cliques, it would be Del and myself. So we share that, at least.

Unlike me, though, the thing about Del is that she's basically just too cool for it. She has friends in college. She does all sorts of interesting stuff outside of school. And she's so focused on getting into design school, I guess she doesn't have much time to waste at the parties and the luncheons and the rest. She certainly wasn't at Amber Brunati's Pink Party. Though I would love to see what she would've worn. She definitely has a signature style.

I can handle making costumes for Del.

"I assume you both can sew?" she says, looking from me to Caris after the crew has further divided up into our respective areas.

"Yeah, I like to make costumes," Caris says. "Me and Robbie do cosplay."

"Precious," Del says. "You?"

I nod. "My grandma taught me. It was a . . . bonding-type activity."

Del's expression says that this kind of information is superfluous.

"We'll meet after school starting next week," Del says, "at the multimedia studio. It's in the basement of this building. That'll be our costume shop. I've already got designs worked up. We need to get supplies, take measurements, get started on construction. Lots to do. Are you with me?"

"Yeah."

"Aye aye, captain!" Caris says, smiling.

Del's lips twitch, like she might almost smile back. "Excellent."

* * *

I cut back through the Grove to get to the PLSG parking lot after we break for the day. Alex is supposed to come pick me up since Dad headed home when classes got out.

Footsteps crunch through the brush behind me. I glance back.

"I'm not following you," Iris says sharply. "As if I would follow you."

"I know." I point to the group of sophomore girls on the path up ahead of us. "I'm not following them either. We all happen to be going back to the same place."

I don't slow down. And I don't think Iris is picking up her pace, but somehow she ends up nearer, almost in step with me.

"So what are you doing on the show anyway?"

I glance over at her, surprised. An actual question, unsolicited.

"Costumes."

Iris snorts.

"What?"

"No, it makes sense. I figured you'd do something that requires little to no skill."

That, of all things, breaks me. Or maybe it's just the one thing added to the massive pile of other things that finally tips the scales.

"Why do you have to do that?"

"What?"

We're basically alone now, distance stretching between us and the group of sophomores up ahead, so there's no one around to witness it if Iris Huang actually succeeds in making me cry. The words just come out: "Why do you have to be so mean? Seriously, what do you get out of it? Is it, like, a rush of endorphins? Is there some chemical released in your head when you're a dick to people? Would

61

your brain light up in the same places as a heroin addict getting a fix?"

My voice doesn't waver. I manage to keep it together.

And somehow, inexplicably, Iris just responds with a huff of laughter.

I'm so shocked, all I can do is blink.

"What?" she says. "That was funny."

"It wasn't supposed to be funny."

"Well, it was."

I don't know what to say to that, so I don't say anything at all. I just turn and head off through the Grove, moving quickly enough to leave Iris behind.

eleven

British lit finds us with another assignment the next week. We're supposed to find "critique partners" to review each other's papers. The mad flurry starts, but I know better this time.

I turn to Sam, but before I can grab her attention, Iris appears and drops a notebook down in front of me.

"Write your number," she says.

I blink at her. I don't know how she moved across the room that fast.

"We need to exchange numbers if we're going to work on this outside of school," she says slowly, like I'm stupid.

"Who said we were partners?"

Iris glances around. "Everyone else has paired up."

And it's true. By now, everyone has.

"We need to show Dennings we can work together," she says.

"So this is some kind of . . . redemption arc?"

"Write your number down, for Christ's sake."

"Maybe I don't want to."

Iris looks at me for a moment and then up at the ceiling. "Please." It seems like the word physically pains her.

Inwardly, I sigh.

And then I write down my number.

I go to the appointed place in the basement of the Danforth arts building after school to meet Del. It's a multipurpose kind of studio—there are big craft tables, some sewing machines, computers, some woodworking equipment.

Big bulletin boards line one wall of the room. When I arrive, Del is pinning sketches to one of the boards. She glances back when I approach.

"We're not staying long," she says. "We're going to the thrift store."

"Field trip?"

"A working trip."

I pick up one of the closest sketches not yet pinned up. It shows a figure in a sort of hoop-looking petticoat, wearing a cutoff blazer and fingerless gloves, with aviator goggles around their head, sort of like Amelia Earhart. *MUSTARDSEED* is printed in all caps underneath.

"I wasn't sure what kind of fairies we were going with," I say when Del catches me looking. "You know, Tinker Bell or, like, bug people?"

"Neither," Del says. "Mr. Palmer wants to set the show in the present day." She points to sketches of Hermia and Lysander, already tacked up. Hermia is wearing a cute white dress with a little jacket over it. Lysander has on black skinny jeans and a motorcycle jacket.

"But the fairies will be kind of . . . out of time," Del continues, pointing to Titania and Oberon and Mustardseed, still in my hands. "A mix of clothes from a bunch of different periods, like they've picked up stuff along the way, and they've lived so long, it's from all different times."

"Huh," I say. "That's cool."

Del actually smiles. "I know, right?"

When Caris joins us, we set off to the thrift store. Del gives us each a list of items to track down.

"Fun!" Caris says, beaming. "It's like a scavenger hunt."

I look through mine quickly. Some are more generic items, like *assorted T-shirts (any size/color), white button-down (one each men's and women's), flannel shirt*, while some are more specific, like *ugly bridesmaid dress*, and *yellow raincoat*.

"How do we know what size?" I say. "We haven't even got measurements from people yet."

"Doesn't matter. We'll probably end up deconstructing most of this stuff anyway."

So we set off on our scavenger hunt. Caris is right—it actually is kind of fun.

She and I are sifting through a bin of neckties (*twenty neckties— greens, golds, and browns*) when she glances up at me.

"Guess what." Caris's eyes shine.

"What?"

"Robbie said Gideon was asking about you."

I frown. "What about me?"

"You know. Just. *About* you." She raises and lowers her eyebrows emphatically.

I think of the Oberon sketch tacked up on the bulletin board. A great cloak, a head scarf, big black boots. The figure Del drew didn't have a face, but it somehow captured that Gideon Prewitt swagger, as if she designed it expressly with him in mind, even before the part was his.

"He . . . he's probably just—" I shrug. "You know. Being polite." I fish a gold-patterned necktie out of the bin and add it to our pile.

"Or he likes you."

That doesn't quite compute. I shake my head. "I'm not his type."

"How do you know?"

"Maybe he's not my type," I amend, because Caris is generous and probably genuinely believes that someone like Gideon Prewitt could actually like me.

"Maybe." She looks up from the bin, eyes dancing. "I don't know though. He may be a little ridiculous sometimes, but something about him works on everyone."

It's then that Del walks past with a shockingly ugly tulle bridesmaid dress in her arms. "Less talking, more finding," she says. Then she pauses. "And for the record, it doesn't work on me."

Caris grins. "Noted." And we get back to sorting.

twelve

We go rock climbing, the cast and crew of *Midsummer*.

It's Paige's idea. A first-week-of-rehearsal celebration. She posts the event online, invites everybody.

I made the mistake of mentioning it to my mom, who was just as enthusiastic about it as she had been about Gideon's birthday party freshman year. She doesn't seem to catch the irony of once again telling me it'll be "a great chance to get to know some of the girls at school" three years later.

"It was just an open-invite thing. I really don't think anyone will notice if I don't go. In fact, they'll notice if I do go."

My mom raised an eyebrow. "Is that a problem?"

"I mean, yeah, it kind of goes against my usual thing."

"What thing?"

"You know. Where I'm not really, like . . . *active* in that way."

My mom gave me a look. "Sexually?"

"Agh! God! No! Socially. Socially active."

"Like . . . in terms of . . . justice and things?"

"Like in terms of going to events! I don't need to go to PLSG stuff. I'd rather hang out with Zoe."

"Yes and play video games and go to Tropical Moose and listen to your bands, I know. But it wouldn't hurt to mix things up. Next year . . ."

"What?"

"Everything'll be a mix-up next year. You might as well ease into it now, yeah? And didn't you have fun at the Pink Party? Wasn't it great?"

That wasn't exactly how I recalled it. But it didn't seem like I was going to get out of this one easily.

And maybe she has a point, some little traitorous voice said at the back of my mind.

"I don't even know how to climb," I said, one last attempt.

"You'll learn," Mom replied simply.

So I find myself at a climbing gym on Friday night. I've never been to one before, but I'd hazard a guess that this one is pretty deluxe. It's a giant warehouse with climbing walls bordering the interior and structures set up in the middle for what Keara Shelton, standing in front of me in line to pay, informs me are for *bouldering*.

"What does that mean?"

"No ropes," she says with a grin.

Those of us who haven't climbed before have to take training on how to belay. To my surprise, Iris is here, and she's among this group, too, hanging at the edges. We get paired up with the person standing next to us, so she gets Kaitlyn Winthrop, who's playing another one of the fairies, and I get a guy named Corey, who's in the crew.

Then we're turned loose in the gym. The people who've been before are already climbing—I see Paige hanging from one wall while Gideon stands below, belaying her. Noah Edelman is next to him, chatting with Gideon. Gideon is laughing at whatever Noah's saying, but his head stays tilted up, eyeing Paige's progress.

Do not take your eyes off the climber, the surprisingly stern college kid who trained us had said. *Do not get distracted. Do not take your hands off the rope. Do not lose focus.*

"Do not pass go, do not collect two hundred dollars," I had whispered to Corey, but he didn't laugh.

Corey has headed off and joined a group of guys already at the wall, so I glance around for a new partner.

Iris is still standing where the beginners' group was assembled. She's watching Gideon watching Paige with a decidedly stormy look on her face.

"Come on," I say to her. Everyone else has already paired off or headed to the bouldering walls. "Let's climb."

"I hate everything about this."

"Iris, you haven't even climbed as high as you are tall."

"Let me down. Now."

"You could literally just step off the wall."

Iris does, but there's not enough slack (I'm a good belayer, actually), so she just hangs uncomfortably in the harness, her toes brushing the mat. I fumble with the rope and she drops down fully to her feet, then flops onto the ground like she's completely winded.

I laugh. I can't help it. Iris glares.

"I'd love to see you try," she says, but it's not quite as cutting as usual.

Iris has to clip in to belay me so I don't launch her into the air. Once she's anchored, I pick a relatively easy path and have at it.

Surprisingly, I like it. Reaching for the next hold, pushing up with my legs . . . it feels good. The muscles in my arms burn, but in a strangely pleasant sort of way.

I'm just over halfway to the top when there's a whoop from below. I glance over my shoulder and see that Gideon has joined Iris.

"Whooooo!" he calls again. "Climbin' Claudia! Owning that wall!" He starts to do a dance with jazz hands.

"What are you doing?" I say.

"Dancing for moral support." He executes an awkward turn.

"I won't see you dancing if I go back to climbing," I say, gripping the holds. I'm a little nervous to let go, to lean back into the harness and just dangle. It's not that I don't trust Iris. But.

"You'll know that I'm dancing," Gideon calls back. "Iris will commentate."

I smile at the wall. Shake out one hand, then the other. Then I keep climbing.

I hear some hushed conversation from below, and then "Gideon's spinning," Iris calls flatly. Like there was an argument she's clearly lost. "Now he's doing some . . . weird shuffle thing—that's not a moonwalk, you're high if you think you're moonwalking right now. Now he's doing like a sort of . . . bouncy kick line. . . ."

"Thank you," I say, grinning as I reach for the next hold. "I feel properly encouraged, thanks."

I make it to the top and Gideon cheers. Iris lets me back down in a jerky fashion that's got the harness digging uncomfortably into the flesh of my hips.

When I get to the ground, I flop down like Iris did, leaning back on my hands, but I feel like I've actually earned it. I've worked up a decent sweat, strands of hair coming out of my ponytail.

"Good job!" Gideon says. "I tried to get Iris to do the wave with me, but she said if she did, it would kill you, so we opted not to."

"Probably a good call."

Iris unclips herself. She's looking off across the gym, but there's something close to a smile on her face.

"Are you guys friends from junior high?" I ask Iris after Gideon has high-fived us both and gone back to join Noah, who is sitting with Alicia on a metal bench in the middle of the room. Neither has climbed yet. Alicia's hair and makeup are spotless, and her workout clothes look runway-ready.

"No," Iris says. "I mean, I know him from school, yeah. But not . . . friends. We were lab partners in eighth grade. He's . . ." Something in her expression softens marginally. She doesn't finish.

"A good egg?"

"What the hell does that mean?"

"I don't know." It's something my mom would say.

I try a couple more paths after that—Iris begrudgingly belaying me—but they're much tougher, and I don't make it to the top again. Iris doesn't even try to get back on the wall.

Iris has gone to the bathroom and I'm eyeing a new path when I hear someone call out from above. Just a few ropes away, Kristina Freeman, who's playing another one of the fairies, is clinging to the wall about fifteen feet up. Pete Salata, one of the Mechanicals, is standing below.

71

"I want to come down," she says.

"No way," he says with a grin. "You have to get to the top first."

"Pete, seriously." Even from here I can see Kristina's arms trembling under the force of clinging to the wall. "I don't like it, I want to come down."

"You just need to try harder."

"I'm not kidding—" There's panic creeping into her voice.

"If I let you down, you won't learn anything."

"Hey—" I start to say, stepping toward him, but out of nowhere, Noah Edelman beats me to it.

"Pete. My dude. How about you let her off the wall because she fucking asked you to?"

"How about you mind your own damn business?" Pete says.

Gideon crosses over then, stands next to Noah. He's a good bit taller than both him and Pete.

"What's going on?" he asks, looking between the two of them, brow furrowed.

"Nothing. Jesus," Pete says, and then fumbles with the belay device. The rope jerks, and Kristina drops a foot or so abruptly and lets out a yelp. "Sorry!" Pete calls, and manages to lower her the rest of the way more smoothly.

When Kristina's feet hit the ground, she stumbles a bit but Gideon is right there, grabbing on to her elbows to hold her upright. She looks close to tears.

"It's all good," Gideon says quietly. "Back on solid ground."

"I didn't like it," Kristina says.

"No harm in that. Let's shake those arms out."

"Just to be clear," I hear Noah say to Pete, "you're an asshole."

"You know, he's not always gonna be around to back you up," Pete replies, his smile at odds with the edge in his voice.

Gideon has started shaking his own arms out, waving them in the air like one of those crazy dancing noodles at a used-car lot. Kristina lets out a weak laugh and then a more genuine one as he starts dancing around in a circle, arms still flailing.

"Yeah. He is," Noah replies evenly.

I'm taking off my harness and shoes to turn them back in at the end of the evening when Gideon approaches me again. He's spent most of the night with Paige and Noah and Alicia, but he bounds up to me now like we're old friends.

"Hey, do you know Jacob Dolby?" he says like he's going to introduce us, but there's no Jacob Dolby in sight.

I shake my head.

"He's having a party tomorrow night."

"Good for him."

"It's gonna be fun. You should come by."

He's got the dimples on display. It's a particularly flirty smile, and he seems as if he's aware of its effectiveness.

"Yeah, maybe," I say.

"I can text you the info." He fishes his phone out of his pocket and extends it toward me. I pause for a moment but then take it and type my number in. "Or I could come pick you up if you want?"

"It's okay. I can drive."

"Cool. Well, I'll see you there."

"Maybe," I say as he backs away, flashing me a double thumbs-up.

"Bye, Iris!" he calls, shooting her a grin.

She just snorts.

"What?" I say, turning to look at her when Gideon has rejoined Noah, gathering their things to leave.

"Nothing," she replies.

Iris and I end up walking out together. Well, not *together*, exactly, but close enough that she's forced to pause and hold the door open for me. Most of the cast and crew have left by now, the parking lot emptying out as the place prepares to close for the night. I start toward my car, but Iris lingers by the front door, pulling out her phone.

"What are you doing?"

"Calling a ride. What does it look like I'm doing?"

"You don't have a car?" Most of the girls in our class do.

"I don't drive," she says primly, pressing the phone to her ear.

"Do you—" I take a deep breath. "Do you want me to drop you off?"

"Why would you do that?"

"Because I'm not a terrible person?"

She looks at me for a moment and then lowers her phone.

"Fine. You can drive me."

"Really? Thank you. How gracious. What a privilege."

Her lips twitch a little, almost a smile.

"Do you need my address for the GPS?" she asks, following me to my car.

"Hate to break it to you, but 2004 Toyota Corollas don't come standard with GPS. You're gonna have to Google-Map that shit for me. Think you can manage?"

"I'll do my best," she says.

It's silent on the ride to Iris's house, in between her clipped directions.

"Climbing was fun," I say eventually, even though I know Iris didn't find climbing particularly fun. "Good . . . bonding activity."

She looks over at me sharply. "We didn't bond."

"I meant, like, for the show. For the cast and stuff."

She doesn't respond. It's quiet for a bit until she speaks again, a bit gruff: "I didn't even want to be in this stupid play. I should've done like you did and fucked up my audition on purpose."

"I didn't . . . fuck up on purpose."

"Wait, so you were for real?" Iris just blinks at me. "You making faces in the dining hall before auditions. That was . . . you acting?"

"What can I say. We're not all talented enough to be Magic Fairy Number Five."

"Hey, I'm *First Fairy*. It's a named character. I have lines."

"Oh geez, let me get the Tony nominators on the phone."

I glance over at Iris. She doesn't smile, but for a moment I think she might. Until her expression darkens.

"I don't want to be a fairy. They all . . . I'm supposed to . . ." A pause. "Almost all my scenes are with Paige."

I don't know what to say—if I should act like I didn't notice Iris sneaking glances at Paige all evening, or just come out and acknowledge it.

I decide to go for it. "Do you still like her?"

There is a split second where I think Iris might Hulk out of her seat and crush me. But then:

"I love her," she says, quiet. "You can't just turn it off like that."

"It doesn't . . . have to be weird between you two."

"What would you know about it?"

"Nothing, I just—"

"I'm sure you've got tons of exes," she says. "Being the pinnacle of charm that you are."

"Do you want to walk home from here?"

"Oh, so that was your plan. Get me in the car and then abandon me somewhere."

She doesn't sound like she's joking.

"I didn't have a plan, there was no *plan*. Not everything is malicious. Not everyone thinks the way you do."

"Not everything I think is malicious."

"What would a pie chart of your malicious to non-malicious thoughts look like? How big a piece of the pie is non-malicious?"

"You know, I think I liked it better when you were afraid of me."

"I was not *afraid* of you."

"Yes you were." A pause. "Everyone's afraid of me. Everyone avoids me."

"That doesn't mean they're afraid. Maybe it just means they don't like you."

Iris doesn't answer, and I feel instant regret. We were doing okay. Iris just said she loved Paige. Iris Huang used the word *love*.

When I glance over at her at a red light, she doesn't look angry. Just . . . contemplative, I guess.

"I didn't mean—"

"It's a left at the next turn," she says.

The next turn takes us onto a road with fancy pillared streetlights lining each side, and we are on it for a bit before I realize that it is in fact the driveway to Iris's house.

At the end of the drive is the largest mansion I've ever seen in real life. Bigger than Amber Brunati's. Bigger than Lena Ideker's, or

Mikayla Jackson's, whose birthday party I went to in tenth grade and whose mother manages a hedge fund.

I glance over at Iris as I pull through the circle drive to the front of the house and come to a stop. She doesn't look over or say thanks. She gets out and shuts the door behind her.

Nevertheless, I wait until Iris gets inside before driving off. Because that's what you're supposed to do when you drop someone off. Even if you drop them off in front of a house roughly the size of a shopping mall. Even if you're not exactly friends.

Iris doesn't look back.

thirteen

My phone dings the next morning:

Jacob Dolby party 8PM see you there!!!!!!!!!

An address follows, along with a startling array of emojis.

"Is that Zoe?" Alex says, looking up from the couch where he's flipping through the dearth of Saturday morning programming. "Tell her she should come over."

"It's not her."

"No? Who else could it be?"

"I have other friends," I say.

"Tell Julia I say hi."

"It's not Julia either!"

Alex just smirks.

"Don't you have to work?"

"Not right now."

"Hm."

Alex keeps odd hours. He works at a grocery store and also picks up random shifts as a busboy when he can, all the while taking classes at Springdale Community College toward his associate's degree.

It's not that he didn't get into college, because he did. He got into a couple state schools last spring. But his grades were thoroughly average, and he couldn't get a scholarship. My parents gave him two options—either take out loans, or go to community college, get his Gen Ed requirements out of the way, save up money, and then transfer.

He didn't know I was privy to that conversation, but I was—our house isn't huge, and positioned at the top of the stairs, you can hear everything anyone says in the living room below.

Through the spindles of the banister, I could see Alex standing in the doorway. My dad had muted the TV.

"This can't have come as a surprise, Alex," my mom said. "We talked about it last year, we talked about it the year before. I don't know what you expected."

Dad chimed in before Alex could: "We made it clear, bud. We've always made it clear. If you want to go to college, you either get scholarships, or you take out loans. No one's saying you can't go. But you've got to be responsible for yourself here."

I couldn't see Alex's face, but the line of his shoulders was tense.

"What about Claude?" he said finally.

I startled a bit, which was silly, because no one could see me.

"What about her?" Mom said. "She knows she's responsible for herself, too."

"What about the money you pay for her to go to Prospect?"

"That's different."

"How?"

"Because of Daddy's job," Mom said patiently. "You know the tuition is on a big fat discount—"

"But not entirely. You still pay part of it. So how is that different? How can you shell that out for Claude, but you can't help me here? Money that you could've paid for me to get an actual college degree, you're paying for Claude to go to high school. It's . . . fucked up."

"*Alex.*"

"It is. It's not fair. And don't say 'life's not fair.' You always say that."

"It's true, though." Dad's voice was firm. "And frankly . . . Claudia earned it. We get the tuition break because of my job, but Claude had to be accepted into PLSG all on her own. It's very competitive, and she had the grades, she put in the time, she got in. Whereas . . ." He sighed. "Al, I'm sorry, I hate to say it, but if you had devoted more time to school like your sister has, we wouldn't be having this conversation, would we?"

"This is bullshit," Alex said finally, and turned away. I stood up fast and raced into my room before he could see me there.

I heard his door slam. When I went back into the hallway, I saw several crumpled sheets of paper on the floor in front of his room. I picked them up, turned one over:

Dear Mr. Wallace, It is our pleasure to offer you a place in the incoming class at Illinois State University. . . .

I knocked on his door.

"Go away."

"It's me."

"I know, go away."

I swallowed. "Do you want my car money?"

"What?"

I cracked the door, stuck my head in. Alex's room was perpetually messy, full of books and unfolded clothes. "My car money," I said. "You could use it for school."

He was lying on the bed, and his face—sunk into a scowl—softened slightly.

"Claude, your car money would barely pay for a semester."

"I'm sorry," I said, leaning against the doorframe.

"Why?"

" 'Cause you're right. They do pay for me to go to Prospect."

He shook his head. "It's not your fault. It's just . . . I just wish things were different. I wish I was smarter."

"You are smart."

"I wish I'd tried harder."

"What are you gonna do?" I asked.

He shook his head. "I don't know."

I think it was difficult for him—first graduation season, seeing where everyone was headed. Then this summer, watching his friends pack up and leave one by one.

But he kept working. He enrolled at Springdale Community College. He's moving forward.

Right now he changes the channel again and glances at me while I save Gideon's number to my phone.

"For real, tell Julia to get online."

"It's not Julia," I say, and hover over the message for a moment, trying to decide if I should I reply.

I decide against it and flop down on the couch next to Alex, reaching for the remote.

"Don't even think about it," he says.

fourteen

We have a movie night that evening, me and my parents. Alex headed out in the afternoon and said he wouldn't be back until late.

We're halfway through when my phone buzzes.

GIDEON PREWITT flashes across the screen.

I grab it and get up.

"Do you want us to pause it?" Mom says, reaching for the remote.

"No, it's okay."

I step into the kitchen, press accept.

"Hello?"

"Are you here?" Gideon says.

It's loud in the background, the pound of music and the hum of conversation.

"I—" I didn't really expect any follow-up on this. I hadn't actually said I would go. It wasn't a *yeah*, it was a *yeah maybe*, which is basically a *no*. "No, I stayed in."

"Aw, really? I thought we were gonna hang out!"

To be honest, I didn't really think he would remember. Gideon

Prewitt, Danforth–PLSG social director apparent, must invite dozens of people to parties every week.

"I'm just . . . kinda wiped. Sorry."

The background noise changes, like Gideon is moving through a crowd, and then it lessens considerably.

"No worries. What did you do today?"

"Sorry?"

"That has you so wiped."

"Oh. You know. Saturday stuff."

"What's Saturday stuff? Typical Saturday for Claudia Wallace."

I blink. I didn't know he knew my last name. I think of what Caris told me at Goodwill—*Robbie said Gideon was asking about you.*

"I ran a 5K," I say.

"Really." He says it like he might believe me, so I go on.

"Actually, I ran twelve 5Ks. Basically a 60K. And then I fought like seven bears. So. You know, I'm pretty beat."

"Seven bears. All at once?"

"No, three and then four."

"That's impressive. I've only ever fought seven bears tournament-style."

"I'm not saying it was easy. That's . . . that's why I'm so tired."

He huffs a laugh.

"What'd you really do?"

I did homework. I went to the grocery store with my dad to get the frozen pizza we ate for dinner. My family is currently watching a several-years-old weepy romance movie based on a weepy romance novel that my mom liked. And in between:

"I, uh. I was playing a game. Battle Quest? Do you know it?"

For a moment I'm afraid he'll scoff or hang up immediately, but he does neither of those things. "I don't," he says easily. "What kind of game is it?"

"An MMORPG, like Final Fantasy or WoW, but it's a lot newer. It's not that popular yet, but my sister and her husband are really into it. They got me into it, too."

"That sounds very cool," Gideon says without a hint of irony. "Very interesting." A pause. "What's an MM-something-something?"

"A massively multiplayer online role-playing game. It's like . . . where you design a character, and you do tasks—quests and stuff— that are part of a larger story arc. You pick a server when you sign up and then you can interact with anyone who's playing on that server, too. It can be people from all over the world. It's cool because it's not like a video game that has a start and a finish that you play all the way through. I mean, there's the story arc, but it's more about . . ."

I realize how much I am talking about this.

"About what?" Gideon says.

"I don't know. Like . . . inhabiting the world, I guess?" To me, it's not so much a game that you play but a place that you go.

"Huh."

It's quiet for a moment.

"Do you—shouldn't you get back to the party?" I say.

"Oh, I bring the party with me wherever I go." And then, "That's the first lyric off my mixtape, just FYI," he says when I don't respond.

I'm fairly sure he's joking, but at the same time, he thought I was the kind of person who could run a 5K.

"So . . . what did you do today?" I ask for lack of anything better.

"Claudia Wallace, you're not even a little bit curious about my mixtape?"

"I'm like sixty-five percent sure you don't have one."

"It's called *Gideon Prewitt: Getting Improvement.*"

"Agh, God, why?"

"Because it sounds cool."

"*Getting Improvement*? What does that even mean?"

"It doesn't have to *mean* anything, it just has to strike a chord with people."

"I'm now eighty percent sure this mixtape doesn't exist."

"But the other twenty percent of you is imagining the cover art, right?"

A pause. Before I can think of a response, he goes on:

"It's a close-up of an iguana wearing a Christmas sweater."

I laugh.

"So," Gideon says after a moment's silence, "I know I blew it with the whole you being at my birthday party thing. But I know you didn't go to Morningbrook with us, I definitely would've remembered."

"Maybe I had a face transplant."

"Maybe you did. But I also feel like I would've remembered if someone in my class in middle school got a face transplant."

"It was the summer between eighth and ninth grade. I kept a low profile afterward."

"What did you look like before?"

"Better," I say. "I had a rare condition. The doctors said I was too attractive. It was detrimental to my health and also society. So they gave me this face instead. For the greater good."

Gideon laughs and then says, "I like this face."

I don't know what to say to that. But then voices rise up suddenly in the background, all talking at once.

"GIDEON!" a deep voice yells above them, followed by a chorus of giggles and several female voices:

"Giiiiiiideon!"

"Come inside!"

"There's the party, right on cue," I say.

"Told you. Hey, listen, do you—"

"I'll let you get back to the fun."

"But this is fun."

"Bye, Gideon."

I just barely catch the last thing he says, "Talk soon!" before I hang up.

fifteen

I wake up earlier than usual the next day and end up doing what I typically do on a Sunday morning—lying in bed, scrolling through various apps on my phone. Blowing through one, switching to another, then switching back to see if anything new has been posted. Which, at roughly eight a.m. on a Sunday, isn't very likely.

Though a number of pictures have gone up from the party last night. Lena Ideker and Sudha Prabhu, heads tilted toward each other, looking seductively at the camera. The two of them, posed similarly, but with Gideon in the center, an arm around each. The caption is three chili-pepper emojis.

The girls look gorgeous—that's nothing new. But I can't help but focus on Gideon. Gideon, pressing a kiss to Lena's cheek. Something in my stomach shifts. Which is absurd. It's so stupid. I don't even know why.

I close the app and get out of bed.

* * *

I go over to Iris's house that afternoon. We have a new assignment for Brit lit, and since we have rehearsals after school, it makes more sense to just work on it now.

I park to one side of Iris's driveway, which is as wide as some major freeways, and head to the front door.

I ring the bell, and Iris answers after a long delay. I wonder for a moment how you even hear the doorbell in a house as big as this. Do they have speakers throughout? Are there cameras? Some kind of broadcast system?

"Come in," she says, but she turns to me right inside the door, so abruptly that I have to back up fast not to run into her.

"My parents don't know about me and Paige," she says in a low voice.

I blink. "You mean like . . ." I match my volume to hers. "You dating, or you breaking up?"

"Any of it. If you say one word to them—"

"I won't," I say.

But Iris continues: "No one will find your body." Then she turns and goes inside.

Awesome. Great. No problem.

I follow her upstairs to her room. She pushes the door open to reveal a huge four-poster bed with ornately carved posts and a big white canopy. Windows on either side of the bed look out over the sprawling lawn.

I step into the room, glancing at the opposite wall.

"Whoa." I can't help it.

The entire wall is covered, floor to ceiling, in images of the same five faces.

"What?" Iris says, crossing over to the bed.

The focal point of the wall is a giant tapestry with *THIS IS OUR NOW* emblazoned across the top, and five boys posing underneath it, grinning with their arms around one another.

"I just . . . you must really . . . I mean, I guess you're a big fan, huh?"

"You could say that," Iris says.

"I . . ." I barely know what to say. This room is probably three times bigger than mine, this wall is expansive, and literally every inch is covered. I knew TION was popular, but . . . well, I didn't know they were this popular with Iris. I move closer. There are magazine clippings, multiple movie posters for the TION documentary, and seemingly every promotional ad and poster available—some, even, in languages I don't recognize.

One face is more prominent than the others. I know vaguely about the band, but I could only name two of the five: Tristan, the "bad boy," and Kenji, the fashion plate, the heartbreaker, and, clearly, Iris's favorite. A life-sized cardboard cutout of Kenji stands in the corner, his hands in his pockets, his smile wide and just a little bit roguish.

"Are we going to work or not?" Iris says abruptly.

So we work. The boys of TION watch us unrelentingly, but we don't speak of them again until I get up to go to the bathroom. There's an en suite attached to Iris's room—I'd have expected no less—and I jump when I flick on the lights.

"Holy shit."

"What?" Iris says from the other room.

I stick my head out the door. "There's . . . another Kenji in here."

"That's *Will You Stay* tour Kenji," she says.

"And that one?" I point to the cutout in the corner of her room.

"That's *All of Us* tour Kenji."

It's a little difficult to take care of business with Kenji's cardboard face grinning at me from five feet away, but I do my best.

"So," I say when I get back out there, because I literally can't keep from saying something. "You really like Kenji."

"Yes."

"You, like, *really* like Kenji."

"It's not like I want to date him," she replies.

"But . . . then what else is there?"

"What else is there besides wanting to date someone? It's fucking sad you have to ask that."

"Not like—obviously I know in general, I just meant, like, in . . . boy band circumstances."

"He is my small son," Iris says, and even though the words coming from her lips are completely ridiculous, her expression is 100 percent serious. "I want him to be happy, and healthy, and to be with people he cares about, and do things that he loves. I want him to know how much he's appreciated and how much he's changed people's lives by . . . just being who he is. And by helping us be who we are."

"Oh."

It's quiet for a while after that. I make an editing mark on Iris's paper, and then once again the words bubble up without my consent.

"It must be hard," I say. "Your parents . . . I mean, them not knowing. About Paige and stuff."

"Oh great," Iris says, looking up from her computer. "Is Straighty McHetero going to give me a lecture on *living my truth*?"

"I—" I blink. "You're right. I'm sorry. None of my business."

Iris frowns down at her notes, and it's quiet for a bit. Until she says, "Sorry. I shouldn't assume you're straight. All I know is that you have an obvious boner for Gideon Prewitt."

I sputter. "I—I don't—"

"Though to be fair you could have had boners for people of all genders in the past and I wouldn't know."

Before I can respond, Iris points to the wall—the massive TION collage. "Which one is your favorite?"

"Why?"

"I want to know."

"I'm not really . . . familiar with them."

"Look at them. Your heart will tell you your favorite."

I start to smile—I think she's joking—but when I glance over, her eyes are solemn.

So I get up and cross over to the wall, zeroing in on an artsy photo of the boys standing on a bridge.

They all stare back with thoughtful expressions—Kenji's eyebrows are pulled down, a little crease between them, like he's examining me deeply. Me, or the photographer, or whatever person he envisioned one day buying this poster.

"I think . . . I think I like Kenji," I say.

"Huh." Iris comes and stands next to me. "Really? You're not just saying that because you want to ingratiate yourself to me?"

"I don't want to *ingratiate* myself to you, God."

"That was an SAT word."

"I know. Do you want me to congratulate you for using it?"

"Is he really your favorite?"

"I don't know. It might be some kind of subconscious conditioning, since his face is literally all over the room, and, you know, he just watched me pee and everything." Something almost like a smile tugs at Iris's lips. "But . . ." I shrug. "He has a certain . . . something."

She nods. "He does." And we both contemplate Kenji for a moment. Then she crosses over to a bookshelf and grabs a book, returns, and presses it into my hands.

"What's this?" I say, even though *Daring to Dream* is emblazoned across the front, and underneath, *Our Words, Our Voices: The This Is Our Now Official Autobiography*. The title says it all. In more words than are probably necessary.

"The first TION book," Iris says nonetheless. "You can focus on the Kenji chapters if you'd like, but it really helps to understand your favorite in the context of the group."

"Oh." Again, I check, but again, this is not a joke. "Uh. Thanks."

She nods briskly. And then "You should go. I have other homework."

Zoe comes over for dinner that night, and the first thing she does when we get up to my room is zero in on the TION biography, which features a black-and-white photo of the TION boys on the cover, all in varying degrees of pensiveness.

"What's the deal with this?" she says, holding up the book and grinning at me.

"Iris lent it to me."

"Okay, multiple questions."

"Go for it."

"You were hanging out with Iris?"

"We're partners in Brit lit."

"By choice?"

"Kind of? She sort of coerced me into it."

"Redemption arc?"

"Exactly."

"And is this required reading? Is that what really goes on at your school?"

"Obviously not," I say with a grin. "Iris loves them. She's some kind of superfan. She has two cardboard cutouts. She has every piece of branded merchandise they've ever released."

Zoe considers the cover for a moment. "Collectible dolls?"

"Yes."

"Bedsheets?"

"Yes, and apparently they come in king-sized, which boggles the mind."

"Bottle opener?"

"Yeah, Kenji's mouth is where you put the bottle top."

"For real?"

"No. But if it existed, she would own it."

"Well, I guess that's . . . her prerogative. Not everyone has our taste."

We start playing Battle Quest, and it's quiet for a bit until I ask, "Would you buy a Drunk Residential bottle opener?"

"No. We love them because of the music, not because we want Jes Peretta's face on stuff. Iris is obviously trying to fill some void in her life with manufactured pop music."

"Maybe," I say. "She's crazy rich you know. Like private island rich."

Zoe snorts. "They're all private island rich at your school."

"Not really."

Before PLSG, I didn't know how many different kinds of rich there were. I guess I thought of it more as a binary—either you had money, or you didn't. I think Zoe, not having witnessed the various gradations of Having a Boatload of Money, still probably feels like that. But apparently there are many different degrees of richness.

There are kids whose parents are doctors or lawyers—"Just normal, I guess," Sam McKellar said when I asked her about it once. Though to be fair, I think Sam's perception of *normal* is different than my perception of *normal*. Sam's mom works downtown as an accountant for Chase Bank. I'm pretty sure the McKellars don't stock up on five-for-ten frozen meals as often as my family does. They definitely have the luxury to think that the grocery-store brand isn't as good as the name brand. Sudha Prabhu is *normal* by Sam's standards, too—both her parents are cardiologists.

Then there are kids whose families own something, or invented something, or are the CEOs of something. "Well-off," according to Sam.

To me, Sam's notion of *well-off* was what I imagined when I thought of stereotypical rich people. They had designer things. They skied. They occasionally suffered from a disregard for consequences, or the crushing weight of trying to live up to their family's expectations. Sometimes both.

If there was a flowchart for *well-off*, it would start with *Is there a child nicknamed "Trey" in your family—called thus because he is the Third?* Yes? Well-off. No? Proceed to next question.

Is there someone in your family with a name that is more than the Third? Callie Ford wins that at PLSG—her brother is Clifford Oscar Ford the Fifth, and they call him "V." Like "five." Like the roman numeral for five.

Does your family own something with their last name on it? Like Amber Brunati. Her family owns a regional chain of fast-food

Italian restaurants called Brunati's Pizza. Lena Ideker's family owns a series of car dealerships—the Ideker Automotive Group. Her dad is on TV on the regular: *Shop Ideker Automotive Group for your new Ford, Volkswagen, Buick, BMW, Hyundai, Subaru, or Volvo!* Lena had her pick for her sixteenth birthday.

Then, past *normal*, past *well-off*, there are kids like Iris Huang.

Where either you don't even really know what their parents do or how they made their money, or else their wealth is so conspicuous that you know exactly how because their name is on a skyscraper or something. "Next level," Sam said. "Just . . . a whole other dimension of rich."

The kind of rich where even rich kids think you're rich.

I can't help but wonder how Iris's family got so rich, so I get online that night and Google a number of combinations of the name *Huang*, and *fortune, Chicago, business, rich*, etc.

Finally, I text Sam McKellar.

Hey do you know what Iris's parents do?

She replies with a link to an article:

MERGER OF BEICHEN RETAIL GROUP AND OMNI INDUSTRIES. "Yun Huang, CEO of Shanghai-based Beichen Group, expands internationally following the acquisition and incorporation of Omni Industries properties. . . ."

Why the interest in Iris? Sam texts. *Looking for a sugar mama?*

I send her the eye-roll emoji back.

If you're in the market, she's a prime pick I guess. She could literally afford to buy us all, put us on a preserve, and hunt us for sport.

Lovely, I reply.

sixteen

Del, Caris, and I go to the theater after school on Monday to take measurements for the costumes.

For the girls, we're supposed to get measurements for the bust, waist, and hips. For the guys, we need measurements for the neck, chest, sleeve, waist, hips, and—the entry on the wikiHow page that gave me the most pause—inseam.

"Measure from the crotch to the back of the heel, where you want your pants to end," it said.

Measure from the crotch, it said.

Thank goodness, Mr. Palmer's plans for setting the play in the present day meant that certain people—the lovers and the court for the most part—would just wear clothes they already had. Or clothes we could buy, like, based off their normal sizes. So that lowered the number of crotches that I would need to be around.

Not that I was pathologically afraid of crotches. I just . . . like to know a person before I *measure from the crotch to the back of the heel where I want the pants to end.*

I start by measuring Keara Shelton, who's playing Hippolyta, for the wedding dress that Del's designing.

While we're measuring people, they're going through the first entrance of the fairies on stage. Before Titania and Oberon show up for the first time, there's a little scene between Oberon's magical servant Puck and the character scripted as *First Fairy*. Iris.

Puck is being played by a sophomore named Aimee Santo. I don't know her personally, but as is the way at PLSG, I've seen her around. She has short, spiky hair and lines her eyes all the way around with dark liner.

It looks like most people have changed out of their school uniforms for rehearsal—the girls are wearing a variety of yoga pants or soccer shorts. Aimee is wearing black jeans with holes in the knees and a big, baggy T-shirt.

Iris is still in full uniform—jacket on, even—and they make an odd picture, standing there onstage. Like Iris is Aimee's weirdly formal aunt or something.

"How now, spirit?" Aimee says. *"Whither wander you?"*

Iris holds up her script and begins to read in a complete monotone, with little pause for punctuation: *"Over hill over dale thorough bush thorough brier over park over pale thorough flood thorough fire."* She speeds up even more:

"Idowandereverywhereswifterthanthemoon'ssphere—"

"Let's hold for a sec," Mr. Palmer says. "Iris, how about we try slowing it down a little?"

He works through the scene with Iris and Aimee a bit, but before long they move on to Gideon's and Paige's entrance. We don't get to stick around to see it, though—Del gestures Caris and me out into the hallway, where we find the Mechanicals running through their lines, and we set about getting their measurements.

We head back to the shop when we're done, and as we're wrapping up for the day, Iris stops by.

She gives Del the briefest glance and then approaches me. "They said to stop by here for measurements?"

"You could've come tomorrow," I say.

"Or never," Del adds. I look over to see if she's joking, but she appears absorbed in her work, pinning scraps of fabric to a dress form.

"I'll measure you," I say, noting the glare Iris sends Del's way.

I pull out my tape and start in on it.

"I saw the scene you guys were doing earlier," I say as I move Iris's limbs this way and that.

"Ugh" is Iris's reply.

"Sounded like you were a little . . . rushed."

"This whole thing is stupid," she says darkly.

"You must've done well enough in the audition to get the part."

"That's different."

"How?"

"It was fine being ridiculous when there were just two people in the room, but here everyone's . . . looking at me being ridiculous."

"It's not being ridiculous, it's acting."

"Oh, thanks. That helps."

I finish the rest of the measurements in silence.

"What?" Iris says when I'm done.

"Nothing."

"No, say whatever you're thinking."

I shrug. I can't help but think of the car ride home from rock climbing, of Iris's quiet admission: *I love her. You can't just turn it off like that.*

"The play is important to Paige, right?" I say. "Like, she's pretty into it?"

"Yes."

"So . . . maybe. You could, like . . . take it seriously and do really well, and . . . show her that it's important to you, too."

She blinks at me. "Why would I do that? Why would it matter?"

I shrug again and loop up my measuring tape.

"I don't even know what this stupid scene is about," she says before I can move away.

"What do you mean?"

"The scene. Like the actual words." Her voice drops. "I don't . . . actually . . . get what they're talking about."

"Oh. Well, that's . . . it's not so complex, is it? You're in the woods, doing your fairy thing—like, running errands for Titania, I guess—when Puck shows up. And you know him, you've heard of him before, and he likes that, so he starts telling you stories about funny stuff he's done. Sort of like he's trying to impress you, but sort of just because that's how he is. That's all."

She looks at me, suspicious. "Did you get the version where it says it all in normal speak on the opposite page? Because we were supposed to get the Folger edition."

"I did get the Folger."

"So how do you understand what they're saying?"

"I don't know. I just read it."

She's still eyeing me suspiciously. "Okay," she says, and then "Help me."

"Sorry?"

Iris takes a deep breath. "Will. You. Help. Me."

I nod. "Sure."

We break down Iris's dialogue and go through it bit by bit, sitting at the bench in the costume shop even after Caris and Del have left. We practice a few times, too, me stumbling along as Puck in place of Aimee Santo.

When we're finished and we've both set our Folgers aside, I glance over at Iris.

"Can I ask you something?"

"What?" She looks suspicious again.

"How did Lucas make it into TION if technically he got eliminated in week three of *Pop Talent*?"

Iris's eyes light up.

seventeen

At Iris's behest, I watch a playlist of videos titled "TION *Pop Talent* Journey," which is not only a compilation of the time the This Is Our Now boys spent as contestants on *Pop Talent*, but also a fan edit of this time, meaning there's a lot of slow-motion replays and editorializing with emotional music.

I can't help it. I fucking love it.

Should I listen to their albums in any particular order? I text Iris that night.

She immediately texts back a detailed order for listening.

I find myself in the studio the next afternoon, working on construction in between taking measurements of the people we missed yesterday. Including Gideon.

He stands in front of me expectantly. "I'm ready for you to measure me!"

Measure from the crotch to the back of the heel, where you want your pants to end.

I glance across the room at Caris, who's chatting with Aimee

Santo. "Or, you know," I say, "I could just . . . like, you could measure yourself and read the numbers off to me, if you want."

"No, I want the full costume shop experience."

"Okay."

Okay.

I unspool the measuring tape. Then I step closer and look down at the expanse of Gideon's chest. He has one too many buttons unbuttoned on his shirt. I think. Maybe it's exactly the right number of buttons.

"Claudia?"

I startle.

"Am I . . . supposed to do something?" Gideon says, looking at me curiously.

"No, just stand there. I mean, you could put your arms out. Like out to the sides."

Gideon obeys. I go about gathering his measurements as quickly and non-awkwardly as I can.

Del comes in during, her arms full of fabric.

"Hello, Delilah," Gideon says, and I'm sure it's accompanied by a sunny smile, but I'm too busy fumbling with the measuring tape around his waist.

"Am I interrupting?" she says in that smoky voice of hers.

"No," I say as Gideon says definitively:

"Yes."

I mark down his waist measurement and then look at the remaining empty spot on the sheet, which I'd purposefully skipped.

I don't want to measure that. There's no way. It's not happening. I can feel my face getting hot already.

"What's your inseam?" I blurt.

"Huh?"

"Your inseam. Like the inside of your legs, like the measurement for—"

He blinks at me. "We can't be properly sure unless you measure it, right?"

"It's the second number of your pant size," Del says, crossing over to us. "Put poor Claudia out of her misery, she obviously doesn't want to get anywhere near"—she gestures widely at Gideon's lower half—"all that."

He tells me the number, and I record it, and Del moves off to the other side of the room.

"Sorry," Gideon says after a moment. "If I made you uncomfortable. I was just trying to be funny. I'm sorry."

"It's okay."

"Noah says I shouldn't try to be funny but I don't know why. I'm the funniest person I know," he declares. "Except for you. You're funnier than me."

"That's not saying much, because you're not funny at all," I murmur, and then blanch. That's not the kind of joke you make around someone you don't know very well. But Gideon just grins at me.

"Maybe I haven't found the right market for my humor. Maybe I'd be really big overseas."

"Maybe."

I put Gideon's sheet on the clipboard with the others. When I look up, he's fiddling with the edges of a bolt of fabric sitting on the table.

"So," he says.

"So?"

"Maybe I'll see you around this weekend."

"Maybe." Like, if he goes to the same grocery store my parents go to? Or if he happens to be in the mood for a Pinky's sub.

"Cool." Gideon smiles as Aimee approaches.

"Hey, can I talk to you?" she says.

"Sorry." I turn back to my stuff. "I'll leave you guys to it."

"I meant you," she says.

"Oh. Uh, yeah. Sure."

"I'll see you upstairs," Gideon says to Aimee. "And I'll see you this weekend!" he says to me with a grin.

"What's up?" I say as Aimee pulls out the stool from the table and takes a seat.

"I heard you helped Iris with her dialogue."

"I, uh. I mean, not really, we just talked about it some."

"Well, whatever you did, you made her not suck. She said you helped her make sense of it."

"She did?"

"Uh-huh." Aimee holds up her script. "So you want to make sense of some more stuff?"

eighteen

PARTY 8PM TONIGHT MELISSA PRATT'S HOUSE!!!!!!

I stare at the message from Gideon in the hall between classes on Friday. It's probably a mass text, and I don't want to be the loser who responds thinking it was just for them. So I don't reply.

IT WILL BE REALLY FUN, Gideon sends a little later.

LIKE VERY FUN CLAUDIA shortly follows.

I blink.

And open up a reply:

Are the capital letters supposed to sway me?

THEY'RE SUPPOSED TO CONVEY THE LEVEL OF FUN. WHICH WILL BE UNPRECEDENTED.

What will be so fun about it?

YOU'LL BE THERE

I smile. And against my better judgment, type:

Yeah okay.

EXCELLENT. GET READY. SO MUCH FUN.

* * *

It's not fun.

Or, really, I guess it's more accurate to say that I'm unable to assess the party's level of fun, because I don't make it past the front steps of Melissa Pratt's house. Gideon and Noah are standing outside when I arrive, next to Alicia and Sudha, who are sitting on a decorative wrought-iron bench underneath an arched trellis.

"Hey!" Gideon waves when I approach. "Hey, hey," and he holds up a hand for a high five, which I slap.

"What's going on?"

"We're just figuring out a game plan," Gideon says. "I've deemed this party unacceptable."

I blink. "You said it would be unprecedented levels of fun."

He shrugs. "Unacceptable is unacceptable."

"What's wrong with it?"

"The cups," Gideon says resolutely.

"The cups," I repeat. I glance at the girls—Sudha is on her phone, but Alicia looks exasperated. Noah is looking at Gideon expectantly, eyebrows raised, amusement pulling at his lips.

"They have Styrofoam cups instead of plastic cups," Gideon explains. "Styrofoam cups are for warm drinks, but they're serving cold drinks in them. It makes no sense. I can't be a part of that."

"So . . ."

"So we're going somewhere else! Where should we go? What do you want to do?"

I don't particularly want to go into Melissa Pratt's house, but I did drive all the way here. And I put on a shirt with like an actual shape to it, which goes against my nonuniform, nonwork clothes policy of maximum comfort and minimal effort.

"Uh, I don't know. Are there . . . other parties? It's not like we can go to a bar." I figure they want to drink, but Gideon shakes his head.

"We're not trying to *party* party," he says. "I don't drink. And neither does Noah."

"There was an incident," Noah says.

"The RumChata Incident of freshman year," Gideon explains.

"What happened?"

"We don't speak of it. But we've both sworn off alcohol forever."

"I mean, not forever," Noah says.

"*Forever,*" Gideon says emphatically. "We took a vow."

"We did take a vow," Noah admits with a sheepish smile.

We go to Steak 'n Shake instead. Sudha opts to stay at Melissa's, but Alicia comes, too.

We get a booth in the corner. Noah heads off to the restroom, and for a moment, it's silent. Alicia is checking her phone. Gideon is staring at the menu. The sights and sounds of Steak 'n Shake press on around us.

"What are you going to get?" Gideon says eventually, looking up at me.

"Um. They have a cookies 'n cream shake that's really good."

His face lights up. "That's Noah's favorite, too!"

Silence again.

"So, uh . . . how long have you known him?" I ask finally, because Gideon asked me a question, and so etiquette-wise, I'm probably obligated to ask one back.

"Noah?" he says. "Forever."

I raise an eyebrow.

"No, really. Our moms have been friends since they were in school, and we grew up together. Like literally, since birth. They put matching outfits on us and propped us next to each other for photos before we could even sit up. So I don't remember meeting him or becoming friends with him. We just always were. You know, like one of those intrinsic facts you've always known about yourself. Like you don't really remember learning your own name, do you? I'm Gideon Prewitt, and Noah Edelman is my best friend."

"I feel like that about my best friend," I say. "But I remember becoming friends with her. It was in preschool. So, you know. I was able to sit up on my own and stuff."

Gideon smiles.

Noah returns, and we order, and eventually we're settled in with milk shakes. Noah and Alicia are talking about some article they'd both read online when Gideon takes a long pull from his shake and then leans forward, resting his arms on the tabletop.

"So I wanna know more about Battle Quest."

"Sorry?"

"Your game. The game you play. Are there fairies in it? Like in *Midsummer*? Could I be king of the fairies in the game?"

"No fairies. None of the races have wings in Battle Quest."

"The races? Like . . . wizard and stuff?"

"Those are classes. There are races—like human, or elf, or troll. But then there are classes, which is like your job or your skill. Maestro, mage, busker, archer, notary . . ."

"Notary? Like a guy who stamps documents?"

"Notary signore. They're a magic class. They use symbols and stuff. To be honest, no one really plays it unless they absolutely have to. In order to get your cavalier past thirty you have to level your notary up to fifteen."

"Which means . . ."

"Um . . . so you can have more than one class on the same character, but you have to build it all the way up, like go through all the levels to gain all the skills. It's kind of like . . . earning degrees in different things? So you can't become a cavalier without a notary minor?"

"Huh." Gideon considers this for a moment, chewing on his straw. "What's your character like?"

"She's a thaumaturge. It's another magic class."

"What's her name?"

"Viola Constantinople. It was the first name I thought of."

"The first name you thought of was Viola Constantinople?"

"Yes."

"I like the way you think," he says with a grin. "Do you play any other games?"

"Other MMOs?"

"Sure."

"No. Just Battle Quest."

"Why?"

"I don't know. I like it. My brother and sister play it, too. And I got Zoe into it." I realize Gideon has no idea who Zoe is. "My—my best friend. From Springdale. We all play together sometimes—my sister's husband joins in, and we raid, do the higher level dungeons and stuff."

"You have a brother and a sister?"

"Yeah. Both older." I fumble with my straw. "Do you have siblings?"

"One sister. Victoria. She's six years younger."

"Did you ever want a brother too?"

"I already have one, remember?" he says, nodding toward Noah.

I smile.

"So," he says. "Do you and your brother and sister and everybody all get together and play? Like on a big TV or something?"

"Oh, no. Everyone has to play on their own screen. At their own house, usually. I mean, Zoe comes over, obviously, but my sister and brother-in-law live in Indianapolis."

"So you're at your house, and they're at their house . . ."

"Yeah, but we usually talk online, like Skype or whatever while we're playing. And we can all text chat in the game and see each other's characters. We get on there and it's like . . ."

Like we're all hanging out. Existing in this alternate shared space.

Time passes in the game—three minutes in Aradana is equal to one hour of real time. So there's dusk. Dawn. Sunsets. Stars. There's weather. There are rivers and lakes and forests and villages and . . . other people, all populating this strange virtual world. It's not tangible. But somehow, when we're there, when we play—it doesn't feel *real*, exactly, it doesn't feel like real life, but it feels like what it is. Something separate, and ours.

"We all like different parts of it," I say after a pause. "My brother likes raiding, my sister likes the side quests and stuff. And I guess I like the idea that . . . you know, that we're somewhere apart but still together." I take a long drink of my shake, and when I look back up, Gideon's gaze is fixed on me. There's something soft about his expression that I don't know what to do with, so I take another

110

drink and then say, "There's also this wizard we really want to fight."

"Sorry?"

"So in the recent expansion—that's like where they add new features and new quests to the game—the rumor is that if you follow a series of side quests correctly, you unlock a secret area in the game: the Island of Souls. On the Island of Souls is the ultimate boss, the Lord of Wizard. If you battle him and win, untold riches await you."

"Untold riches? What does that even mean?"

"I don't know. No one's actually beat him yet."

"For real?"

"Well, there are rumors online of people doing it but nothing definitive. We've been trying really hard to get there though."

"I'm sure you'll do it," Gideon says, swirling the straw around in his shake. "Can anyone play?"

"Sure."

"I want to. Let's go to your house and play right now."

"Well, I mean, you have to get the game and, like, design your character and all that. And like I said, you have to play on your own computer, it's not like we could all play on mine or something."

"Oh." He looks disappointed. But only for a moment. "Let's see a movie then. Noah, movies?"

Noah starts to search on his phone as I look askance at Gideon. "It's, like, ten thirty already."

"So? It's Friday."

"Won't your mom care if you're out that late?"

"She's at work right now," he says.

"Gideon's mom is a *very* successful exotic dancer," Noah adds, eyes on his phone.

"Dude."

"Gideon's mom is an ob-gyn," Noah amends.

"Yes, she's busy bringing new life into this world. And it conveniently coincides with my little sister sleeping over at a friend's house tonight, which means I don't have to go home, which means we should see a movie."

"What about your dad? Where's he?" I ask before I can think better of it.

"Tokyo," Gideon replies. "On business."

"He's a *very* successful exotic dancer," Noah says, and I smile.

"Pulling in some serious yen?"

"So many."

"Guess there's not much he can do about you pushing curfew then," I say. "But unfortunately, my mom is not actively pulling a human out of another human, and my dad is in this time zone, so I should probably get home soon."

Gideon grins.

nineteen

When I get to the costume shop on Monday, Del holds up two over-sized fake flowers—one purple and one white.

"For me?" I say, and she makes a face.

"You want to run these upstairs? Give them to Tara Schmidt. Do you know her? She's stage manager."

I know Tara Schmidt in the same way that everyone knows everyone at PLSG. I have had at least three classes with her, and I know at least two things about her—in this case, that she plays the piccolo and is stage manager for this play.

I take the flowers and head upstairs. When I duck into the theater, it appears they're running through the start of act one. I find Tara sitting toward the front with Mr. Palmer, a big binder open in her lap.

She lights up when she sees the flowers and whispers a quick "Tell Del thanks!" before shifting laser focus back to the proceedings onstage.

When I leave the theater, someone calls my name. Paige is standing at the end of the hall, and she gestures me her way.

"Got a second?"

I head toward her.

"I heard that you're helping people with their lines," Paige says when I'm closer.

"Um . . . not on purpose?"

"But you get it." She's got a script in one hand and she holds it up. "Like what it's trying to say."

"Sort of? I don't know. I just read it like everyone else."

I also watched the movie adaptations I could find online. And I read some articles about it. Just casual research. I did the same thing when I wanted to know more about the *Titanic* or collected filmography of Fred Astaire. When I'm interested in a thing, I want to know about that thing. Extensively.

It is a process that may or may not be happening right now with a band called This Is Our Now. Hard to say. It's still in the early stages.

"Maybe you could help me and Gideon with our first scene," Paige says, gesturing to an open classroom door a few feet away.

Ask the director, he knows what he's doing, I think. "If you want," I say instead, and follow her inside.

I watch Paige and Gideon's first scene together—the meeting of Titania and Oberon in the woods. They've been fighting over the fate of a changeling boy; Titania was friends with the boy's mom and wants to raise him, but Oberon wants him to join his crew instead. As a result of their fight, everything in the world—weather, seasons, time—has gone sort of haywire.

Paige and Gideon have both changed out of their uniforms. Paige is wearing athletic shorts and a T-shirt from some kind of charity run. Gideon is wearing jeans and a patterned shirt. Neither of them look like fairy royalty. And yet, when they start the scene, they each adopt a kind of . . . royal air about them.

Paige is good. Very good. I don't remember seeing her in any school plays previously, but she really seems to know what she's doing. She doesn't trip up around the language. She's expressive and confident.

And I don't know what I expected from Gideon, but as soon as they start, he goes from goofy and dimply to . . . strong and commanding. He seems taller. His voice seems deeper.

They seem like . . . well, like the King and Queen of some kingdom. The fairy kingdom, in this case.

"What do you think?" Paige says when they finish.

"It's good," I say, because it really was.

But Paige's expression urges me on, because it seems like good is not good enough for her.

"It just . . . I don't know. Really, I don't know anything about anything, but I guess I'd just say . . . it seems really serious right now."

"It is serious, isn't it?" Gideon says. "They're fighting."

"Yeah, but . . . okay, don't get me wrong, their relationship is obviously super dysfunctional. But I feel like they kind of live for the drama, you know? Like they kind of love it? That's part of their dynamic. And also . . . it seems like there's genuine feeling there, between them. Or they would just get bored and move on, instead of always coming back for more." I make a face. "At least to me. That's how I read it, I guess."

"No, that makes sense," Paige says, nodding. "Right?"

Gideon nods.

"How would you play that in the scene?" Paige says. "What would you do?"

"I'm not an actor."

"But what would you want to see?"

I shrug. "I don't know. Like . . . sparks, I guess. Almost like they're sparring. But . . . in a hot way."

Inwardly I cringe. Sparring in a hot way. Brilliant.

But Paige just grins. "Okay. Yeah."

They start the scene over.

There's a back-and-forth this time. There's more fire to it. Gideon grins on "*Am not I thy lord?*" and Paige's eyes widen, she holds a hand to her heart, feigning surprise.

"*Then I must be thy lady.*"

She's sharp from there, calling Oberon out for courting Hippolyta, describing all the repercussions that their fight has had on the mortal world. But she softens, talking about the mother of the changeling boy, the time they spent together before her death. It's sweet, and sad. Melancholy, even as she glances to and from the script for lines.

Gideon's standing tall and proud at the beginning of that last speech, but by the end of it, it's almost as if he too has softened. He steps closer to Paige, reaches for her wrist, and clasps it lightly. When he speaks, his voice is almost gentle:

"*How long within this wood intend you stay?*"

"*Perchance till after Theseus' wedding day,*" she says, and turns to him, eyes wide and imploring. "*If you will patiently dance in our round and see our moonlight revels, go with us.*" A slight shake of her head. "*If not, shun me, and I will spare your haunts.*"

It's good. This is good stuff.

Yes, my brain says.

Gideon looks at Paige for a moment. Drifts closer, like he almost can't help it. Paige rests a hand against his chest, and for a second it looks as if they're going to kiss.

ALSO NO, my brain replies.

They linger for a moment, just inches away from each other, until Gideon speaks: "*Give me that boy and I will go with thee*," and suddenly it's like he flipped a switch. Paige pushes him away, all fire and brimstone.

"*Not for thy fairy kingdom—Fairies, away! We shall chide downright if I longer stay*." And she storms offstage, which, in this case, takes her just a few feet to the right, before she turns and looks at me expectantly.

They both do, like they weren't just about to make out in front of me.

"Yeah," I say, and my voice comes out a little too loud. "Yeah, like that."

Paige beams.

twenty

Lena Ideker hosts a party for the cast and crew on Friday night.

"All these freaking cast bonding activities," Iris said when I mentioned it after rehearsal on Wednesday. She had come to the shop to go over her scene with Puck again. "I don't want to bond. I specifically want to not bond. What's the opposite of bond?"

"Alienate?"

"I want to alienate."

"Well, you're pretty good at it."

"*Hey.*"

I grinned.

Iris didn't say if she was coming or not, so it's a bit of a surprise to see her standing in Lena's massive kitchen, holding a soda and glaring openly at the room.

I consider going over to her when Gideon intercepts me.

"Claudia! You're here!"

"Yeah. It said cast and crew, right?" *Right?*

"It did. And you are. Cast and crew, I mean. Or crew, specifically. Do you want something to drink?"

"I'm good."

"We're hanging out in the family room," he says. "Noah and other people. Del's here, too! She never comes out. You should say hi."

I follow Gideon to the family room, where indeed Noah and Del and a few other people—Alicia, Paige, Madison Lutz, and a couple guys who are both Mechanicals in the show—have congregated, sprawling out on a giant U-shaped leather sectional. I've never seen a couch that big before, but apparently they exist.

There's a massive TV hanging on the opposite wall—more like a small movie screen—and it's currently showing the opening credits of a Pixar movie.

"You weren't supposed to pick until I got back!" Gideon says.

"Majority rules," Del replies. She's holding a cup of something in one hand and a TV remote in the other. She holds the drink up to me in acknowledgment when I sink down onto the cushion next to her. "We also decided we need popcorn and we voted you go find some," she says to Gideon, "since you're the only person here who actually likes Lena."

"*Delilah*," Paige chides from Del's other side, but Gideon jumps up.

"I will not return without popcorn. Who's with me?"

Paige looks toward Gideon, smiling. "I'll go," she says, getting up, and they disappear into the other room.

It's quiet for a moment, the opening credits ending, the movie starting, but then I catch Madison leaning over to Alicia in my peripheral vision. "Would *literally* not return without popcorn," Madison says in a low voice, and they both snicker as Alicia pulls out her phone.

Del must notice me looking, because she tilts her head toward me.

"They started a Heartmark account," she says. "JustGideon-PrewittThings. It's where people post all the strange things Gideon says or does."

I frown, and Madison shakes her head.

"Not in a mean way, not to make fun," she says. "We love him, obviously. It's just . . . sometimes he says or does something so random it's like he's a life-form from another planet who's failing at blending into life on earth but trying, like, *really hard*, and you just have to share it with other people."

I glance at Noah, because surely he wouldn't let people make fun of his best friend in earnest, but he just nods. "It's true. He does at least one JustGideonPrewittThing a day."

"Like what?"

The group explodes with them, the movie temporarily forgotten.

"He doesn't like green M&M's even though they all taste the same."

"One time he said towels shouldn't be too soft."

"I've seen him cry at two movies, and those movies were *Spy Kids* and *Spy Kids 2*."

Del chimes in late: "He prefers cereal to be soggy. I've heard him talk about it. He pours the milk in and legit lets it sit for like ten minutes before eating it. If I didn't know him, I'd be, like, what kind of serial killer shit is that—"

"Pun intended?" Noah says with a grin.

"Ugh, no. I mean straight-up, weaving a sweater out of your shower-drain hair, serial killer nonsense. But with him, it's not, it's just . . ." She shrugs. "A Gideon Prewitt Thing."

I blink. "I don't know what to do with this information."

"But aren't you glad it's been collected somewhere for future use?" Madison says with a grin.

"If you ask me," Del says, "the most valuable piece of information is to never get him started on the fact that he has the same name as a Harry Potter character."

"Hashtag it's spelled different, hashtag I had it first," Madison and Alicia say in unison, and then break into giggles.

Paige and Gideon return eventually, when focus has returned to the movie, and they're each holding several bags of microwave popcorn. They hand them out and then sink down onto the free section of the sofa across from Del and me, whispering to each other about something.

I realize I am not very interested in watching this movie.

"I'm gonna grab a drink," I say to Del, and she *hmm*s noncommittally, more engrossed in Pixar than I expected her to be.

Iris is still in the kitchen when I head back through, though now she's engaged in conversation with Lena and a couple of other girls from our class.

I go to grab a soda off the island in the middle of the kitchen, but I don't really want it, and, anyway, something about Iris's expression puts me on alert.

I can hardly believe it, but the unflappable Iris Huang looks . . . flapped.

"Honestly," Lena is saying, and though she's smiling, it belies the sharpness in her tone. "I don't get why you're even here."

"Yeah and I don't get why your face is like that," Iris replies, but it's not her best, and she seems to know that.

"Why don't you run along and play with your own friends?" Lena says. "Oh. Wait. I know. It's because you don't have any."

"I have friends," Iris says, but it lacks the usual acidity.

"No, Iris. You don't. What you had were people who put up with you so they could hang out with Paige."

Something flashes across Iris's face, just for a second, and then it settles into a blank expression.

But I see it. I see her grip on her drink tightening.

"Name one person who likes you, and not because of Paige, and not because your dad could buy them a Major League baseball team," Lena continues. "Name one person who genuinely, actually, likes you for you."

It would be very easy to walk away right now. Or to stand and do nothing. But it would be very hard to feel okay about that later.

I swallow. And I step forward.

"Me," I say. "I do."

They both look at me. Lena blinks, clearly surprised, but then her lips curve into a smile. "Sorry, who are you?"

She is full of shit, and we all know that, because there are only fifty girls a grade at PLSG, and even I could name all of them. Lena herself sat next to me in chemistry sophomore year, and we were in the same reading group in world literature.

"Iris's friend Claudia." I grab Iris's wrist. "Let's go," I say, and guide her away.

She follows, but when we reach the hallway, she shakes out of my grip roughly.

"I don't—that wasn't necessary," she says with a glare.

"She was being a jerk."

"I didn't need you to do that."

"I was just . . . trying to be nice."

"Well, don't. I don't need you to feel bad for me."

"I don't."

"I don't need you to lie then."

"I didn't."

I'm not entirely sure whether that's the truth. Iris just blinks at me, and I continue anyway. "We're . . . friends. Kind of. Right?"

She's still frowning at me, but it's a different kind of frown, a considering sort of one.

"I . . . guess."

"Okay. So. That's that."

Just because we are newly declared kind-of friends does not mean that Iris wants to spend the rest of the party with me. She disappears after that and I don't see her again.

I don't really feel like going back to the family room (*like watching Gideon and Paige all night*), so I go out to the backyard instead. It's quiet out there and landscaped to high hell. A pool sits in the center of the yard, a big rectangle lit from within and sparkling, though it's too cool to swim. The whole pool deck is in brick, with big cushioned lounge chairs along one side. Ideker Ford must be doing pretty well. That or Ideker Volkswagen, Buick, BMW, Hyundai, Subaru, or Volvo is picking up the slack.

I take a seat on one of the lounge chairs and watch the water ripple until I hear a door open and shut behind me.

I glance over as Gideon sidles up to the chaise next to mine.

"I thought you were coming back," he says.

I shrug. "Just wanted a little quiet."

"Mind if I sit?"

"Why would I mind?"

"Don't want to disturb the quiet," he says with a crooked smile.

I gesture to the seat and he sits, stretching his legs out in front of him. He's got on a pair of old-looking brown leather boots that are kind of at odds with the sneaker-of-the-month culture pervasive at Danforth and PLSG. "Smooth job answering a question with a question by the way. Super ninja deflecting skills."

"I'm a level fifty deflector," I reply.

"Out of how many levels?"

"How many levels do you think?"

"Deflected!" he says, throwing his arms in the air like he's blocking blows. Then he settles back in his chair. "So."

"So . . ."

"If you could have one superpower, what would it be?"

"That's like the most cliché question in the world," I say.

"Because it's a good question!"

"There are literally only two responses. Either you want to fly and that means you're outgoing and free-spirited or whatever, or you want to be invisible and you're an introvert."

"What if I want to do both? What if I want the power of invisible flight?"

"Like Wonder Woman's plane?"

"Yes, I want Wonder Woman to ride me around the sky."

I snort.

"Okay," Gideon says with a grin, "take the normal answers off the table. What non-cliché superpower would you pick?"

"You say yours first."

He presses farther back against the cushion of the chaise and contemplates the sky for a moment. "I would want the power to listen to my favorite songs again for the first time," he says finally.

I look over at him. "Seriously?"

"Is that weird?"

"All the superpowers in the entire universe. Anything you could possibly dream of. And all you want is to listen to your favorite songs again for the first time?"

"Why, what would you pick?"

"No, don't deflect, that's my thing. Why? Why that?"

He shrugs. "It's the best feeling. The first time. Why wouldn't you want to take something you love and go back to the very best part?"

"Maybe I don't think the first part is the best part. Maybe I like the part later on. Hearing a song so many times you know all the little ins and outs of it. Experiencing something so many times that you can just . . . live in it. Maybe I like that better."

He looks at me for a moment and then nods. "Okay. Yeah. I can see that." A pause. "Now you have to pick one. But it has to be unconventional. No flying or invisibility. No super spit."

"Is super spit conventional?"

"You know what I mean. What would you pick?"

I think about it for a moment. "I would want the ability to see the future."

"Why?"

"Because it's sort of an all-encompassing power, isn't it? You could see what numbers are going to win the lottery. What stocks are going up. What choices you should make to have the best life you could ever possibly have."

"I mean, sure you could make money off it, but how would that make it the best life you could possibly have? Beyond money?"

I shrug. "I feel like if you can see the future, you'll never make a wrong decision. Because when it comes time to decide something, you just look into the future of all the possible outcomes, and pick the thing that will lead to the best one."

Gideon considers this for a moment. "I would hate not having surprises," he says finally. "I would hate feeling like everything was predetermined."

"But it's not. You're determining it by . . . looking ahead and picking the best thing."

"Maybe the best thing's not always the best thing. Maybe shitty things have to happen to get you to the right place."

"That sounds like something someone who's never had shitty things happen to them would say."

He frowns. He's about to speak when the door bangs open behind us.

"GIDEON PREWITT, GETTIN' INTO IT," someone bellows.

"That's a way better title for your mixtape," I say as a guy I don't know comes up behind Gideon and engulfs him in a bear hug.

"This dude right here," the guy says, "is a fucking treasure."

I watch Gideon stand and turn to embrace him fully. The guy thumps Gideon soundly on the back, bro-style, but Gideon just hugs him in a surprisingly earnest kind of way.

"You're very drunk," Gideon says when they pull apart.

"Gonna drive me home later?" the guy says.

"Of course."

The guy looks from Gideon to me and then back again, eyes widening. "Did I interrupt?" He drops down to a loud whisper. "Was magic happening?"

Gideon looks embarrassed, meeting my eyes for a second and then looking away. "I mean . . ."

I can't tell if he's embarrassed because magic was not actually happening, or because I'm the person being implicated in the magic.

For a moment, it's very awkwardly silent.

"I, uh, think I'm gonna head back in," I say finally, sliding off my chaise and standing up. "Getting kind of cold out."

"Gideon is very warm," the drunk guy says too loudly. "He's known for. Warmth. If you need someone. To warm you."

Gideon looks like he wants to melt into the ground.

"See you guys inside," I say, and head in.

twenty-one

Zoe is over at our house, gaming with Alex, when I get home from the party.

"You're later than I thought you'd be," she says, setting her laptop aside.

"Wanna play?" Alex says, but Zoe stands, grabbing my arm.

"I want to hear about this party."

So Zoe and I get ready for bed, and I tell her about the party and about Gideon. After the awkwardness of the drunk guy's interruption, I ended up back with the movie-watchers. When Gideon joined us again, minus the drunk guy, he started toward the spot where Del and I were sitting, hovered awkwardly for a moment, and then moved back to the empty spot beside Paige.

"He sounds goofy," Zoe says. We're lying in bed and I've got my teddy bear, Mr. English, in the crook of one arm.

"He is. Kind of. But also not?" I shake my head. I think of Madison's description: *a life-form from another planet who's failing at blending into life on earth but trying, like,* really hard. "He's like a benevolent space prince. From a planet with three suns that are all named after him."

"Really."

"Yeah, and when it rains, they call it the 'prince's tears' in their native tongue, which is so beautiful it makes you cry instantaneously."

Her lips twitch. "Is the space prince looking for a space princess?"

I look up at the ceiling. "If he is, he'll pick someone more suited to his station in life. Like, you know, an imperial senator's kid, or a royal from a neighboring planet. Not a . . . humble trash robot."

"They have trash robots on this planet?"

"They need an infrastructure for waste removal like everyone else."

"And you're the trash robot?"

"I didn't say me exactly. I'm just . . . saying." Magic doesn't happen with trash robots. I think that would be widely accepted on Gideon Prewitt's hypothetical planet.

It's quiet.

"Do you like him though?"

"Everyone likes him."

"Yeah, but do you?"

I fumble with Mr. English's bow tie.

"He has a weird sense of humor," I say. "I like that. And . . ."

"What?"

I shake my head. "Also, his laugh is way too goofy for someone as attractive as he is."

"What's an attractive laugh? Like what would be a suitably hot laugh for him?"

"I don't know." I try to demonstrate. Like some kind of throaty chuckle.

Zoe's shoulders start shaking, suppressing her own laughter.

"What? I'm trying. Like—" I lower it a bit, try to get it deeper and gruffer.

She throws a pillow at me, laughing out loud now. "You sound demented. Truly."

"Thank you. I try."

"What's he look like?"

I blink. I could grab my phone and find any number of pictures of Gideon Prewitt from any number of parties or games or school functions. But I realize that I already have a picture of Gideon in my room. It's from his fifteenth birthday party.

There was a photo booth at the arcade, and everyone was queuing up to take photos with him, like he was some kind of celebrity. I got in line behind Madison and Ainsley and forced my way into their photo op, because there was no way I was going to go into the booth with Gideon Prewitt alone. That was just way too embarrassing. I didn't know him at all. And he was too good-looking. I was certain I'd say something stupid, because when have I ever not said something stupid?

We took four pictures, and when we divided them up, I got the first one, because no one else wanted it. It was the only one you could actually see me in.

Madison and Ainsley and I had crammed ourselves into the booth. Madison sat on Gideon's lap, and Ainsley was squished beside him. And there was me, hunched over in the top corner, mostly obscured.

Madison was grinning at Gideon, Ainsley was pulling a funny

face. Gideon was laughing, his mouth wide, his eyes squeezed shut. You could only see the top of my face, really, the rest of it blocked by Ainsley's head as she leaned forward. But you could tell from my eyes that I was smiling.

I hung this picture in my locker for the remainder of freshman year. Even now it's still tucked into the bottom seam of the bulletin board hanging over my desk. It made no sense, really, to keep it, because I didn't know Gideon then, and I've never been all that close with Madison and Ainsley either.

But I guess it looked how some little part of me wanted things to look. Even if it was just for a second. Like some TV version of high school.

I get out of bed and grab the picture, return, and present it to Zoe.

"It's old," I say. "But it gives you a general jumping-off point."

"Bawww," she says, considering it for a moment. "He's a cutie. Look at his floppy hair."

"He's taller now," I say, even though a photo-booth photo in no way conveys height. "His hair is longer but somehow less floppy, if that makes sense."

She glances over at me. "It's okay if you like him."

"I don't like him."

"You just like his creepy laugh."

"I didn't say creepy."

"You said he is so hot but his laugh is so creepy. You said he laughs like a deranged cartoon villain but you want to have his children."

"Zoe."

She cackles.

twenty-two

Iris comes up to my locker on Monday and thrusts something in front of me.

"Do you want this purse?"

It's a small, coral-colored bag with a long thin strap. I blink at it and then at Iris, who is openly glaring at me.

"Sorry?"

"I got it online. I don't like the color."

"What's wrong with the color?"

"The pictures were shit. I thought it was orange. This is basically pink. I hate pink. I never want to see pink again."

"I . . ."

"Do you want it or not?"

"You could just return it."

"It was final sale."

"I couldn't . . . I mean, maybe you'll change your mind—"

"I will literally throw it away, Claudia."

I take the purse.

"Okay. Geez. Thanks." I look at it. It is definitely a hundred times nicer than my current purse. "Thank you."

She just grunts and heads off down the hall.

I Google the bag that evening. It is indeed on final sale. It also retailed at $498.

I pick it up off my desk, carefully, like it's live ammo. I have never owned any one thing this expensive.

I'm still holding the bag when my mom comes in. It's now in my lap, and I'm petting it absently, like a small dog. Like it's a sentient being.

"Where did that come from?" Mom asks.

"A girl from school. She didn't want it anymore."

"It still has tags."

"It was final sale."

Mom narrows her eyes. "Are you in a Bling Ring?"

"Sorry?"

"Like on TV. When the kids break into celebs' houses, steal people's Rolexes and whatnot."

"I'm not in a Bling Ring," I say.

The corners of her lips twitch. "Good. Though I can't decide if I'm relieved or disappointed."

"Disappointed?"

She wiggles her eyebrows. "I mean, you could've stolen me a Rolex." And then, "Make sure you do something nice for the friend with the purse," she calls over her shoulder as she heads out.

twenty-three

I don't know if watching the TION documentary counts as doing something nice for Iris, but I watch it regardless.

Normally I would invite Zoe over for this kind of thing, but I think about what she said when I mentioned Iris liking them—*She's obviously trying to fill some void in her life with manufactured pop music.* I'm not trying to fill any kind of void. But . . . I can't help it. I like TION. I like their music. It's upbeat and happy, and even when it's not—even when it's some kind of cheesy ballad—it works, somehow. There's an earnestness to it and also some kind of element of . . . fantasy, I guess. They're creating a world where you dance all night long and party till dawn and drive with the windows down and kiss in the rain, and maybe it's not realistic, but it's appealing. Maybe it's a little like the photo-booth picture from Gideon's birthday party—a snapshot of a different life. Some kind of idealized version of how things could be.

Zoe got into Battle Quest because of me, and I got into Drunk Residential because of her, and we've gone back and forth so many times over the years, trading interests and introducing each other to new stuff. But this is one thing that I don't think she'll understand.

This is one thing, ironically, that I can talk to Iris about.

It's remarkable—Iris could go on for hours about TION. If I just barely bring them up in conversation, she'll show me videos of old interviews, behind-the-scenes posts, screenshots of the boys' tweets from days or months or years ago. She has an almost alarming knowledge of what any one of the TION boys are doing at any given moment—it's easier, I guess, because they're touring right now, but she knows that Kenji and Lucas are in Los Angeles while the other boys are staying in Sacramento before the show there. She follows an array of TION update accounts, all the while disparaging update accounts, which *shouldn't be trusted, but still monitored nonetheless.*

"I'm going to start an update account for myself," I say at school on Wednesday. Brit lit has been canceled so we have a free period.

"No one would follow it," Iris says, not looking up from her homework.

"Thanks."

"Just being honest."

It's quiet for a bit as we both work.

"So . . . I watched the TION movie the other day," I say eventually, eager to shift to something that's not calculus homework.

Iris looks up with a frown. "You should've told me."

"Why?"

"We could've watched it together."

"I . . . figured you'd seen it."

"Of course I've seen it. I love it. I would live in that movie if I could." A pause. "It's just . . . fun sharing fandom stuff with other people."

I nod. And suddenly I recall a conversation at Amber's Pink Party—Ainsley and Madison discussing a band that had just appeared on a late-night show. *Kenji looked damn good,* Madison had said, but Ainsley had disagreed. *What was that jacket? He looked like a disco ball.*

"I think Ainsley and Madison like TION, too."

Iris makes a face. "Ainsley says she only likes *Will You Stay* tour Kenji. It's insulting."

"Why?"

"If you only like one version of your favorite, then they're not your favorite," she says primly, and I can't really argue with that.

I go to the auditorium to give a few costume pieces to Tara during rehearsal the next day, and to my surprise, Mr. Palmer spots me and gestures me over.

He's onstage, going through a couple of fixes with the couples for their big scene, but he leaves them with a "take five" and leads me off to the side.

"You're Claudia, yes?" he says.

"That's me."

"You've been doing a little coaching, from what I've heard. A little *text work*, as we say."

I blink. Am I going to get in trouble? For like . . . horning in on directorial territory?

"Not on purpose, I just . . . you know, a couple people asked me about stuff—"

"No, I think it's fantastic," Mr. Palmer says. "I love the initiative. And I would absolutely love it if you have some time to maybe do a little bit of one-on-one coaching with, uh, with our lovely Helena." He gestures to where Lena is standing, chatting with the guy playing Demetrius.

Lena, who I had an awkward confrontation with in the kitchen of her own house at the last cast get-together. Lena, who pretended not to know who I am, because I am so far beneath her notice.

"I think she would really benefit from some . . . close reading of the text," Mr. Palmer continues.

What can I say, really? *No thanks, I'd rather do literally anything else.* I guess it's for the good of the production, at least.

"Um . . . sure. Okay."

"Excellent. I'll have a chat with her after rehearsal today. Thank you, Claudia! This'll be a big help."

"Hopefully you can work miracles, because from what I've heard, she's been a total disaster," Del says when I mention my new assignment from Mr. Palmer. She's working on Mustardseed's bodice, and Gideon and Noah are keeping her company, though they should both be off rehearsing their monologues.

"It hasn't been that bad," Gideon says.

Del snorts. "I heard she can't remember her lines, so she keeps paraphrasing and making shit up."

"To be fair, she does have a lot of lines."

Noah makes a face. "She's been lobbying to make the *l* in 'Helena' capital in the program so it's HeLena, because it would be 'so funny, like do you get it? Do you get why it's funny?'" His Lena impression is startlingly true to life.

"I mean, I guess it's accurate," Del says. "A mashup of her name and where she's from. Lena plus hell."

I let out a choked burst of laughter before I can stop myself.

Gideon grins but still manages to look disapproving. "She's trying really hard, I think."

"You know, her dad donated money for the production," Del says.

"Why, Delilah," Noah says, fake scandalized, "are you implying that's why she got the part?"

"It's not *not* why she got the part, that's all I'm saying," Del replies with a knowing look.

I have my first meeting with Lena after school the next day.

She doesn't acknowledge anything that happened at her party. She just smiles pleasantly at me when I walk up to her in the hall of the arts building and starts chatting about rehearsals as we get situated in the same small classroom where I saw Paige and Gideon run their first scene.

We start going through lines, beginning with her first scene, where Helena runs into Lysander and Hermia as they're making plans to run away and get married.

I read her first cue: *"Godspeed, fair Helena! Whither away?"*

"Call you me 'fair'?" she says in sort of a broad, generally enthusiastic tone. *"That 'fair' again unsay. Demetrius loves your fair. O happy fair!"*

We get through Helena's first big speech and then stop to discuss. How it's not like Helena is just having a nice chat with Hermia— she's upset because the guy she's into likes Hermia instead. "She wants to know what Hermia's doing to get Demetrius to like her," I explain.

Lena rolls her eyes. "I mean, I get it, sort of. I guess I just don't really relate to her at all. She's throwing herself at this guy who's not into her in the slightest. It's pathetic." She examines her nails. "She should get with Theseus, at least he's a duke."

"Theseus is engaged to Hippolyta."

"Engaged is not married, that's what my mom always says."

I have to stifle a smile.

"It is kind of messed up when you think about it," I say. "Lysander and Demetrius both get put under spells to fall in love with Helena, but Lysander's gets taken off, and Demetrius's doesn't. So maybe that's actually the only reason he likes her at the end."

"She deserves better, that's all I'm saying," Lena says, and then picks up her script. "But I guess I'm stuck with her."

We go through the rest of the scene, breaking down Helena's monologue at the end, and while it's hard to get Lena to sound anything other than generally upbeat, she seems to be making some sense of it at least.

"Mr. Palmer says we should meet again next week," Lena says when we're gathering up our things to go. I think she's trying to sound casual. "Just to brush up a few more spots. But you're probably working with other people, too, right?"

"I . . ."

"Because it's not like I need special help."

I nod. "Sure."

"To be honest, this is kind of amateur stuff. I just wrapped up a *professional* acting job, you know."

"Really."

"It was a commercial for my dad's company." She waves a hand. "Not like I've never done one before, but it's been a long time. It was all fine and good when I was younger—like that always helps, you know, plug a cute little kid in there, up the *aww* factor or whatever—but then when you're in junior high it's just not the same, you know? So my dad said I had to wait until I was eighteen till I could do another one, and then I could be proper eye candy."

I text Zoe this direct quote that night.

I'm sorry, I can't respond, she replies, *because my brain has spontaneously combusted.*

Right?

Gross-out city, Zoe says.

Wrong on many levels.

The levels have levels of wrongness.

twenty-four

There is an annual fall carnival called Fall Fun Fest—lovingly referred to as Triple F—that is an oddly big deal at Danforth and PLSG. I remember going with my dad when I was a kid, but ironically I haven't gone to one since I started high school. I had no plans to change that, until Alicia catches up with me on my way to the studio after school on Thursday.

"So Noah invited me to Triple F," she says without preamble, "but I kind of said we should make it a group thing. So do you want to come and hang out with Gideon?"

I blink. "Why don't you just ask Sudha? Or Madison?"

"Because I'm asking you."

I pause outside the door to the costume shop. I can see Del through the glass, pinning fabric onto a form. "Yeah, I don't know. . . ."

"Come on. It'll be fun."

She makes *fun* sound more like a threat than a promise, but then she tries to dial it back with a smile.

"Um. Okay. Yeah."

"Great. I'll text you," she says, already moving away.

"You don't have my number."

"I'll get it from Gideon!" she calls, rounding the corner and disappearing.

Iris texts me that night:

Are you going to Triple F?

The question of the day, clearly.

Yeah, I reply. *Alicia invited me.*

I pause and think about Iris in the kitchen at Lena's—*Name one person who genuinely, actually, likes you for you.* And Iris's responding silence.

I type *Want to come with us?* and hit send before I can second-guess it.

Not really, Iris replies a second later.

Then why did you ask me if I was going?

There is a long pause. The little text bubble appears, and then disappears, and then appears again.

Fine. I'll go.

So we go.

Alicia is standing inside the front gate when we arrive. Her nonuniform outfit looks like she's ready to be photographed and featured on a fashion blog with some pretentious caption quote like *I'm just really inspired by the world around me—people, places, feelings, things. Dress by Alice+Olivia, shoes by Steve Madden.*

Alicia waves when she notices me, but her face does something strange upon seeing Iris.

"I need to grab some tickets," she says, and grips my arm. "Come with me, Claudia," and she pulls me in the direction of the ticket booth.

"Why the hell would you bring Iris?" she says when we're in the vicinity of the booth.

"What do you mean?" I brace myself. If Alicia is going to talk shit about Iris, I'll have to say something, and it goes against my deep-seated desire to avoid Making a Scene.

"Why would you bring Iris on a double date? Who does that?"

"This isn't a double date."

"Uh, yeah, it is."

"You said it was a group thing! 'Group thing' does not mean 'double date'!"

"Well, it was implied."

"You should have said the words 'double date'!"

"You should have warned me before you inflicted Iris on us!"

"Hey," I say, but the tone of my voice must be enough, because Alicia grimaces.

"Sorry. Okay. It'll be fine. Let's just—"

But it's then that Noah and Gideon stroll through the gates, spot us, and wave. Gideon slow-motion runs toward us, like we're reuniting in a romantic movie. When he reaches us, he hugs Alicia and then holds his hand up to me for a high five.

"Are you ready to put the 'fun' in Fall Fun Fest?" he says as I slap his palm.

"I can at least put the 'trip' in 'Triple F.'" A pause. "By being clumsy, I mean. Not by, like, sharing drugs with the group." Three sets of eyes are on me, and I can't stop myself from talking. "I don't have any drugs. In case you were worried. Or, in case you were . . . expecting me to have drugs. . . ."

Gideon grins.

And then, by mercy, Iris appears at Alicia's elbow. "How long can it possibly take to get tickets?"

"Oh, yeah, hey," Alicia says. I know she's faking nonchalance, but she's pretty good at it. "So we just ran into Iris, and she's going to hang out with us. Because she doesn't have anyone else to hang out with."

Iris's face darkens.

"I invited her," I say.

Gideon looks from Iris to me to Alicia and back, his expression confused. But it clears quickly, and he claps his hands.

"I need three funnel cakes like yesterday. Claudia, can I buy you a funnel cake?"

"That's okay."

"You don't like funnel cake?"

"I do, just, you don't have to buy me one. But we could stand in line together."

He smiles. "I'll take it."

twenty-five

We get funnel cake. And play those ringtoss games that are clearly rigged, though I manage to win a tiny stuffed dragon—purple with electric yellow trim—that's kind of hideous. I offer it to Iris, who makes a face, and then to Alicia, who looks at me like I'm crazy.

"I'll take it," Gideon says, and my face must do something odd, because he looks a little embarrassed. "You know, if everyone else is just . . . willing to orphan it like that."

I extend the dragon toward him and he tucks it in the front pocket of his jacket, so its little head is sticking out.

"His name is Balthazar," he informs me.

"Oh really?"

"He's small right now but one day he's going to grow as big as the Chrysler Building."

"I don't think he'll fit in your pocket in that case."

"Hey, I could grow as big as the Chrysler Building, too. My mom says I'm not finished growing."

"Yeah, you're just a few thousand feet off."

"There might be, like, a vat of toxic waste I could fall into sometime in the future."

I smile as we join the others in line for the Ferris wheel.

"Nope," Alicia is saying as we reach them. "Absolutely not."

"They're perfectly safe," Noah says.

"Seven people a year die in Ferris-wheel–related accidents."

"Seriously?"

"Yes. I read it online."

"I don't think that's a real statistic," I say.

"Seven people. A year." Alicia's tone brooks no argument.

"They're so fun though," Noah says. "You can see everything from up there."

"I'm fine down here, thanks."

"But—"

"What if it detaches and rolls away? Have you ever thought about that?"

"I can honestly say I haven't," Gideon murmurs to me, and I grin.

The line moves forward, the couple ahead of us gets on, and then the next little bench opens up.

"Come on," Noah wheedles, holding a hand out to Alicia as he climbs the steps.

"Absolutely not," she says.

"We're holding up the line," Iris mutters.

"Here, get in." I step forward, urging Noah into the car and sliding in next to him.

"But who's gonna ride with me?" I hear Gideon say as the Ferris wheel attendant pulls the bar down over us.

We lurch to a start. I look back as the wheel slows, and see Gideon and Iris getting on behind us.

Next to me, Noah is quiet.

I glance over at him when we're almost to the top, the wheel still pausing to load on new people. All of Triple F is laid out below us.

"Nice view," I say, for want of anything better.

He grunts in response.

The wind rocks us back and forth a little, the metal creaking under the seat.

"Sorry," he says after a moment. "Sorry I'm no fun. I just . . . I kind of wanted this to be, like, romantic. Like me and Alicia."

"Ah."

"You know, like we'd get to the top, and she could be like, 'it's so beautiful,' and I could be like, 'yes, it is,' but I'm looking at her and not the view? Or maybe she's a little scared of heights and she holds on to me or whatever?"

"I'm sorry," I say. "I didn't mean to ruin something so cliché for you."

One corner of his mouth lifts up, a wry half-smile.

I look out over the fair, yellow-and-white-striped tents dotting the ground below us. "If it makes you feel any better, you were right about her being scared. It kind of backfired though, because she seems, like, pathologically afraid of this whole situation."

He huffs a laugh at that.

Behind us, not too far off, a loud cackle rents the air. I glance back and to my surprise it's Iris, her head thrown back, laughing with abandon. Next to her, Gideon looks slightly confused, but pleased nonetheless, at having elicited such a response.

Then the wheel lurches and begins to turn again.

147

*   *   *

We play a few more crappy carnival games. Noah wins a baseball hat that says *I'D RATHER BE BOWLING* across the front. We get another funnel cake, and although Alicia insists she's stuffed and more fried food would be absurd, she eats at least half of it.

We make it through pretty much everything, all the way to the back edge of the fair, where a little go-kart course is set up, marked off in the parking lot by stacked-up bales of hay.

"Ooh." Alicia grabs Noah's arm when we near the course. "I love these. And there's no line!"

I glance at Iris. "Want to?"

"Not really," Iris replies as Alicia and Noah run ahead. "But can we note that Alicia's pretty full of shit, because I feel like go-karts are probably a hundred times more dangerous than Ferris wheels."

I grin, glancing over at Gideon. But his face is pulled into a frown, and before I can speak, he's moving ahead, advancing quickly on Noah and Alicia, who've reached the track and are giving their tickets to the go-kart guy.

Gideon says something to Noah that I can't hear, and Noah replies equally quietly, while Alicia puts on her helmet and picks her go-kart.

When Iris and I reach them, Gideon and Noah are still conferring.

"—don't think you should."

"Yeah, well, good thing it's not up to you," Noah says.

"Are you being serious right now?" Gideon says, and he sounds oddly . . . agitated.

"Yup," Noah replies. He glances at Alicia, already strapped into her car, and then takes the helmet out of the guy's outstretched hand.

148

"Not happening," Gideon says, and reaches for the helmet himself, but Noah pulls it back and jams it on his head, clambering into the car. "Not happening," Gideon repeats tightly, trying to grab the seat belt out of Noah's hand as he goes to clasp it.

"Leave me alone," Noah says, pushing Gideon's hand away and fastening the seat belt.

"I will sit on you," Gideon says, and normally I would laugh, but nothing about this seems funny. There's a desperate edge to his voice. Alicia is eyeing them, confused, and the go-kart guy looks annoyed.

"Like hell you will," Noah says. "Get out of the way."

"Kid, can you get off the course?" the go-kart guy says.

"I saw your hands this morning."

"I don't know what you're talking about."

"I *saw*," Gideon says. When Noah just stares, he turns to the go-kart guy, almost frantic. "Look, can you just—"

"Let's get a move on." The guy claps a hand on Gideon's shoulder and tries to guide him away. Gideon just shakes him off and moves back toward Noah.

"Seriously—"

"Yeah, seriously," Noah says, clipped, and I'm reminded suddenly of the steeliness he used on Pete Salata during rock climbing night. It's weird to see it used on Gideon. "You're not my mom. You're not in charge of me. At all. So back the fuck off." And then Noah pumps the gas and drives away.

"Not fair!" Alicia cries, flooring her pedal and peeling off after him.

I look over at Gideon. His hands are balled into fists at his sides. On the track Noah lets out a whoop and makes a sharp turn, rounding a corner and disappearing with Alicia just behind him.

Gideon stands a moment longer and then stalks off.

Iris is frowning. "What was—"

"Stay here, okay?" I say.

"And do what?"

"Just . . . make sure Noah doesn't die."

"Why would Noah die?"

"I don't know, but . . . stay. Okay?"

Iris doesn't scoff, for once. She just nods, eyes serious. "Yeah, okay."

With that, I turn and head after Gideon.

I find him not too far away, standing off to the side of the last row of concession booths. His back is to me, his head down.

"Gideon?"

I think he's mad, but when he looks back at me, there's pure panic in his eyes.

"I don't—why would he—" Gideon shakes his head, breathing fast and shallow.

"You're gonna give yourself a stomachache," I say, which is something my mom would say and entirely unhelpful in this situation. So I step closer. "Hey, come on, come here." I don't say "it's okay" because I don't know if it is. I honestly don't know what's going on, but something is obviously wrong.

I must've been four or five the first time I remember Julia having a panic attack. We were at the mall and she was arguing with our mom about a T-shirt she wanted. My little-kid memory cuts out, but suddenly we were standing by the restrooms while Julia sat on the floor with her back against the wall, her face buried in her arms, while my mom kneeled next to her and counted, deep breaths, five counts in, and five counts out.

"Can I?" I say, reaching toward Gideon. Sometimes Julia didn't like being touched, but sometimes she said it helped, warm circles drawn on her back, or gentle pressure on her temples.

He nods, shuffling closer, and I put my hands on either side of his face, resisting the urge to thread my fingers through his hair and instead resting them lightly atop it. His skin is clammy, and there are tears forming at the corners of his eyes as he squeezes them shut.

"Deep breath," I say, and repeat my mom's often-chanted words: "One two three four five in, one two three four five out." And then I demonstrate, in long, out long. Gideon tries to follow. I do it again, we breathe again, and again, and finally he opens his eyes.

He drops his head—if we were any closer, our foreheads would be touching—and covers one of my hands with his own.

"Sorry," he says, quiet, still a little choked. "I freaked out. Sorry."

"Don't worry about it."

"I just . . ."

I shake my head. "We'll sort it out," I say, because that's vague enough but hopefully at least a little bit comforting. "Don't worry." And I try not to think about the weight of his hand on top of mine, or how soft his hair feels under my fingers.

We stand like that for a bit. Until someone clears their throat behind us. I turn.

It's Noah, standing with his hands shoved in his jacket pockets. "I'm sorry," he says.

I let my hands fall from Gideon's face.

"I'm sorry I was a dick," Noah continues. "I'm just . . . tired."

"Then let's go home," Gideon says, his voice rough.

"Not that kind of tired," he replies.

"There you guys are!" Alicia rounds the corner, picking her way delicately through the grass and holding a pretzel. She is now wearing the *I'D RATHER BE BOWLING* hat, and under different circumstances, I would appreciate the absurdity of that. "Here," she says, thrusting the pretzel at me. "Iris said you wanted this. Why you couldn't get it yourself, I have no idea."

Iris follows quickly behind us, and her face says *Sorry, I did my best*.

I smile. "Thank you. It was, uh, there was a carb emergency. But it's okay now."

"It was three-fifty," Alicia says.

"Awesome. Do you take American Express?"

Next to me, Gideon gives a weak laugh.

"Maybe we should call it a night," Iris says. No one disagrees.

twenty-six

I go to the theater to drop a few more things off with Tara on Monday afternoon. They're rehearsing the big scene with the lovers, so the court and most of the fairies are off running lines, the Mechanicals are down the hall practicing their play-within-a-play, and Gideon and Aimee are sitting in the house, ready to insert themselves into the scene after Mr. Palmer has worked out what he refers to as all "the business" with Hermia, Lysander, Helena, and Demetrius: who's running where, who's holding on to who, etc.

I hand the pieces from Del over to Tara. And on my way out, I can't help but pause by where Gideon and Aimee are sitting, toward the back of the house.

"What's up?" Gideon says quietly, smiling at me. There's a seat between them, but he's got his arm resting across the back of it. His fingers could brush Aimee's shoulder if either of them moved an inch.

"Not much. I just, uh." I glance at Aimee. I don't want to embarrass Gideon. But I keep thinking of him at Triple F, breathing fast. Near tears. "Just . . . wanted to see if you were okay."

"I'm fine," he replies brightly. "A-okay."

I pause, not sure if I should really ask, but I do anyway: "Are you and Noah okay?"

"Yeah." Although he's smiling, there's something slightly artificial about it. Some kind of forced chill. "We're awesome."

Aimee looks between us, amusement in her eyes. "What kind of weekend did you guys have?"

"Nothing," Gideon says, and then makes a face. "I mean, we had a weekend, obviously, but it was fine, nothing happened."

I look at him for a moment and then glance away. "Right, okay. Just checking."

I head off. When I reach the very back of the auditorium, I look back to where Gideon is sitting. He's got his head bent toward Aimee, whispering something. She cocks a look at him and then smiles and whispers a reply. Then they both turn to face the action onstage.

"Did Gideon seem okay in rehearsal?"

I can't help but ask as I drive Iris home after rehearsal that afternoon. All the planets had aligned just right, meaning that I actually have the car for once.

She gives me a look. "I don't, like, monitor him."

It's quiet.

"He seemed fine," she says begrudgingly, after a bit.

We don't talk much the rest of the ride. When we arrive at Iris's massive mansion—villa, compound, whatever—she pauses with her hand on the car door, halfway out.

"Something wrong?" I ask.

"You could—I mean, my parents are working. You could. Hang out. If you want. We could watch the *Will You Stay* tour movie."

It's just . . . fun sharing fandom stuff with other people. I look at her for a moment, but she's staring intently at the dashboard.

"Yeah. Okay."

It turns out Iris's house has a movie screen–sized television like Lena's, though it's not in the family room. Instead, there's a specially dedicated "media room."

Iris stops by her room to grab a pillow and then we head to the media room to watch the concert movie of TION's second tour, which I haven't seen. *Will You Stay: Live from São Paulo.*

The opening montage shows the stadium, packed to bursting with fans. Screams reverberate through the media room as TION takes the stage for the show opener.

"You know, they're coming here next month," I say when we're a couple songs in. Kenji is on-screen, belting out the chorus to "Here and Now."

"I love how you think I didn't know my favorite band in the entire world is coming here next month."

I don't acknowledge that. "Are you going?"

"Paige and I got tickets," she says after a pause. "We were gonna take her little sister. She loves them, too."

"Oh."

It's quiet.

"I miss her," Iris says, and when I glance over, her eyes are glued to the TV. "I miss hanging out with her."

On-screen, Lucas blows a kiss to the audience, and the camera cuts to a group of girls jumping up and down—some screaming, some crying, all of them with their hands extended toward him.

"There's so much I want to tell her. I never thought about that.

Like if you break up with someone. So much random stuff I think of during the course of a day that I would tell her if I could. But I can't. She doesn't want me to. She hates me."

"She doesn't hate you."

"She broke up with me."

"You kind of forced her to."

"What?"

"You . . . prompted her. I was there, remember?"

"You said you couldn't hear anything. You said you were peeing loudly."

"I lied."

"I knew it," she says wryly, with a shadow of a smile. It disappears after a moment. "If it hadn't been then . . . she would've done it eventually. I would've driven her away at some point."

"Why?"

"Because I'm inherently unpleasant, Claudia." I can't tell if she's joking.

"Why for real?"

She doesn't speak, and for a moment, I think that's it. End of conversation. But then she glances over at me, hugging her pillow—with a TION case, of course—to her chest.

"Do you know how we met?" she says.

twenty-seven

According to Iris, her and Paige's story begins on the first day of seventh grade. It was Iris's very first day at Morningbrook Academy, and she was terrified.

"I didn't know anybody," Iris says. "I was really shy."

"I find that hard to believe."

"Why?"

"Because. You're you. You just . . . say and do whatever. You give zero fucks."

She shakes her head minutely, and her voice is quieter when she replies: "I give a lot of fucks."

Paige, on the other hand, has never been shy. I didn't know her in junior high, but by Iris's account, she was fun and funny and wonderful in seventh grade, and since long before that probably. She laughed easily and often. She was everyone's friend. And on the first day of seventh grade, she sat next to Iris in biology.

"We just . . . clicked. She was my best friend. We were *best friends*. I never got along with anybody like that before. But then everybody said . . . someone started a rumor saying that I liked her. They'd be like, 'Just look at the way Iris looks at her, she's so gone on her.' And I was. I did like her like that. But I didn't think that she . . . I was scared, you know? I didn't think she'd ever like me back. So I would say no, I would tell everyone they were wrong. And, just . . . over time, like . . ." She shakes her head. "We just kind of drifted apart. She's the kind of person that everyone wants to be around, and I'm . . . not. By the time we got to Prospect, we didn't really hang out much at all. She would still be nice to me, you know, like wave to me in the halls and stuff, but . . . it was different."

But then.

It was the night of a party, sophomore year. Iris walked in on Paige making out with another girl.

(I give a comically loud gasp here, and Iris hits me with her pillow.)

"I was so surprised, I dropped my purse and they both turned and saw me, just standing there like a complete idiot, but they didn't—" She cuts off, shakes her head. "I remember it so clearly, I remember being surprised and shocked and whatever, but also like so annoyed, because they didn't break apart all the way. Paige still had her hands in the girl's hair, she still—" A pause. "Anyway, I left as fast as I could. It was Jackie Casella's house. Have you ever been there?"

"No."

"It's in the French Palladian style. Way too ostentatious if you ask me."

"I'll keep that in mind when I design my chateau."

Iris tells me how she reached the end of the driveway—it was a long driveway—before she realized she had left her purse right where it landed. On the floor in the hallway.

She just couldn't fathom it. Paige was kissing a girl. Paige was *kissing*. A *girl*. Paige kissed girls. That was a thing Paige did. Her Paige.

"But she wasn't my Paige. We hadn't even hung out in ages, she didn't . . . she was that other girl's Paige. And the idea of that just . . . I realized I was crying. I was crying, and I had to go back inside and get my purse to call someone to pick me up. But I couldn't go back inside like that. And I couldn't go back upstairs—what if they were still there? What if Paige had seen me, shrugged, and then kept on making out with that other girl because she didn't even care?"

Iris had convinced herself that that was most certainly what was happening. Paige's hands in someone else's hair, her smile pressed up against someone else's lips: it was terrible, it was—

"But then someone said my name. I turned around and . . . there she was."

Paige, haloed in the glow of the floodlights lining the front of the house.

"You dropped your bag," Paige had said, holding up Iris's purse. She blinked and then stepped closer. "Why are you crying?"

"I'm not," Iris replied, and took the purse.

"I can see you. You're crying right now."

"No," Iris said, even though it was idiotic, and then she riffled through her purse for Kleenex that she didn't have.

Paige clasped her hands together, biting at her bottom lip for a moment. "Are you mad at me?" she said finally.

"Why would I be mad?"

"You always seem mad at me. You never talk to me."

"You don't talk to me either."

"I try to. Sometimes. I just . . ." She shrugged. "It got hard after a while."

"Why?"

"Because." She took a deep breath. "Because I liked you, and you were always saying that you didn't like me." The expression on her face was pained, and it nearly broke Iris's heart all over again. "Every time someone would say something about us being into each other, you'd get so mad. I thought that you—I thought you would hate it if you found out that they were half right."

Everything twisted and rearranged itself in Iris's mind. Settled into something she almost couldn't believe was real. Something she had never dared to hope for.

Iris shook her head. "I wouldn't. I . . . That would be very hypocritical."

"Why?" Paige said, though Iris suspected she knew why.

"Because I like you, too. If you still . . . I mean, you said 'liked' like past tense but it's still, I still. Present tense. I mean I know that you"—she gestured in the direction of the house—"have someone now. That's okay. I just . . . just so you know. I like you, too. And I'm sorry that I ruined it. I didn't think you'd ever feel the same way. I thought I was making it easier for both of us."

Paige looked at her for a long moment, and maybe everything was twisting and rearranging itself in her mind, too. "I don't have someone now," she said finally.

"Sorry?"

"I don't have anyone." She gestured back to the house, too. "We were just messing around. She doesn't—she just likes fooling around, like at parties and stuff. So I don't have anyone. Officially."

"You could have me," Iris said. "Officially." Her heart felt ready to beat out of her chest.

Paige nodded. And then she moved toward Iris, moved close and wrapped her arms around her, rested her face in the crook of Iris's neck even though Iris was smaller. Iris breathed in, breathed out. Everything smelled like Paige.

"Do you want to be my girlfriend?" Iris whispered.

"Yes." Paige pulled back a little, still so close that Iris could see the tears clumping her eyelashes together. She nodded. "Yes. Do you want to be mine?"

"I probably wouldn't have asked if I didn't," Iris said, because she couldn't ever pass up an opportunity to be a smartass.

Paige just smiled, wide and radiant. It was all Iris could see.

"We were together ever since then," Iris says. "We didn't . . . we didn't kiss that night. We wanted to do it proper, like go on a date and all that. So we went out the next day, and ever since we were together. Up until Amber's party."

"Who said 'I love you' first?" I ask, because we're this far into it anyway; why not go whole hog?

Iris makes a face at me. "Nosy."

"Her?"

"Me."

I tilt my head back, looking at the can lights embedded in the ceiling of the media room.

"I've never said that to someone else," I say.

"And I'm the cold one?"

"I mean, like, in a romantic way. Obviously I've said it to family. And Zoe."

"Who's Zoe?"

"My best friend."

Iris considers this for a moment.

"How do you know when you love a friend?" she says finally.

I shrug. "How do you know when you love your girlfriend?"

"You just do."

"Same, I guess. Or not, I don't know. Seems more straightforward with friends, don't you think?"

"No," Iris says, and when I glance over at her, her eyes are closed. "Well, I don't know. Paige was both, I guess." A pause. "I think . . . I don't know, I think she helped . . . balance me out."

"She's the velvet glove," I murmur.

"Is that a euphemism or something? Because, I mean, we both have velvet gloves."

"Oh my God, I meant like that saying. Iron fist, velvet glove? You're the fist, she's the glove."

"Still sounds unseemly."

"Get your mind out of the gutter."

"I'm sorry. I can't focus. I miss her velvet glove."

"Gahhhh."

She smiles, but it quickly fades. "I miss everything about her. I thought . . . I thought maybe it would get easier. Or like, maybe it would get harder and harder every day until I hit a certain point and then it would, like . . . recede, you know? But it hasn't yet. Maybe it never will."

I don't know what to say. I just give a hum of assent.

She looks over at me, clutching the TION pillow to her chest, and her eyes shine. "I miss her when she's sitting three rows behind me in class. I miss her when I see her talking to Sudha at lunch. I miss her in the play." She shakes her head. "That fucking play. Pretending I'm a fairy and she's the queen and I, like, serve her or whatever. Follow her. Adore her." She shakes her head. "It's not hard to pretend to love her. It's the rest of the time, having to pretend like I don't."

"Iris—"

"You know, I always knew that she was better than me. And I knew that her friends knew, too. I knew when she told them about us, they said 'we don't care that you like girls. But do you have to like *that* girl?' And I was always so scared that she'd figure it out. That she'd see what everyone else saw."

Iris loosens her grip on the pillow and looks down at the boys' faces, fixed into smiles with varying degrees of sincerity.

She thumbs at Kenji's cheek and then presses a kiss to it absently before holding the pillow tightly again.

"When we broke up, and she said . . . she said that thing, about wanting me to be better?" She glances up at me. I nod wordlessly.

"I know she was right. I should be better. But I don't know how. I don't know how to not be selfish, you know? How to not fuck things up. How to . . . talk to people about . . . feelings and stuff."

"Are you serious?"

"Yeah, I'm serious."

"You're literally doing it right now."

She looks at me for a moment, face scrunched up in thought. "This doesn't count," she says finally.

"Why not?"

"Because. I don't know. It doesn't." A pause. "You're not people. You're . . . Claudia."

"What does that even mean?"

"I don't know. It means what it means."

"Great contribution, Iris."

She throws the pillow at me, suppressing a smile.

twenty-eight

Zoe comes over for dinner the next evening, and we sit around the table doing homework after we've cleared the dishes away. My parents have the TV on in the living room, some home renovation show, and my dad is snoring lightly on the couch, my mom in her chair, working on a baby hat. It's the fourth she's knitted for Julia's baby so far. *My first grandbaby,* she's always eager to say.

"Is it weird," Zoe asked once, "that she's going to be a grandma but she's also still your mom?"

"I think a lot of grandmas are also still moms?" I replied.

"You know what I mean. Like she's still actively mom-ing you."

"I don't know. I never really thought about it."

"What if she loves the new grandbaby more than you?" Zoe said with a grin.

"Oh, she definitely will. I've accepted that."

I know that's not the truth, but it's funny all the same. In terms of the excitement hierarchy, my mom's anticipation of the baby nearly rivals Mark's.

Zoe's an only child, so her mom becoming a grandma depends

solely on Zoe. When we were younger, my mom preferred we hang out at our house, because Zoe's parents work a lot and she didn't like us being at their place alone. Nowadays we do it mostly by habit, and because Alex is here, too, and then we can all hang out, if Alex is in the mood.

This evening, Zoe looks up at me after a while, tapping her pencil against a page of half-finished calc problems. "So what'd you do at Iris's yesterday?"

I don't think Zoe will understand about *Will You Stay: Live from São Paulo*. So I just shrug. "Not much. Watched a movie."

"So you're like, actually hanging out with her now. No homework pretenses or anything."

"Yeah." A pause. "Is that weird?"

"Weird that you want to hang out with Iris who you hated, or weird that you have a friend that's not me?"

"Both, I guess? More the second one."

"No." She clicks her mechanical pencil until the lead is long, then holds down the top and presses the tip against the page, pushing the lead back in. "Of course not. You should hang out with lots of people. You should have a lot of friends."

"We have friends besides each other."

"I know." Zoe certainly does. Most of her friends were my friends, too, at one point—the group of girls we hung out with in junior high. But I can't help but think of what Lena said to Iris at her party—*what you had were people who put up with you so they could hang out with Paige.* Maybe it was a little like that? But maybe that's not fair. I'm not there with them every day the same way Zoe is.

"I just mean, like. Ones you make on your own," she says. "Without me."

166

I don't point out that I did make one friend all on my own—Will Sorenson. Because look how that turned out.

Zoe was the one sitting with me on the couch, running her hands through my hair while I cried an embarrassing amount because I would never wear the dress I bought for Will's junior prom, and he would never kiss me again, and *I thought, I thought, I just thought that he really* . . .

It's quiet now, for a moment, until Zoe taps her pencil against her notebook page once more. "Have you guys done differentials yet?" she says, and we talk math for a good while after that.

twenty-nine

I get a text in the middle of the night a few days later.

I grope for my phone through the darkness and see the notification. It's from Iris.

SDFJKEFLEWFDKNJ is all it says.

Iris? I reply.

The texts begin appearing in rapid succession.

NWEW SDINGEL DROPESD

NEWW SINGLEW

KENJI

KENJISS VERRSE

IM DYIGN

IM DEADD

FEJKGGKJGREKJG

AWSWOPEFWJKLFSNVFKLEW

I call her, and she picks up on the first ring.

"Are you okay? What's happening right now?"

"New single just dropped! A new single! From the new album! It's the best thing I've ever heard! You have to listen to it!"

"Okay, I—"

"Right now!" Iris says, and before I can say another word the opening chords of what can only be the brand-new TION single are playing over the phone.

It has a great hook. Catchy and upbeat but with a little edge to it. A slightly more grown-up sound, maybe, than the singles from their last album. Kenji's verse is a thing of beauty—he hits this falsetto on *I want to start a scandal, baby* and then drops back down on *I do, I do, just say that you do, too,* ripping out a giant note on the last word leading into the chorus.

When it's done, Iris tells me it's called "Scandal Season" and is the first single from TION's still as of now untitled fourth album. We listen to it again, and then talk about it more, and then listen again twice more for good measure, not counting all the times that Iris replays Kenji's verse. By the end we're singing along: *I do, I do, just say that you do, too.*

Eventually, I burrow further under the covers, the phone still pressed to my ear, sleepiness settling in again.

Iris, too, sounds quieter, silences extending between comments about the song.

"I wonder what Paige thinks," she says eventually. "I wonder if she knows it's out." A beat. "Maybe you could ask her."

"I can't call Paige at one in the morning."

"Obviously I don't mean right now, geez."

I pause. "You know, just because you broke up doesn't mean you can never speak to her again."

She doesn't reply.

"You there?"

"Yeah," she says, and then it's quiet again.

"I'll ask her," I say.

"See if she thinks it's better than 'Without You.'"

"I will." I shut my eyes. "I should sleep soon, I think."

"Can we listen one more time?"

I smile. "Yeah, okay."

thirty

Gideon's eighteenth birthday party happens.

His house is sizable. It's not an Iris-style mansiony-mansion, but it definitely speaks to the Prewitts being *well-off*, at least according to the Sam McKellar scale of personal wealth.

Gideon answers the door, face splitting into a smile when he sees me.

"You're here! You came!"

We haven't really hung out outside of rehearsals since Triple F. I shift back and forth on the front steps. "I am. I did."

He opens the door wider to let me in. I imagine there isn't going to be a table for gifts, so I hand him the card I brought as I step inside.

"Can I open it now?" he says, shutting the door behind me.

"If you want. It's nothing special—"

His eyes gleam as he opens the envelope. "Is it a gift card to Outback Steakhouse?" And then he flips open the card, which has a cartoon dog on the front. (I deliberated over it for way too long.) "It is!" he says with delight.

"It's eighteen dollars for your eighteenth birthday. I had to go there and everything because they don't normally make gift cards for eighteen dollars." He looks up at me with his lips pressed together, amusement in his eyes. "Most people probably would've just rounded up to twenty," I say. "But, you know. I wanted to be consistent."

"I love it, thank you," he says. "Maybe you could go with me and we could share a Bloomin' Onion. Throwing up in the parking lot afterward would be super optional."

I can take only one more moment of the Gideon Prewitt stare. I focus on the wall behind him. "Yeah, no, you should take Noah. Relive that magical evening."

There's a pause. When I glance back at him, his expression is unreadable. But it quickly clears.

"Well, come on in. There's food. My mom made meatballs."

I follow him through the foyer and into the massive living room, which gives way to the massive kitchen. Noah is sitting on the couch with Paige, Sudha, and Alicia. Caris and Robbie are sitting on the love seat catty-corner to them, and a few guys from the play are sitting on the floor in front.

A woman stands in the kitchen, stirring a big pot. She turns when we approach.

"Mom, this is Claudia," Gideon says.

"Oh." Her expression brightens. She lowers the flame on the stove and sets the spoon down. "*This* is Claudia," she says with a smile.

Gideon leans against the counter. "Mom. Please."

"It's so nice to meet you, Claudia, I've heard a lot about you."

I glance at Gideon. "Really? Because of the Bloomin' Onion incident?"

"What is the Bloomin' Onion incident?" Dr. Prewitt looks between us, her smile widening.

"You should try the meatballs," Gideon says. "They're really good. Prewitt family specialty."

"Yeah, that would be great."

Dr. Prewitt fixes a plate for me, asking about school and the play as she does, and then ushers us off to join the others.

"No Iris?" Gideon says as we move into the living room. I take a seat on a plush armchair. It's big enough that it could fit both of us, but he settles on the ground next to it.

"She wasn't feeling well," I say. That's the official story Iris told me anyway, but really I think she didn't want to go to a party with Paige there, especially one that Gideon had described to us as "small, just close friends, very intimate"—he waggled his eyebrows a few times and then grimaced—"was that creepy? Sorry if that was creepy."

Paige looks my way from her spot on the couch. I give her a little wave, and she smiles.

Suddenly two girls dash in and plop down on the floor next to Gideon. They're both younger—eleven or twelve, maybe—and the one nearest to Gideon resembles him.

"Is this your girlfriend?" she says, leaning into him but looking my way.

"This is my friend, Claudia, who is a girl," he says, wrapping one arm around her. "Claudia, this is my little sister, Victoria, and this"—he gestures to the other girl—"is her best friend in the whole wide world, Casey."

"Stacy!" the girl squawks. Gideon claps a hand to his forehead.

"Yes, of course. This is Tracy."

"Gideon, geez," Victoria grumbles, ducking out from under his arm. She turns to me. "Are you in the play, too?"

"I'm working on the costumes."

"Oh. You know, Gideon said the costumes are really good."

I nod. "Yeah, the girl who designed them is super talented. I'm just doing the sewing."

She considers this for a moment and then, "He said they're sewn *very well*." Next to her, Gideon buries his face in his hands.

"Hey, Vic, how about you and Macy go get some punch, okay?" he says, muffled.

Victoria grins and gets up, pulls Stacy to her feet. "We'll be back!"

Noah settles in next to Gideon. "Was Vic trying to wingman you?" I hear him say. I look down at my plate of meatballs, feeling a little flush of embarrassment like at Lena's party when the drunk guy asked whether there was "magic happening."

We all talk and play games and eat Prewitt family meatballs, and in general it's . . . nice. And absolutely nothing like Gideon's giant birthday bash of freshman year.

I head to the bathroom partway through the evening—I got detailed directions this time, and hopefully no one decides to end their relationship right outside the door while I'm in there—and I pause in the hallway as I pass a cabinet with a host of photos sitting atop it. The largest is a silver-framed family portrait of the Prewitts on the beach, wearing white shirts and khakis, posing in the setting sun. Gideon's dad looks a bit older than his mom—he's got gray-white hair, impeccably styled. One of his arms is slung around Gideon's shoulders, the other around Dr. Prewitt's waist.

Another frame sits next to that one, a dual set of school photos of Gideon and Victoria that look pretty recent. Beside that is a small round frame with a picture of two babies in it—one of those department-store portrait type things. They can't be more than a year old, sitting on the ground next to each other in front of a blue background, wearing little matching white-and-blue sailor suits.

I pick up the frame to get a closer look.

One baby is bigger than the other, with a round face and very little hair, and his mouth is open wide in a laugh. The other baby, with dark hair and eyes, is staring solemnly at the camera. Or, presumably, at whatever stuffed toy was being held up behind the camera.

It's clearly baby Gideon and Noah. Best friends since forever.

I put the picture down, a small smile on my lips, and reach for the frame sitting behind that one, partially obscured.

This one's a picture of Gideon alone, maybe three or four at the time. He's wearing pajamas patterned with sheriff's stars and proudly clutching two *Toy Story* dolls: Woody in the crook of one arm, and Buzz Lightyear in the other. He's smiling big, all chubby cheeks and gappy teeth.

It makes something bloom in my chest. Some fondness, unbidden.

I startle when someone rounds the corner suddenly, and the frame slips from my hand, knocks the edge of the cabinet, and falls to the floor facedown.

"Oh gosh." It's Paige. "Sorry, I didn't mean to startle you."

"It's okay." I kneel down and turn the frame over. The glass has cracked.

Great. Excellent. Not only was I creeping, but there's now evidence of my creeping. There's collateral damage as a result of me being a creepy creeper.

I glance up at Paige. Her gaze snaps to a spot behind me just as someone else enters the hallway.

"Dr. Prewitt," she says, and I turn, the frame in my hands, as Gideon's mom approaches. "I'm really sorry." Paige grimaces. "I knocked it right off the cabinet, I'm such a klutz."

"No big deal, hon. Let me take that. Looks like it's mostly big pieces, but we should vacuum just in case—" She goes to take the frame from me, but her eyes widen. "Oh, honey, you've cut yourself."

I look down, and it appears I have, just the tip of my pointer finger, a couple of beads of blood blooming from it.

She takes the frame and sets it aside. "Doesn't look too deep," she says, examining it from several angles. "We've got a first-aid kit in the bathroom under the sink. Let's get you cleaned up."

"I can do it," Paige says, stepping around the glass zone, guiding me by the elbow past Dr. Prewitt and into the nearest bathroom.

She turns on the faucet and lets it run for a moment, tests the temperature; meanwhile, I stand there holding my finger like a useless git. It's starting to throb.

"Why'd you do that?" I say as Paige moves my hand under the faucet, even though I'm perfectly capable. "Why'd you say you broke it?"

"You had panic eyes."

"Sorry?"

"You know." She looks at me, face stricken, eyes wide. Then her expression softens back into an easy smile, and I'm reminded once again that she's a pretty great actor. "Panic eyes."

"I just . . . didn't want . . ."

For Gideon to know that I was creeping on pictures of him as an adorable kid? For Gideon to know that I think he was an adorable kid? For Gideon to know that I think he's adorable now?

"No problem, I got you," Paige says with a wink, switching off the faucet and grabbing a wad of toilet paper. She presses it to my finger and then goes under the sink for the first-aid kit.

"Thanks," I say weakly. I watch as she searches through the kit, and suddenly I remember my one a.m. promise to Iris. "Um, hey, so . . . have you heard TION's new single?"

Paige looks up at me, surprised. "It's so good! I've been listening to it nonstop."

"Do you, uh, think it's better than 'Without You'?"

"Oh, definitely," she says. "It's a whole new sound for them, I think it'll really help them break through." A pause as she unscrews the cap on a tube of antibiotic ointment. When she speaks again, it's a bit hesitant: "But I think . . . I still think 'Breathless' is better."

"Oh."

"Just . . . in case anyone was wondering." She glances up at me.

And then Gideon appears in the doorway. "I heard there was an injury," he says, brow wrinkled. "You okay?"

"I might lose the finger," I say, but he doesn't smile, just steps into the bathroom while Paige applies some Neosporin.

"Lemme see."

"It's fine."

"My mom's a doctor, I should probably look."

"Your mom who's a doctor already looked and said it was fine," Paige replies.

"I think you're supposed to get a second opinion on this kind of thing," Gideon says as we all watch Paige wrap on a Band-Aid.

"All done!"

"Thanks," I say again. "Sorry."

"For what?"

Being a nuisance. Property damage. Coming to this party in the first place. I just shrug.

"Your bedside manner needs work," Gideon says as Paige starts putting the first-aid kit back together.

"Why's that?"

"You didn't even kiss it to make it better. That's like an integral part of the process."

"Good point," Paige says, and then claps Gideon on the shoulder. "As the child of a doctor, you're probably more medically qualified for that part of the process than I am." Then she swiftly stows the kit away and slips past Gideon, throwing me another wink before she heads out.

Leaving me. And Gideon. In the bathroom. Alone.

"Should I . . . ?" he says after a moment, glancing at my hand, which I'm now cradling to my chest for no reason at all. The pain's settled to a dull twinge.

"You don't have to."

"Want to." He shifts closer. "But not if you don't want me to," he says, quieter, and oddly serious.

I swallow. "It *is* an . . . integral . . . part of the process."

He smiles a little, takes my hand in both of his, points my finger, and raises it to his face. I feel the warmth from his mouth, the press of his lips on top of the bandage.

I never think about my hand being small. I never think of any part of me being small, really, but it looks small in Gideon's.

He lowers my hand but doesn't let go. I try to say "Thanks" but the word sticks in my throat, comes out more like "Thurnk."

He just smiles, and I realize how close we're standing.

"Gideon, Mom wants to—" Victoria sticks her head through the door. I back away abruptly, bumping into the sink behind me. Gideon grabs my elbow to steady me.

Victoria looks all too knowing. But she simply says, "Cake time," and then disappears.

thirty-one

I text Iris that night:

Talked to Paige re: "Scandal Season." She said it was better than "Without You" but not as good as "Breathless."

The little text bubble pops up instantaneously, indicating that Iris is typing.

The three little dots pulse for a while until a message appears, much too short for the time spent crafting it.

Were those her exact words?

I mean not like exact exact but I said do you think it's better than "Without You" and she said yes definitely and then she said she still thinks "Breathless" is better.

She still thinks? She said that she still thinks it's better?

Yeah basically?

SHE BASICALLY SAID IT OR SHE ACTUALLY SAID IT CLAUDIA

You do not need to scream at me, I type, frowning.

Sorry, she replies, and then right after: *I'm sorry.*

Why does it matter?

"Breathless" was our song.

Huh.

Yeah.

So . . . what does that mean? Does Paige still like you or is "Breathless" just categorically a better song than "Scandal Season"?

Oh my God I'm going to poke you.

Good luck trying.

I meet Iris after class on Monday so we can walk over to Danforth together.

When I near her locker, I see she's there, backpack on, arms folded. But she's not alone.

I'm already too close to turn around and disappear when I clock Paige, standing a few feet away from Iris, her bag on one shoulder and an envelope in her hands.

"You don't have to . . . prove anything," she's saying as I reach them.

Iris just stares. "I'm not trying to."

"Well, then . . . take the tickets." Paige extends the envelope toward her.

"It's Lexy's birthday," Iris says simply, arms still folded across her chest.

Paige looks at her for a long moment and then opens the envelope and takes one ticket out, holding it to Iris.

Iris just shakes her head. "Take your mom."

"Iris—"

"For Lexy. She'll like that."

Another long look from Paige. I might as well have been painted on the lockers behind me.

"But you love TION," Paige says finally, her voice soft. "And they're sold out, you can't get more—"

"I'm not taking the tickets," Iris says, turning back to her locker, grabbing a book, and shutting it with a snap. "So if you don't want them, then give them away, or tear them up, or whatever. But they're yours, and I'm not taking them back."

And then she walks away.

I follow Iris, catching up with her on the path between the lit building and the gym.

"You just gave Paige your TION tickets," I say, even though we were both there.

"Yes."

I blink. "Are you going to get new ones?"

"You heard her, it's sold out."

It's quiet for a moment.

"But couldn't—I mean . . ."

"Spit it out, Claudia."

"Your parents could get you tickets, right? You know . . . pull some strings?" With a house that big, and a corporation that large, surely the Huangs had strings to pull?

Iris looks over at me. "It doesn't work like that. They don't just give me whatever I want whenever I want it."

I think about Iris's room, the various Kenjis and the tapestry, and the purse she gave me because she didn't like the color. I don't have to say it out loud—it must come through all too clear.

"Yeah, I know that's how it seems. But it's not how it works. Not all the time, anyway."

"So you just . . . gave her the tickets, even though you knew you couldn't get new ones?"

"I bought them for her." A pause. "I bought them for us, to go together with her little sister. And there is no us anymore. So they might as well go."

It's quiet as we cut through the Grove.

"That was really nice of you. To do that," I say finally.

"I didn't do it to be nice."

Would it be weird to tell Iris I'm proud of her? Because I am, oddly. Proud.

"Why are you looking at me like that?" she says.

"No reason."

She eyes me suspiciously. "Don't fall in love with me. Gideon would never forgive me."

I start to sputter a laugh, but then, "Wait, what?"

"We're gonna be late" is all Iris replies, picking up her pace.

thirty-two

"We've got ticket tag going for those coveted TION tickets, five chances a day to play—seven, eight, one, four, and five! Call in and tell us the name of the last person to win and you could score tickets to see TION on the Heartbreakers tour at Soldier Field! We've got your hookup here on 103.5 the Jam so stay tuned...."

"What are we doing?" my dad says.

I hold up my phone, the number already dialed and ready to go, seven o'clock the morning after Iris gave Paige the tickets. "We're trying to win TION tickets. I can't technically win 'cause I'm not eighteen. So will you call?"

"You and Zoe have a new favorite band? How will Drunk Residential feel losing their two biggest fans?"

"They're not for me and Zoe." The commercial break ends and the deejay comes back on and requests the twenty-seventh caller. "It's happening! Call now!"

I hand my dad the phone and hope for the best.

* * *

We don't get through at seven, and the line is busy again at eight. I can't try at one or four, but I stalk the 103.5 Twitter page and manage to find the name of the last winner in their mentions to try again at five. I make Alex call when he comes to pick me up from rehearsal. The deejay actually answers to say we're caller twenty and to keep trying, but that's as close as we get.

I try again on Wednesday morning with no luck. But I'm determined. I want to do this for Iris. And if I'm totally, brutally honest, maybe I want it a little bit for myself, too.

A few of the fairies come to the shop on Wednesday afternoon to try on their costumes. Del beelines to Gideon and Aimee immediately, handing them each their things.

When Gideon reenters the room, he's wearing tight jeans, tall boots like a pirate, and a battered-looking dress shirt. There's a scarf wrapped around his head, his hair tumbling out from under it. He is wearing a half dozen or so necklaces of varying length and a long cloak, which I know Del has spent a lot of time on.

Del makes him spin around and examines him for a moment. Then she steps up and unbuttons two of the buttons on his shirt. Steps back, looks, then unbuttons one more so the shirt falls most of the way open.

Gideon throws his hands over his chest. "Delilah Legere," he says, scandalized.

She smiles slightly. "Better."

"Do I look hot?" he says, striding away and then back, the cloak billowing out behind him. "I feel like I look hot."

"You look good," Del replies.

Gideon's eyes dart to me, almost in question.

I nod and then force myself to speak. "Not bad."

He grins.

"Don't cut your hair," Del says.

"I like it long," Gideon replies. It looks good, undeniably—soft, curling nicely under his ears.

"Good. You cut it, I cut you."

"Yes, Ms. Legere."

Del pats his cheek and then heads off.

Gideon watches her go. "You know those people where it's like, you know they could kill you, but it would be a privilege to die by their hand?"

I smile.

Are you playing Battle Quest right now?

I get a text from Gideon that evening.

Yes . . .

Where are you?

At my house.

No like in the game.

The Central Square, I say, and then frown. *Why?*

He doesn't respond right away. I don't think much of it; I get up and retrieve a bag of microwave popcorn I had going, and then I steer Viola Constantinople to the merchant stalls to pick up some scrolls for a side quest. After I finish with the merchant, a buxom elf named Trippola Lightyear approaches me, and next to her, a level-one human notary signore named—

I almost choke on my popcorn.

>Viola Constantinople: Is that you for real?

186

>Gideon Prewitt: yesssssssssss

>Gideon Prewitt: codeword bloomin onion

>Viola Constantinople: Gideon you can't name your character after yourself

>Gideon Prewitt: why not?

>Gideon Prewitt: I have a great name, everyone says so

>Gideon Prewitt: It's the same name as a harry potter character you know

>Gideon Prewitt: it's spelled different though

>Gideon Prewitt: and I had it first

>Gideon Prewitt: btw you haven't said hi to Iris yet

On-screen, Gideon Prewitt begins dancing wildly.

>Gideon Prewitt: shit I was trying to gesture

He lunges and then executes a triple turn.

>Gideon Prewitt: shit shit shit

A few feet away, Trippola Lightyear stands motionless.

>Viola Constantinople: Iris is that you???

Trippola Lightyear does not respond. But my phone buzzes a moment later. It's Iris:

I don't know how to type in the game

Meanwhile what the fuck is Gideon doing

On-screen, Gideon Prewitt is bowing in supplication.

>Gideon Prewitt: Jesus all these buttons are too close together

>Gideon Prewitt: how do I stop emoting

>Gideon Prewitt: Claudia how do I make the emotes go away

>Gideon Prewitt: Claudia

>Gideon Prewitt: the emotions

I can't help but grin.

thirty-three

"Why are you a notary signore?" I ask when I see Gideon outside the arts building the next day. He and Noah are hanging around out front when Iris and I arrive.

"Because it's a noble profession," Gideon says before leaning down and pulling Iris into a hug. "Hello, First Fairy!" He's a good bit taller, so when he straightens up, still holding on, Iris's feet dangle off the ground.

"Unacceptable," Iris says, kicking out weakly, but she clasps her arms around his neck, and when he whirls them around, I can see her smile.

"He wanted something, and I quote, 'obscure as shit,'" Noah says.

"You were in on this?" I say as Gideon lowers Iris back down. She punches him lightly on the arm.

"Who do you think consulted on character design?"

"And you let him name his character after himself?"

"He has a great name, everyone says so."

I snort. "You two. Honestly."

We head inside, Gideon holding the door for us. I let Noah and Iris go ahead, and turn back to him as he enters.

"You got Battle Quest," I say.

"I did."

"How come?"

"Because you like it," he replies, and then makes a face. "So, you know, it must be fun. I just . . . figured I'd try it."

"And Iris too?"

"Iris was so on board." He glances at her and Noah walking ahead of us, chatting. "I didn't want to be the only one starting out. And she said you've been really supportive of those guys she likes? The This Is Where We Whatever?"

"This Is Our Now."

"Yes."

"You have a little sister and you don't know TION?"

"Vic is weird, she only likes the Beatles and German techno and YouTubers who do acoustic covers of dubstep songs."

"Eclectic."

I part ways with them at the auditorium and head down the hall to the classroom where I'm supposed to work with Lena.

She's already in there, her script in front of her, but she closes it when I walk in.

"I'm off book!" she declares.

She is not off book.

We're going over some of her longer speeches in Act 3. I think her delivery has definitely improved, but she keeps mixing words up, dropping lines here and there.

"I swear I had it last night," she keeps saying. "I did it so good."

189

When I prompt her for the fourth or fifth time, she drops her head into her hands.

"I'm never going to get this."

"You just . . . need some more time with the text," I say, because it's something I've heard Mr. Palmer say in rehearsal.

"There are just so many words, and they're so weird, and I'm not . . ." She shakes her head, frowns down at her script. Reaches for her phone, picks it up, puts it back down.

"What?"

"Helena's supposed to be tall, and she's supposed to be pretty," Lena says. "And that's why they picked me. That's the only reason they picked me." She looks . . . oddly upset. "I'm not, like, totally oblivious. I know that's the only thing I've got going for me. God doesn't give with both hands, that's what my mom always says." In a small voice: "I know I'm not good at this."

I shake my head. "You shouldn't . . . that's not true. You must've given a good audition. They must've seen that you have . . . raw talent."

"Do you think so?" she says, eyes shiny.

"Yeah. Yes." I nod. "Very raw."

She nods too, looking down at the script. "Yeah," she says. "You're right. I bet you're right." And when she looks up, it's almost as if she's seeing me for the first time. "Would you like to come to my commercial-viewing party?"

"I—sorry?"

"My commercial is premiering on TV, and we're hosting a viewing party for family and close friends. Would you like to come?"

190

"Um . . . sure. Yes."

"Great!" she says with a sunny smile. "Lots of cast members are invited, but not everyone, so don't spread it around."

"I won't," I say when it seems like I'm supposed to respond.

"Let's try it again," she says, picking up her script.

thirty-four

Iris, Gideon, and I go back to Aradana that night.

After spending so much time with our guild—with Zoe and Alex and everyone—it's odd to be hanging out with different people online. To see Viola Constantinople with, well . . . new friends.

We set up a conference call online so we can talk while we play, and I lead them around and help them kill the monsters in their creature logs. It's the quickest way to level up.

"How come we have to zap them with shit for ages and you just shoot one spell and they keel over?" Iris says after our encounter with a pack of miniature wargs.

"Because I'm level fifty, and you're level three."

"Can I just pay to be a higher level?" Iris asks.

"Where's the fun in that?" Gideon says, and on-screen, avatar Gideon Prewitt runs into a wall.

We're crossing through Blaze country—a sort of outback area to the west of the capital city—when we come upon the entrance to a cave that is glowing faintly. The sun has just gone down in Aradana.

"Ooh, I read about this!" Gideon exclaims. "This is an instance, right? We're about to go into one?"

"Did you, like, read a book on gaming?" I say.

"I read the Internet. It told me all about it."

"You read the entire Internet?"

"Yup. I also learned a lot about Communism and sleight of hand magic."

"What's an instance?" Iris says.

"Yeah, Gideon, tell us all about it."

"Well," he says, and even though I can't see his face, I somehow know he's smiling. "It's essentially like . . . you know how when we're in the market or somewhere, we can see all the other players? Like Joe Schmoe elf guy walking around with his lizard friend? An instance is a special area of the game—like a dungeon or something— that you go into, and when you do, it sort of duplicates itself, so you're the only ones in there. You're all alone, just you and your people. In theory, another group could enter the same dungeon, but you wouldn't see them and they wouldn't see you, because they're in a different instance of the same place."

"Not bad," I say.

"Fifty bucks says you have the Wikipedia page open," Iris says.

"I don't!" Gideon squawks. "I happen to have studied thoroughly."

"Trying to impress someone?" Iris says.

"The glowing cave awaits!" Gideon says abruptly. On-screen, avatar Gideon moves forward, and we're all sucked into the instance.

Later on I'm waiting for Gideon and Iris to each finish a one-on-one battle against a zombie captain—another instance that they each had to enter alone—and as I'm standing there on the Blaze, a group comes up the hill behind me. A couple elves, a troll, and a humanoid dragon carrying a large broadsword.

His name floats above his head:

Alphoneus Centurion.

My stomach drops.

"Jesus Christ," Gideon mutters. "I keep punching this guy and he keeps zapping me. Why are his zaps so powerful?"

"I think you have to kill the little skull guys first," Iris says. "They're, like, recharging him or something."

I am barely paying attention. Inexplicably, I'm waiting for my chat window to ding. For Will Sorenson to acknowledge me. But that's absurd—he doesn't know that this is my character. He doesn't even know that I play Battle Quest.

"Fucking yes!" Iris lets out a whoop. "Got him."

Trippola Lightyear materializes next to me.

"How?" Gideon says. "God. He keeps—shit. Okay."

"Go for his lower half, that's where the zaps are coming from. His dick is like a lightning rod."

"If his dick were like a lightning rod, it would be drawing in the zaps, not shooting them out."

"His dick is jizzing electricity, is that better?"

"Iris Yiwei Huang, I am appalled."

"How do you know my full name?"

"I'm all-knowing."

"No, really."

"My mom met your parents at a school thing and—fuck fuck fuck he just let out this giant burst—"

"You're almost finished then," Iris says. "He did that right before he died."

Then the chat window does ding. Alphoneus Centurion is addressing Trippola Lightyear.

>Alphoneus Centurion: Greetings, traveler!

>Alphoneus Centurion: We are recruiting for our guild, the Legion of the Hunt. Are you currently affiliated with a guild? Would you like to join our merry band?

"Claudia, what is this guy talking about? Am I supposed to say something?"

"Ahh, got it!" Gideon says, and then avatar Gideon Prewitt reappears on-screen as well.

>Alphoneus Centurion: Greetings, traveler!

He repeats the guild invite to Gideon as well.

"What is this? Should we say no?" A pause. "Claudia? You still there?"

"Uh, yeah."

"What should we do?"

I clear my throat. "Just . . . say no."

"Are you okay?"

Alphoneus Centurion is still standing there. Neither Iris nor Gideon respond, so after a moment, he and his group move on.

"Yes," I say, and try to shake myself out of it. "Yeah, I just . . . I know that guy."

"That troll guy?"

"The dragon guy." It sounds so stupid, and I have no idea why I'm telling them. "We dated."

"Like . . . in the game?" Gideon says.

"Like in real life, asshat," Iris replies, and then a pause. "Right? Or have you actually . . . dated people in this game . . . ?"

"In real life," I say, though it is possible to marry someone in Battle Quest. It gets you some perks, the main one being that you can teleport together. Mark's and Julia's characters are married, and Alex has suggested it to Zoe more than once, but she always makes a face: "I refuse to be tied down."

("It'll be more efficient though!" Alex replied. "And it's not like I can freaking marry Claudia."

"Maybe I'll marry Claudia," Zoe said.

"Fine. Just someone marry someone in a non-incestuous manner so that we can transport places faster.")

"What happened?" Iris says.

I change Viola Constantinople's cloak for the sake of having something to do. "We broke up." The truth, again, unbidden: "He broke up. With me."

"What?" Gideon says. "Why?"

On-screen, Trippola Lightyear begins arming a flaming arrow.

"What are you doing?" I say.

"I'm gonna shoot him," Iris replies simply.

"Iris! You can't just shoot players indiscriminately!"

"He dumped you; he deserves to die."

"That's—"

"In the context of the game," she amends. "His stupid character deserves death in the game."

"You can't do that. It'll make you a player killer, we won't be able to get into any of the towns, and—"

"Don't care, worth it," Iris says as Trippola Lightyear levels her shot.

"If Paige had a character, you wouldn't want me to shoot her with a flaming arrow, would you?"

Trippola's hand stills on her bow. "No."

"So. Maybe it's like that."

"Is it?"

A pause. Iris and Paige obviously cared about each other. And they seem to care about each other still, even now. It wasn't a one-way street. "No," I say.

"Arrows away," she replies.

"Iris, seriously—" But as Trippola goes to fire, Alphoneus and his group disappear in the distance.

"Hold on, there's a spell I could do," Gideon says. "I could do . . . Sharp-shooter and enhance your aim, or I could do Summoner and bring him back—"

"You can do neither, because you're level three," I say. "Look, I appreciate the thought, but it's fine, okay?" It's quiet. "I should probably go, it's getting late."

"Are you sure you're—" Gideon starts.

"Yeah, okay," Iris cuts him off. "See you at rehearsal."

"Night, Claude." Avatar Gideon Prewitt vanishes, and Gideon's name disappears from the call window as well. But Iris's doesn't.

"Wait," she says.

"What?"

"Tell me about the dragon guy."

"Sorry?"

"Gideon's gone so we're . . . girl talking. This is girl talk."

"Is it?"

"Jesus, Claudia, just tell me what happened."

"There's nothing to tell."

Silence. I check again to see if she's hung up. She hasn't.

I sigh. "It's nothing. He was my first boyfriend." My only boyfriend.

"And?"

"And . . . what? I don't know. He liked me. And then he didn't." I swallow. "Or maybe he never did, I'm not sure."

"What do you mean?"

I have never told another person this, not even Zoe, but for some reason, inexplicably, it leaves my lips now: "When we broke up, he said he felt *regular* with me."

"What does that even mean?" Iris says.

"I don't know." Except I know exactly what it meant. "I was . . . really sad about it though. I thought . . . like, for a while after, part of me thought that maybe he would change his mind. Like he would realize he made a mistake. Isn't that stupid?"

"No."

"It is." I shake my head, even though she can't see me. "But it doesn't seem right to me that you can feel so horrible and the other person doesn't feel—anything. I hate that you can think that everything's good, you can think they mean what they're saying—even *they* can think they mean what they're saying—but they don't. And you give them whatever part of yourself and it doesn't even mean anything to them in the end. And you can't get it back." I swallow. "It sucks. I hate it."

Silence.

I take a breath. "Sorry. Rambling."

"You're not." A pause. "Do you want to play a little while longer?"

"Yeah, okay," I say, and it comes out almost normal.

thirty-five

It's Alex who finally, *finally* gets through at 103.5. He has a brief on-air discussion with the deejay, who makes borderline offensive comments about how two tickets to see TION couldn't possibly be for him.

"Actually, they are," Alex says defiantly, because that's who he is. "I love TION."

"Really now. Who's your favorite?" the deejay says with an air of derision.

"Kenji," I whisper.

"Kenji," Alex replies. "He's my guy. I love him. I would trust Kenji with my life."

"Okay then," the deejay says, his line of joking effectively squashed. "Right on, I guess."

Alex has to stay on the line to give his information, and he agrees to pick up the tickets for me at the station when they come in.

"Thank you," I say, for the tenth time.

"Just keep it in mind in case I need something in the future," he says with a grin. "We're talking massive favor here."

"Yeah, yeah," I reply.

Iris is oddly stoic when I tell her about the concert tickets. I didn't expect her to jump up and down, to . . . squeal or anything like that, but I thought she'd do more than just look at me solemnly for a moment and then nod. Although she does say thank you, so I consider that an achievement.

I go to Iris's house to pick her up in the afternoon, the day of the concert. A housekeeper lets me in, and I climb the stairs to Iris's room. When I stick my head through the doorway, she's standing in front of her full-length mirror, turning back and forth to admire both sides of the jacket she's wearing.

"Is that . . ."

"Kenji's jacket from the 'Stop My Heart' video?" she says without looking over. "Yes and no."

"Explain."

"It's the jacket but not his exact jacket. I bought one just like it. It's Valentino."

"It's nice."

"Of course it is—Kenji chose it," she says, adjusting it in the mirror, then running her fingers through her hair. "I have something for you to wear, too."

"Kai's gym socks? Josh's headgear?"

"Ha," Iris ducks into her closet and emerges a moment later with a long scrap of purple and gold paisley fabric. "Kenji has this scarf," she says. "He wore it in Japan." She gestures to me. "Come here."

I step toward her. "You really don't have to—"

"You're just borrowing it. For the night. So you don't feel left out."

I wouldn't have felt left out otherwise. I'm not sure many other girls at the concert will be wearing Kenji's Japan scarves. Or maybe they will, who knows?

"Lean down," Iris says, and I do. I expect her to wind the scarf around my neck, but instead she ties it around my head like a headband. A crease between her brows appears as she tugs it back and forth a little, settling it, and then adjusting my hair just so. "There," she says, stepping back. "Just like Kenji."

I look in the mirror. It's not *just* like Kenji. But coming from Iris, I think that's an incredible compliment.

I realize she's waiting for me to say something.

"Thanks," I say. "I feel like . . . like Japan Kenji."

She grins. "It's one of the best Kenjis to feel like."

I swing back home to get my dad, since "I don't know about you and Iris driving alone downtown" was my mom's only protest to tonight's activities. So Dad drives us into the city and lets us listen to TION the whole way. He even bops his head a few times and destroys the chorus to "Without You," their first big radio hit that even people's dads know.

He insists we go to his favorite Korean barbecue restaurant for an early dinner—the kind of place where you get to cook your own food on a little grill sunken into the center of the table. I'm kind of unsure what the me/my dad/Iris dynamic will be like, but it's surprisingly okay. She asks him about what it's like to teach at PLSG. He asks her about her dad's company. They both make fun of me perpetually overcooking the meat.

"Beef à la Claudia," Dad says with a grin. "Charred to perfection."

After dinner he drops us off a few blocks away from the stadium—the streets are clogged with traffic—and we walk the rest of the way.

We join a huge crowd when we arrive. I glance at our tickets as we slowly filter into the stadium.

We go up. And up. And up, looking for our section number.

And when we finally find our section and step out into the stadium, the stage could not be farther away. The boys of TION will be approximately the size of ants to us. They'll be boy band–shaped specks in the distance. Even the jumbotrons look like postage stamps from up here.

I feel like an idiot.

It's not like I thought the seats would be particularly *good*. Like obviously not on the ground level or anything. But I didn't expect them to be this terribly bad, and I'm very certain that the seats Iris originally had were probably way, way better.

Iris just stands there, looking at the stadium below, her expression unreadable. Finally she turns to me.

"We can see everything from up here," she says, and if the smile that breaks her face isn't genuine, it's the best lie she's ever delivered in the whole of our acquaintance. "The rainbow-light fan project is going to look so good."

"Yeah."

"And we're right at the front of our section. So maybe if they shoot up here, Kenji will see us."

"Maybe," I say.

She just smiles at me and heads down the stairs toward our seats.

thirty-six

"My name is Kenji Ko, you're Chicago, and we are This Is Our Now."

I have never heard such earsplitting screams in my life.

"Thank you for joining me and the boys here tonight." A camera tracks Kenji as he makes his way down the catwalk extending from the stage out into the audience. The other boys are trailing somewhat behind him, Josh and Lucas pausing to wave to people here and there, Kai stopping Tristan to point out a sign in the audience. Iris has her phone out, and even though they're tiny-sized from here, she takes a picture every time Kenji appears on the jumbotron.

"I can see all of your beautiful faces here in the front," Kenji continues, and a massive cheer erupts, "and on the sides, and in the back, way up there, way up, way up!" Our section joins the cheering, Iris letting out an incredible whoop. "Well, I can't see your faces up there, exactly, but I know you're there, I know you're beautiful, and I love you." As the rest of the boys catch up, getting into place and slipping their mics on to their stands, Kenji grins, bright and devastating. Iris snaps another picture.

"This is 'Scandal Season.'"

The show is incredible.

We jump around to the fast songs, we sway to the slow ones. During "If Only," a sweet ballad, the boys sit onstage, backed only by acoustic guitar. Phone screens dot the stadium like a mass of constellations, like the night sky reflected.

But it's during an upbeat song—"Carry Me," one of my favorites on their second album and what my mom would refer to as "a total bop"—that I look over and see that Iris is crying.

"Are you okay?"

She looks at me, surprised almost, like she had forgotten I was there, and then nods. "I'm happy," she says, and gives a watery smile. "I'm just really happy."

We meet my dad after the concert is over and head back home. It's mostly quiet on the ride, but whenever Iris or I say something, we speak way too loudly. Dad doesn't seem to mind.

I feel tired in the best way possible.

Dad doesn't comment when Iris directs him down the drive leading her to mansion. He just pulls up to the front of the house and puts the car in park.

"Thanks for driving us, Mr. Wallace," Iris says, unclipping her seat belt and getting out of the car. "And thank you," she says, ducking her head back in and looking at me, eyes bright. "For everything."

"No problem."

She goes to close the door.

"Wait," I say, and she pauses. "Your scarf." I go to pull it out of my hair.

"You should keep it," she replies, and then shuts the door.

My dad waits for Iris to get inside, ducking his head to get a better view of the house. "This place is something else," he says.

In the hierarchy of praise from my dad, *something else* ranks among the highest. Ironically, it can also rank lowest, depending on context. A truly annoying coworker might be *something else.* But usually it's something wonderful, or impressive, or unique— something apart from everything else, singular and rare.

"Nice to see you with a new friend," Dad says as he pulls away from the house.

For some reason, I don't protest that I had friends before. Or really, that I have all the friends I need in Zoe. I just nod. "Yeah."

thirty-seven

The "viewing party" for Lena's commercial is held the Friday after the TION concert, in a private room at Brunati Notte. It's the upscale version of Brunati's Pizza (which offers *fast casual Italian dining, family-style pizza from our ovens to your table*, at least according to the commercials).

Lena's commercial for the Ideker Automotive Group is airing during an episode of some network crime procedural. There's a projector set up, ready to stream the show on the wall of the dining room, and the place is near packed to bursting with Lena's nearest and dearest (and me).

Del is here, to my surprise, and of course dressed better than most everyone else, in a stunning red jumpsuit. "What?" she says when I cock an eyebrow at her. I kind of thought she hated Lena. "Have you eaten here? The food is worth the cost of admission."

"What's the cost of admission?"

"An evening with Lena," she whispers loudly, eyes gleaming, and then her gaze shifts to somewhere over my shoulder. I turn and see Gideon and Noah waving us over from a table across the room. The place isn't huge, but a number of tables have been crammed in. A big buffet is set up along one wall, and the waitstaff are currently bringing out chafing dishes.

"So what's the plan?" I say after we greet Gideon and Noah and take seats at their table. "Do we really have to watch the show?"

"Are you kidding?" Gideon says. "This is my favorite show. I'm here exclusively to watch this show."

"What's it called?"

"I don't know, something about murder. Or doctors. Doctors who murder? The lawyers who defend them?"

We get food—which really is incredible, Del is right—and when the Doctors Who Murder show comes on, Lena's father informs the room that the commercial will be aired at 8:27.

At 8:25 the room hushes, during an ad for toilet bowl cleaner.

And then suddenly Lena appears on-screen, wearing a skintight satin minidress and posing awkwardly next to a BMW.

"Come to Ideker Automotive for all your car needs," she says.

It cuts to a shot of her walking stiffly in front of a row of Volkswagens. "We've got everything on your must-have list. Luxury. Reliability. Affordable." She gestures and pivots. "Industry standard."

I glance over at Gideon and find he's looking at me. His gaze darts back to the screen, but there's a small smile on his lips.

When the commercial ends, the room bursts into applause. Lena stands and hugs her parents like she's just graduated medical school. When she finally pulls away, they all look a little teary-eyed.

"This is such a huge moment," her mother says to the room at large. "And the start of something big for our Lena."

"We're so proud of you, Cookie," Mr. Ideker says, pulling Lena back into a hug.

My phone vibrates in my purse. I try to check it discreetly.

You look like your eyes are screaming.

I sputter a laugh. I look up at Gideon, and he beams.

Can you blame me? I reply. *What was that?*

It had everything on my must-have list, he says. *Informational. Ingenuity. Creative.*

I laugh harder.

Shhh, Gideon sends, *please don't distract me, my favorite show in the world is back on and I don't want to miss it.*

Suddenly my phone dings from another number. A group text to me and Gideon.

Will you guys stop? It's gross and some of us feel left out.

I look up and Noah catches my eye. He makes a face.

"At least let me in on the joke."

"Gideon's just being mean," I say.

"You laughed though!" Gideon replies.

Lena makes her way to our table soon after that—she's been doing the rounds all evening. She sits down in Del's empty chair, looking at us expectantly. "So. What did you think?"

"You were fantastic," Gideon says, and it sounds so authentic that I wonder if some part of Gideon actually believes she was fantastic.

Noah just nods. "What he said."

Lena looks at me. "Great," I say, bobbing my head, and I can't physically refrain from it: "Watchable. Excellence."

Gideon lets out a strangled laugh that turns into a cough.

"Jesus, G," Lena says, handing him a glass of water. "What's gotten into you?"

He takes the glass and drinks, shakes his head, chokes out: "Sorry. Sorry about that."

Lena smiles, then reaches out to adjust the collar of Gideon's shirt.

"What would you do without me?" she says. Then she looks across the table at me. "You know what, I would kill for a Shirley Temple. Claudia, do you want one?"

"Um, sure."

"Great, will you grab me one, too?" she says, and after a pause, lets out a laugh, slapping her palm against the tabletop. "Oh my God, you should see your face right now. I'm kidding, oh my God, can you imagine?" She stands. "We can go together."

I stand, too, just as Del returns to our table with another plate of food.

"Do you want something to drink, Del?" I ask.

"She's fine," Lena says, taking my arm in hers and leading me away.

She is wearing a satin minidress that's very similar to the one she wore in the commercial, though this one is black and perilously low-cut. We go up to the bar in the dining room, and she smiles at the bartender.

"Hi, she'll have a Shirley Temple, and I'll have a Jack and Coke, please."

The bartender smiles. "Can I see an ID?"

Lena leans in, voice smooth and silky: "Can't you just take my word for it?"

He evaluates her for a moment and then nods. "Coming right up."

Is it really that easy? Are some people just living charmed lives?

I don't even want a Jack and Coke, but I'm fairly certain that if I said *Can't you just take my word for it?* to some random bartender the answer would be a definitive no.

"Won't people wonder why your Shirley Temple isn't pink?" I say as the bartender moves about, preparing our drinks.

"I'm allowed to change my mind, aren't I?" Lena says, like it's the simplest thing in the world. Then she rests her elbows against the bar and considers me for a moment. "So you and Gideon seem pretty close, huh?"

The abrupt change in conversation surprises me. "Uh . . . yeah. I guess."

"I don't mean to make it awkward," she says, leaning toward me a little just like she had to the bartender. At this close range, I can see the expert precision of her eyeliner, the flecks of light catching off her highlighter. "It's just something I've noticed. You're sort of his new thing."

"I'm not anyone's thing."

"Oh, you know what I mean." She waves a hand. "I've known him a long time, and I know what he's like. He gets these . . . *obsessions*, you know? Like one day he wants to learn Spanish and run with the bulls and everything's about that until the next week when he wants to study abroad in Germany. He's dying to get some shirt he's seen on TV and then he gets it, wears it once, and forgets about it. Even the whole theater thing—being in the show, it was just a whim. Before theater, it was lacrosse. Before lacrosse, it was jazz band. Sometimes I feel like he doesn't know how to like something for more than ten minutes." She turns her eyes briefly to the ceiling, gives a small sigh—the picture of fond exasperation. "Don't get me wrong, I adore him. We all do. But that's just how he is. He loves something until he doesn't, you know?" She gives me what she clearly thinks is a Worldly and Knowing look. "I mean, like, he used to buy albums on vinyl for the *aesthetic*. I've been in his room. He doesn't even have a record player."

There are too many things to feel at once: an irrational surge of jealousy (*why was she in his room? What were they even doing?*); a flush of shame, because even though she's not saying it, I feel like she's making fun of me in some way; and somehow, secondhand embarrassment for Gideon, because he sounds ridiculous when she describes him like that. Just . . . mercurial, and oddly . . . foolish.

And then I feel guilty for feeling embarrassed. Like I'm betraying Gideon somehow.

The bartender returns with our drinks.

Lena picks up her glass, smiling at me as she goes to take a sip. "Be careful there. Just a word to the wise. We girls gotta look out for each other, right?"

She takes a drink and then makes a face. "This is just Coke," she says to the bartender. "There's no alcohol in here."

"Oh, there is," he replies. "You just have to take my word for it."

thirty-eight

I return to the private room with Lena, clutching a Shirley Temple that I don't even want. There's a table set out now with an array of desserts on it—cannoli and cakes and little tiramisus—and Noah and Gideon have joined the group lining up to get some.

I set the drink down at our table, grab my purse, and leave.

My stomach is churning. *The food was too heavy,* is what I tell myself as I fumble with my coat check ticket. *I ate too much, too fast.*

I riffle through my wallet for money to give the coat check guy—I've seen my parents do it, on the rare occasion we've had a fancy dinner out; I know that you are supposed to tip the coat check guy—but I can't find money, and my hands start shaking for some reason. I'm scrounging around in the bottom of my purse and the guy is just looking at me, amused, until someone steps up beside me.

I glance over. The jumpsuit, the slicked-back hair, the eyebrows that could kill a man. Del.

She holds a bill in the guy's direction, mutters "Thanks so much," and takes my jacket from him.

I put it on as I move toward the exit. I get past the hostess stand, but Del stops me in the vestibule out front.

"Hey."

"Thanks for that," I say. "I'll pay you back."

"What is it?" Del replies.

I shake my head, and I know my mouth is doing that thing, that barely contained waver that only tells of tears.

"Come here." She takes my arm, leads me to the side, by an ornate bench and a ficus in a gold-rimmed pot. Then she closes me in a hug.

I'm embarrassed. I should fight it. But it's too nice, too warm, too comforting, so I just turn into her and hug back.

"Shut up," she says, but I haven't said anything.

Finally she pulls back, keeps her hands on my arms, looking at me like my mom would, and there's the question that she doesn't even have to ask.

"Lena said—"

"I fucking knew it," Del says. "I knew she was trying to get her hooks in you."

"No, look." I shake my head. She already has murder in her eyes. "It's not—she just—it's not because of what she said, I'm not . . . it's just . . ."

"What?"

I can't answer, though, because I see Gideon spot us from inside the dining room, and then he's headed our way.

"Hey, dessert's out," he says when he reaches us. "I was . . . What's wrong?"

"Nothing," I say, but that's not good enough for him, I know that. "I don't feel well. I think . . . maybe the food, or maybe I'm . . . just tired, I don't know. I'm gonna go."

He frowns. "I'll drive you home."

"It's okay."

"I'll drive your car, and someone can come pick me up."

"No, just . . . stay here and have fun."

"I won't have fun if I'm worrying about you. Let me take you home."

"I don't want you to," I say, and it comes out sharp.

"Dude," Del says, looking at me.

Gideon just blinks once, twice, a wrinkle appearing between his brows.

"I don't want you to," I say again, quieter. "It's okay, I'm okay." And I go.

thirty-nine

Zoe is there when I get home, gaming with Alex.

"You have to tell me literally everything," she says. "You promised."

I shake my head. "Tomorrow. I feel gross now."

"Was it the food, or was the commercial really that bad?" she says with a wry smile, but I just wrap an arm around my stomach.

I was mean to Gideon for no reason. I was mean and even still, he texted me a few minutes ago—*Did you get home ok?*—and I haven't responded.

"Let's just play," I say, and we meet up in Aradana, but not before I bite the bullet and text back a *yeah*. Gideon doesn't reply after that.

Julia and Mark are online, too, so we clear some dungeons until we start making careless mistakes, Zoe probably because she's tired, and me because my mind is too full of other things.

So we go to bed, and after Zoe mumbles *g'night* I think that there's no way I'll ever get to sleep, but somehow I drop off right away.

When I wake up a couple hours later and stumble out of bed to hit the bathroom, I realize that Zoe's not there.

I stick my head out into the hall, but the bathroom door is open, the light off.

I step out, and I realize that the door to Alex's room is cracked just a bit. I can hear sounds.

Smacking sounds. A wet pop. A small . . . sigh . . .

Ew is my very first thought. Jesus. I don't need to hear Alex . . . doing whatever Alex does.

But then.

Two sighs. Two voices.

It doesn't . . . compute. Yet at the same time, all at once I know exactly what's going on.

I rewind through it in my mind at hyper speed—*Tell Zoe she should come over* and *Is your brother around?* All those times coming home and she's already here, but Zoe being here has never been unusual. She's like the School Days portraits on the kitchen wall, the curtains in the living room my mom sewed when we were little, a feature of our house, something that belongs. Zoe has always belonged—*one of those intrinsic facts you know about yourself*—and when I come home and Zoe's already here, it's because she's waiting for me. I thought she was waiting for me.

I stand there for a moment, paralyzed, before crossing the hallway back to my room.

When Zoe slips back in an hour or so later, I am still awake.

She pauses when she sees me, her hand on the doorknob as she's shutting the door.

"You're up," she says, voice scratchy.

"You too."

"I couldn't sleep. I was just . . ."

"What? You were just what?"

She knows I know. I know she knows I know. But neither of us speaks for a long moment, and it's hard not to feel stupidly melo-dramatic, like somehow something hangs in the balance.

"What do you want me to say?" she says finally.

Just tell me. "Say what you were doing."

She crosses her arms, leans back against the door, directs her gaze at the ground. "Claude . . ."

I shake my head. "You should've told me."

"I didn't . . . know how you'd react. And at first I wasn't sure if it was—like if we were just messing around, or if . . ." She shrugs. "Or if it was, you know. For real."

"How long?"

"What?" she says, even though the question was perfectly clear.

"How long?"

"Since the summer. Since we got out of school for the summer."

"Holy shit, Zoe."

"I don't know what to say," she says again, which is not the thing I want her to say, which is *sorry, I'm sorry, I'm so so sorry.*

"That must've been really funny." I can't help how bitter it sounds. "'Oh gee, Claudia has no idea, what an idiot, she's so oblivious—'"

"Claude—"

"I see you almost every day," I say. "We text each other what we fucking had for lunch, but you left out the part where you and Alex are . . . doing whatever?"

"Because I thought you might freak out."

"So were you going to tell me after you guys broke up, or at your engagement party?"

217

"God, this isn't—you're overreacting."

"I am UNDERREACTING, ZOE."

She tries to shush me, holding her hands up and looking at me with wide eyes. "Look, I'm sorry," she says. "I'm sorry that you feel . . . hurt by this."

"That is a crap apology."

"I shouldn't have to apologize for liking him."

I shake my head, and flash on us doing homework after dinner. *You should have a lot of friends. Ones you make on your own. Without me.* "Is that why you were happy me and Iris are friends? So, like, I'm out of your hair more often? So you could fool around behind my back?"

"What? No!"

"'Make other friends, Claudia. Go out with other people, Claudia. Get out of the house so me and Alex can make out and do all the stuff—'"

"You're being ridiculous—"

"I think you should go home." I can barely control my voice. "I think Alex should drive you home. Or, you know, you can go sleep in his room and have fun explaining that to my parents in the morning."

"You're being ridiculous."

"And you're being a shitty friend."

She looks at me for a long moment.

"Fine," she says finally, and grabs up her stuff. She doesn't slam the door on the way out—neither of us want to wake up my parents. I hear her pad across the hall, knock lightly on Alex's door. It swings open and shut. Shortly, I hear them both leave.

I squeeze my eyes shut and fall back across the bed.

forty

Only one set of footsteps returns to the hallway a little while later, pausing outside my door. There's a light knock. It's still dead early, not even four a.m.

"Claude?" Alex says quietly.

I don't reply.

"I'm coming in."

The door opens and closes. I refuse to open my eyes.

"I know you're awake."

"Fuck you."

"Claudia. Geez." He fumbles with the light switch, and when I finally look over he's standing there by my dresser, jacket still on over his rumpled pajamas.

"How could you?"

"We were gonna tell you."

"What are you even doing? Why are you even with her?"

"I love her, Claude," he says, and there is an earnestness to it that only serves to freak me out even more.

"No you don't," I say, sitting up. "You love Smash Bros., and chili-cheese fries, and . . . *yourself*. You don't love Zoe."

"I've always loved Zoe," he says with that same intensity, a pleading look in his eyes. "But it just . . . changed. Recently. It became . . . stronger, and different, and better. I'm better because of her."

"You are eighteen fucking years old and you sound like an idiot."

"I'm trying to—God, why do you have to make things so difficult? Why can't you just be cool about this? For once in your life, be cool and just . . . let me explain."

"Explain what? That you were bored because everyone you know went off to school so you started dating my friend and lying to me about it?"

"I didn't lie, we never *lied*—"

"It's not my fault you couldn't go to college because you're lazy."

He looks at me, and for a split second I flash on a moment in the play I caught at rehearsal last week—the scene where Hermia and Helena are about to fight. Sudha is so good at that part, her eyes narrowing, her back straightening—*Ay, that way goes the game.*

"You can't bear the idea of her having something outside of you, can you?" he says, eyes blazing. "You can't stand the idea that she might move on from you. That you might not be the sun that her life fucking orbits around anymore."

"That's bullshit, because, if anything, I've moved on from her."

This is not even remotely true, and we both know it. He shakes his head. "Come on. Like I wasn't in school with her for the last three years. Like I don't know how many friends she has there. A whole *life* without you, Claude. You want to talk about lazy? You're

220

the laziest person I've ever met! You made one friend in preschool and then stopped trying!"

"Fuck you," I say again.

I think he's going to say more, but he just stands there for a moment, and then walks out.

forty-one

To defeat those who serve the Lord of Wizard, you must follow three basic rules, young warrior.

Viola Constantinople stands in the heart of a cavern, deep within the Mountains of Gelbreth. The crystal in her hand casts a pool of light, but the cavern walls are too wide, the ceiling too high, to illuminate more than a small patch around her.

Havil the Wise stands before her.

Tell me what I must do, Viola says.

It's always odd to see your character speak. You spend so much of a game like Battle Quest running around accomplishing tasks for people—take these scrolls, find these elves, deliver these coins—and for all the nonplayer characters that talk to you in the game, you rarely ever talk back. But when the preprogrammed cut scenes take over, suddenly you're not in control of your character anymore. Suddenly Viola is her own person.

First, the kill, Havil says. *It must be clean, it must be swift, it must be complete.*

Havil tells me what to do. And when the scene ends and I appear back outside the entrance to the cavern, my chat window dings.

>Selensa Stormtreader: what ru doing up this early?

I blink. I could ask Julia the same.

>Viola Constantinople: Couldn't sleep. You?

>Selensa Stormtreader: same. ru ok?

>Viola Constantinople: no. you?

>Selensa Stormtreader: no

I go to Indianapolis in the morning to visit Julia.

I know my mom would flip out if I drove all the way there alone. So I plan to take the bus. But. I need a ride to the station.

As soon as it's barely considered morning—I never did fall back asleep—I call Gideon.

Iris doesn't drive, after all, or else I would've called her. Funny how that happened.

Gideon actually picks up the phone. I was ready to leave a voice mail, unsure if he'd be awake, unsure how not to sound sketch as hell in a text.

His voice is rough with sleep. "Claudia? You okay?"

"Yeah." No. "Yeah, sorry. I just . . ." Tears prick my eyes. I don't know why. I'm still upset about Zoe and Alex, obviously, but somehow his voice makes me feel . . . like I've come undone, I don't know, and I still feel terrible about last night at the restaurant.

"What is it? What's wrong?"

I swallow. "I need a favor."

"Anything."

Gideon comes to pick me up. I walk down to the corner of our street and stand outside the house there.

A tree used to sit square in the front yard. It's long since been taken down. It was old and twisted, a large hollow in the front, branches splaying out like arms.

I was, in fact, terrified of this tree as a kid. I don't remember my first encounter with "Spooky Tree," but apparently at one of my earliest Halloween outings with Alex and my parents, I burst into tears at the mere sight of it.

"It was the most precious thing." My mom has told the story time and time again: "Your brother—just a little guy himself, mind you—runs up to the tree and kicks it and goes, '*Stop scaring my sister!*'"

That's Alex. He kicked Spooky Tree for me. He was fearless.

I wanted to be like Alex when I was little. You'd think it would be Julia. I did want to be like her a little, I guess—I liked playing with her makeup, I liked putting on her clothes and clomping around in her big boots. But Julia's eleven years older. When I was starting second grade, she was starting college.

Alex is just one year older, and he's always been cooler than me, smarter and funnier; he always knows what to say. Where he went, I followed.

Gideon pulls up to the curb in a shiny SUV.

"Morning," he says with a small smile when I open the door and pile in. His hair is messy, and he's wearing a hoodie and pajama pants.

"Sorry to wake you up," I say, and busy myself clipping in my seat belt. "Sorry, I just . . ."

"Don't be sorry," he says quietly. He doesn't go to take the car out of park. "I don't know if I feel super awesome about leaving you at a bus station, though."

"I'm just going to visit my sister."

"I've seen the TV movies. You could disappear, and it'll haunt me, and then you'll show up like fifteen years later totally changed, and like . . ."

"Pretend I don't know you but secretly I'm obsessed with you and your family?"

"Something like that." A pause. "I would totally watch that movie, by the way." Then he frowns. "But I don't want to live it."

"Literally, I'm just going to take a bus to Indianapolis."

"I'll drive you there."

"Gideon."

"It's only three hours. We can, like . . . listen to an audiobook or something. My mom just got *The Brunelleschi Scrolls*. She said it's supposed to be like *The Da Vinci Code* but more convoluted. Apparently, there's this monk who wants to—"

"I just want to take the bus," I say, against my better judgment. "Just . . . by myself."

He nods. And looks forward. Nods again.

"Yeah. Okay. But I'll wait with you until it comes?"

"If you want to."

He does. And when the bus comes, we stand up, and he sways toward me a little. I get the feeling he wants to give me a hug. Like we're parting for some significant period of time. Like we're . . . people who hug each other good-bye.

But he keeps his hands in the pocket of his hoodie, a half smile on his lips.

"Be safe, okay?"

I nod. And then I hug him.

Just briefly, so quick that he barely has time to take his hands out of his hoodie and hug back.

"Thanks for the ride," I say, and then board the bus.

I listen to TION on the ride. Mostly their first album, which is arguably the most upbeat, the most pop-sounding. Boppy songs about partying all night, interspersed with ballads about love as deep as oceans. I sink into it all, try to pick out which band member is singing what part—something that I've improved at doing, and Iris is near genius at.

I don't have much data left, but I watch a couple of videos, too—behind-the-scenes vlogs released before the start of the current tour. One of them features all five of the boys, squeezed onto a couch that's really too small to accommodate them, talking to the camera about the theme of the tour.

"The management and, like, the people in charge," Kenji says. *"They said we shouldn't call a tour 'heartbreakers,' that it wasn't good branding or whatever, if the fans think, like, we'd break their heart. They don't want you to think that. But we always said we were gonna stay true to us, and that's us. We're not perfect guys; we're, like, real, and that's real, you know—getting your heart broken. Nothing's realer than that."*

"Yeah, and who said it's even us? Who said we were the heartbreakers?" Josh says with a cheeky grin. *"Maybe it's them, you know? Maybe we named it after the people who broke our hearts. Or the people who will."*

I call Julia when I arrive, and she greets me at the bus station, her belly rounder than it was the last time I saw her. *An egg with legs,* my mom had said. *That's how I looked when I was pregnant, that's how Juju is going to look. Like she's trying to smuggle a basketball under her shirt.*

We go to Julia and Mark's apartment, a little place just north of downtown. Mark's working all day, so it's just the two of us. I sit on the couch, and Julia makes us lunch. Really, I should be the one cooking—isn't that a thing, aren't you supposed to give pregnant people a rest?—but I'm in too much of a stupor to be properly considerate. So I let Julia heat us up some chili on the stove, and I shut my eyes against the sting of the onions she's chopping up.

She brings two bowls out for us when she's done, and is extending one toward me when her leg catches the side of the table; she jolts, and both bowls go flying, sending chili spilling across the floor. She lets out an aborted "AH!" and then we both stare at the chili-strewn carpet for a moment, until she promptly bursts into tears.

I haven't seen Julia cry in years. Not even at her wedding. Her voice got a little wobbly as she said her vows, but that's all.

But now Julia starts crying and crying and I forget my onion tears and my Alex-and-Zoe turmoil and I remember that Julia was also playing Battle Quest at four o'clock this morning, she was also not okay but she didn't say why, just that the baby was fine and everything was fine, it was "all okay but you could come over if you want, you could come visit for the weekend. If you want."

Julia sinks awkwardly down onto the floor and starts scooping the chili up with her hands, still crying, and I can't help but sputter a laugh.

"Literally, what are you doing? We'll get some paper towels."

"We won't get our deposit back," she sobs.

"That's why you're crying. Because you won't get your deposit back."

"What are we going to eat for lunch?" she says, looking at me totally serious, eyes big and wet, lip quivering.

"Julia, Jesus, it's okay." I get on the floor, too, and pick up one of the spoons, trying to scoop up some chili, though this doesn't seem like the most efficient method. "We'll call one of those rug doctor guys like on TV. We'll get McDonald's."

She shakes her head. "I don't know what I'm doing, Claude."

"You're making it worse is what you're doing. At least use the spoon."

She sits back, and it can't be comfortable, can it? Carting a human around in front of you like that. She rubs her nose with the back of her arm.

"I don't think I can do this."

"Maybe we could use the vacuum?" I start to get up, to grab some paper towels, but the look on her face stops me.

"I mean any of it."

"Any of what?"

"This. The wife thing, the mom thing." Her mouth twists unhappily. "Mostly the mom thing."

"Because you spilled lunch?"

"Because I'm not . . . wired right."

"What are you talking about?"

"I'm supposed to be an adult," she says haltingly. "And like adult things. I'm supposed to . . . care about stuff that's bigger than myself, and I'm supposed to want to, you know, fucking . . . be the best person I can be for my kid, but what if I—what if I'm defective? What if they made me wrong? And I can't do any of that stuff? What if I can't . . . *feel* . . . any of that stuff? What do I do then? I can't even be an adult properly."

"It's going to be okay."

"Not helpful."

"Okay," I say, sliding a bit closer. "Maybe it's . . . maybe you're right. Maybe you're not built for every single one of the adult things. But it doesn't have to be one way, does it? It's not like there's a mold or something. It's not like it's prescribed."

"But it is! Society prescribed it! I'm supposed to eat whole grain pasta and bust a nut saving money on car insurance!"

"Look. Jujube—"

"Do not fucking come at me with Jujube right now—"

"No, listen, I think . . ." I pause. "You're going to be a mom."

"That's great, Claude. Did you forget you were supposed to qualify that with something?"

"No, because whether or not you're a good one isn't decided by some . . . committee, or something. Or society. Or anything. You decide that. You choose what kind of mom you want to be. You choose . . . what kind of adult you want to be. Right? So maybe you're an adult who plays Battle Quest. And spills chili sometimes. Maybe you get things wrong occasionally. Maybe that's okay."

She shakes her head. "It just feels like . . ." Her voice is small. "Sometimes it just feels like I'm faking."

"Maybe everyone feels that way."

She blinks at me, eyes still shiny. "I'm just scared I'm gonna mess this kid up."

"You won't."

"How do you know?"

"Because I just do." I look down at the carpet for a moment and then halfway smile. "In case you forgot, I came here so you could help me with my problems, not the other way around."

"Ugh, okay." She sniffs, presses the back of her wrist to her eyes, and when she lowers her arm, she's composed again in that Julia way of hers. She gets to her feet, and we both stare at the chili for another moment. "Let's fix this," she says. "And then we'll fix your Alex and Zoe thing."

We try to clean up as best we can. I get down and scrub the rug. The stains are huge. Julia's right—they probably won't get their deposit back. But maybe Mark could rent one of those carpet cleaners or something.

We get McDonald's for lunch and sit on the couch and eat while watching a TV show where a woman tries on several wedding dresses that make her feel magical, but unfortunately her family hates each of them in different and creative ways. And only when the woman has finally said YES to her dress does Julia put her Big Mac box aside, mute the TV, and look over at me.

She doesn't even have to ask.

"They didn't tell me," I say.

"That sucks, I know. But what else?"

"What do you mean, what else?"

"What's the rest of the problem? Because there's more to it than that, right?"

I shove the last handful of fries in my mouth and chew unhappily. She's not wrong. "It's different," I say finally. "Everything's gonna be different."

"How?"

I shake my head. "I can't tell her anything now without thinking she might tell him. And same with Alex, I can't—he's supposed to be *my* brother, and she's supposed to be *my* friend, and it's like . . ." I stare resolutely at the TV screen. "It's like I'm losing both of them."

"But you're not."

"But it feels like I am. They're a thing now. They have their own thing, apart from me."

"Yeah, people have things apart from you. Shocking. You know Mom and Dad dated before we were born, right? You know that I existed for a good eleven years before you did?"

"That's not . . . I don't—"

"Hey." A different sister might slide down the sofa closer. Put her arm around me. But Julia just blinks at me, shakes her head minutely. "This is happening. It's happened. They're together. So you can be okay with it. Or not. But they're still gonna be together."

"What if they break up? What if it gets weird and Zoe doesn't want to hang out with me anymore?"

"So you don't want them to be together, but also, you don't want them to break up."

"I just—" I mash my fists against my eyes.

"You don't want anything to change," she says. "You don't want to get left behind."

I nod. "Give me some Mom advice," I say when I can speak again. "Get some practice in."

"Ask Mom for Mom advice, geez. I have seventeen years before I have to deal with this shit with my own kid."

I huff a laugh.

"It'll be okay," Julia says.

"But everything's gonna change."

"That's not always a bad thing, is it?"

I shake my head begrudgingly.

"That's the spirit," she says, and unmutes the wedding dress show.

forty-two

My dad picks me up from the bus station on Sunday. I get a long lecture about going to Julia's without permission (because apparently leaving a note and then calling them from the bus was "more like asking for forgiveness than for permission"). It finishes off with a "You know you can talk to me about anything, you know we're here for you . . ." which implies that they know about my freak-out.

Alex is gone when I get home. We eat dinner. My folks watch *Wheel of Fortune*.

Before I left her place, Julia gave me a Tupperware of cookies she had baked. "You can give them to Zoe," she said. "Difficult conversations are at least one and a half times easier if there are cookies."

"I don't know if I'm ready to talk."

"Then give them to Gideon," she replied. "You can thank him for getting up at ass o'clock and helping you get here."

I sit in my dad's car in the driveway for a bit, staring at the cookies in the passenger seat.

And then I drive to Gideon's house.

I knock on the front door, but then I figure it's so big they may not hear, so I press the doorbell. It's quiet, and I feel like a complete and total idiot—I should've called or texted, I should've said something and now I'm here and even if I leave right now and take the cookies with me, I will still know the private shame of having come in the first place.

I'm considering bolting when the door swings open and reveals Victoria.

Her face brightens on seeing me. "Claudia!" She turns and bellows back into the depths of the house: "GIDEON. CLAUDIA'S HERE."

When she turns back, her gaze drops to the Tupperware in my hands. "What'd you bring?"

"Cookies."

"Did you make them? For Gideon?"

"Um. My sister did. Not, like, *for* Gideon exactly, but I thought maybe . . ."

Gideon appears at the end of the hallway in sweatpants and sock feet and rushes our way, sliding the last few feet and catching himself on the doorjamb before he pitches clear through the door.

"Claudia, hey! Hi. I was just. We were just—"

"Watching the Disney Channel," Victoria helpfully supplies.

"That is . . . exactly what we were doing," he says, looking a little chagrined but pulling out a smile all the same. "What are you doing here?"

"I, uh, I just wanted to drop these off."

His eyes light up upon seeing the cookies. "Did you make them?"

"My sister did. They're just the break-and-bake kind."

"Those are my favorite."

"No they're not," Victoria says.

"Hey, how about you head upstairs and start getting ready for bed?"

"It's seven o'clock."

"How about you head upstairs and just . . . stay there?"

They look at each other for a long moment and seem to be having some kind of nonverbal sibling communication. Finally Victoria sighs and steps away from the door.

"I get half of those cookies."

"Deal," Gideon says, turning back to me as Victoria retreats. "Come in. Want to hang out?"

"Um, sure. I can for a little bit."

"Great."

I follow him into the house and to the family room, where the TV is currently showing *High School Musical 3*. He shuts it off.

"We can go in here," he says, leading me back down the hall to a door at the end. "It's, uh, you know. Quieter."

He opens the door to reveal the biggest home office I've ever seen. It looks like something out of a movie—all warm wood paneling and shelves lined with books. Thick curtains and paintings and a fireplace with a leather couch and two club chairs situated in front of it.

I watch as Gideon goes over to a table up against the far wall, between two big picture windows.

"My dad keeps his record player in here. He lets me use it whenever I want," he says. "Sometimes I—"

He stops himself.

"What?"

He looks sheepish. "It's not like I really think vinyl sounds so much better. Sometimes I just want to come in here 'cause my dad's here. I don't get to see him a lot." He busies himself flipping through records on one of the shelves to his left. He turns and holds one up. "Do you know them?"

It's Drunk Residential's third album.

I nod.

He puts it on and then his eyes widen. "Sorry. I forgot about the cookies. I don't know how anyone forgets about cookies." He reaches out and takes the Tupperware from me and then gestures me over to the fireplace seating arrangement. I watch as he sinks down onto the leather couch.

I pick one of the club chairs adjacent to it.

"So I . . . I just wanted to thank you. For taking me to the bus station yesterday."

"No problem. I'm always up for a trip to the bus station."

I raise an eyebrow.

"If you're the person who needs to go to the bus station. Then I'm up for it," he amends with a grin.

I don't know what to say to that, so I look at the painting over the fireplace, which depicts an ocean scene. The colors are vibrant, but it's oddly calming somehow.

When I look back, Gideon's tearing into the cookies. He extends the Tupperware my way, but I shake my head. "Did you have fun with your sister?" he asks between biles.

We watched a lot of TV and ate a lot of junk food and played a lot of Battle Quest. It was our version of fun.

I nod, and then it's quiet.

"Do you want to play Connect Four?" Gideon says. "I'm kind of amazing at it."

"I know," I say, and he gives me an odd look. I flush. "I read it on JustGideonPrewittThings."

Gideon groans. "You tell one person you like soggy cereal and suddenly you're a fucking meme."

"You know, the crunch is kind of the thing people like best about cereal."

"No, the milk and the cereal working together is the thing people like best about cereal. Why wouldn't you want maximum interaction between the two most essential parts of the meal?"

"Is cereal a meal?"

"The way I make it, it is."

I can't help but grin.

"I will make you Froot Loops. You'll never go back."

"Okay. Make me some Froot Loops right now."

"Right this second?"

I nod.

Gideon makes us bowls of cereal, but while it's sitting on the counter "marinating," we go back to his dad's office and play a round of Connect Four. Drunk Residential is still playing.

He wins the first game. "I feel like vigilance is key," he tells me as we go to retrieve our cereal. "It's my best strategy for Connect Four."

"It's glorified tic-tac-toe. You realize that, right?"

"They added a fourth objective. You need to achieve thirty-three percent more than in tic-tac-toe, plus they've dimensionalized it. It's three-dimensional!"

I don't mention JustGideonPrewittThings again, but apparently the entry I had seen—*Weirdly passionate about Connect 4*—is entirely accurate.

I go for a spoonful of the cereal as we stand at the kitchen counter. It's soggy and terrible. My face likely communicates that.

Gideon frowns. "Not good?"

I chew. Sort of. It's not really required. "I kind of definitely prefer it the old-fashioned way."

"I'll make you more."

"I don't want to waste it," I say, though I don't want to eat it either.

"I'll eat yours, too." He makes a new bowl and presents it to me, and then carries both my old one and his back to his dad's office. "So crunchy cereal only. First entry for JustClaudiaWallaceThings."

"Ugh. No one would follow that account." It's the same thing Iris said about my "update account," and it's not wrong.

"Why not?"

" 'Cause there's nothing to say."

He makes a noise of outrage.

"*Crunchy cereal only* is the first entry!"

"I think it's confirmed that like ninety-nine percent of the population likes crunchy cereal only."

"I need to see some literature on that." He sinks back down on the couch, and this time I join him. "I would follow JustClaudia-WallaceThings. There are so many of them."

"Name three."

"I will name *six*."

I purse my lips, trying to suppress a smile. "Okay. Go."

"Number one, looks good in yellow."

"That's a bit subjective."

"Some Gideon Prewitt things are subjective. *Sings better than you would expect but not as good as he thinks he does?* Subjective."

"That's mean. Who said that?"

"Why, are you going to fight them?"

"I could."

"I don't doubt that." He grins. "Number two, wants to slay the Lord of Wizard, has all the skills to do so. Number three, uncommonly good at Shakespeare. Number four, master deflector. Number five, super smart—see number three, uncommonly good at Shakespeare."

His gaze darts back and forth between me and his cereal bowl.

"Number six, best laugh. Ever." His eyes land on me, fix there for a moment. "When you make Claudia Wallace laugh, you feel like you've earned something."

I swallow. I want to look away, but I can't. "It's like a snort," I say. "Like a snort chortle. It's a snortle."

He moves a little closer. "Is that a Pokémon?"

"Gideon—"

"Do you want to go to Homecoming with me?"

I blink. PLSG and Danforth have Homecoming together, alternating which campus hosts each year. I've never gone. Junior prom with Will Sorenson was going to be my first foray into school dances.

I surprise myself with my answer: "Yeah. Okay."

"Awesome." He smiles. "Now tell me that second bowl isn't the best cereal you've ever had."

forty-three

"I'm not going," Iris says when I mention Homecoming to her on the way to rehearsal on Monday.

"Why not?"

"Because it's lame."

"Is it?"

She glances over at me. "Have you ever been?"

I shrug. "Not really my thing." Though I loved when Zoe would tell me about her Homecomings. Somehow it always seemed like putting everyone in formal wear and adding a deejay upped the chances for Major Drama. School Dance Drama was a whole different breed than your average, run-of-the-mill Drama. Even though I didn't want to live it, I always liked hearing about it.

Though right now the thought of Zoe makes something in my stomach twist. We haven't talked since Friday night. I didn't see her online once this weekend.

"So what's Homecoming like?"

"You have to wear a stupid outfit and listen to stupid songs and dance stupid dances," Iris says.

"Geez, don't hold back. Poor Homecoming's not even here to defend itself."

"It sucks." She fumbles with the strap of her book bag. It's quiet for a moment. "Unless . . ."

"What?"

"Unless you really like the person you go with. Then it sucks less."

"Hm."

"Maybe you should give it a try," she says as we make our way up the path to the arts building.

"You should come."

"I'm not gonna third-wheel you and Gideon."

"It's not . . . it isn't like a *date* date." I reach for the door.

"Claudia, I will bet you ten thousand dollars Gideon considers this a *date* date."

"I don't have ten thousand dollars."

"Good, because you'd lose it," she says before we part ways.

Thursday rolls around. I still haven't talked to Zoe, and the door to Alex's room has been shut every time I've gotten home, and stayed shut for the remainder of the evening.

But come Thursday, rain or shine, without fail, Zoe and I go to Roosevelt-Hart to volunteer. So I put on my blue shirt and I drive to her house.

She's sitting on the front steps, waiting for me.

She gets into the car, wordlessly, and I pull away from the curb.

The radio is on, some generic club song playing, all sirens and whistles. I switch it off without thinking.

"I like that song," she says finally.

"No you don't."

"I could."

I don't acknowledge the possibility of her liking something without me knowing about it. I don't turn the radio back on either.

It's just as quiet on the ride home until I pull to a stop in front of Zoe's house. She unclicks her seat belt and pauses, her expression blank.

"Alex and I broke up," she says.

"What?"

"See you next week." She gets out of the car.

"Wait, what?" I switch off the car and jump out. "Why did you do that?"

"Why do you think, Claudia?" She turns, halfway to the front door.

"I didn't want you to break up."

"You didn't want us to date either."

I hear Julia's words: *So you don't want them to be together, but also, you don't want them to break up.*

I shake my head. "I didn't—look, I just, I needed to—"

"It's done, Claude. It's fine."

"It's not fine."

"I'll see you," she says, and goes inside, shutting the door definitively.

I could knock on the door, or just follow her in, but I don't even know what I'd say. I can't act like this isn't what I wanted because maybe some small part of me did. I get back in my car, rest my head against the headrest, squeeze my eyes shut.

* * *

When I get home, I hear music coming from Alex's room. I knock lightly on his door. "Alex?"

He doesn't answer.

forty-four

Homecoming is a thing that happens.

Gideon picks me up. He's wearing a black suit with a ruffly shirt that should look terrible but somehow does not look the least bit terrible.

I wear a dress I wore to my cousin's wedding last year. It's nothing particularly special, but Gideon tell me it's "Beautiful. Radiant. Excellence," and I can't stop smiling.

He gives me flowers—pink tulips—and we stand in the kitchen while my mom puts them in a vase and exclaims over them as if he'd brought them for her.

She lets us go after she's taken our picture several dozen times. "Have fun, and don't stay out too late. Back by twelve, okay?"

"Okay."

"Do you have your phone?"

"Yes."

"And Gideon's driving safe, right?" she says expectantly, like Gideon was planning to run us off the road.

"Gideon's prepping for the Indy 500. We're going to do a few laps around the block, practice for pole position."

"That's not true," he says, eyes wide.

"No worries, Gideon, I know exactly how sarcastic my daughter can be. Have fun, okay?"

Gideon takes my hand. "We will," he says, and we leave the kitchen.

I look down at our clasped hands in the hall, and Gideon hesitates, loosening his grip as if to let go.

"Is this okay?"

I give his hand a squeeze. "Only because it's Saturday."

"Does that make a difference?"

"Yeah, I mean, hand-holding on a Tuesday is pretty risqué."

His lips quirk. "It's also a quarter moon, you know."

"What happens on the quarter moon?"

"I turn into a quarter werewolf."

I grin.

Danforth's gym is transformed for the dance, and everyone in it is transformed a bit, too. Themselves, but now in formal wear.

We run into people we know and say hello like we don't see each other's faces five out of every seven days, like we hadn't just seen one another a day ago in class. It's kind of funny.

Alicia greets me with a kiss on each cheek. I had no idea we were so cosmopolitan. Or that we were that friendly. But she smiles at me and compliments my dress and then slips her arm through Noah's. He's a good few inches shorter than her in her heels, and they make a striking pair.

"You guys look adorable," she says to Gideon and me both.

"Thanks. You too," I say, because that seems like the kind of thing people say. Alicia flags down someone to take a picture of all of us, and as she's flipping through her phone afterward, she says, "Iris was looking for you, by the way."

"She's here?"

"Uh-huh." A new song starts up. "Ooh, I love this one! Let's dance." She grabs Noah, and off they go.

We find Iris sitting on the bleachers, her purse on her lap. She brightens a little when she notices our approach.

Even in the dim twinkly light of the gym, I can see her dress is very pretty, and very pink.

"I didn't think you were coming."

"Yeah," she says. "I thought I'd just . . . check it out. Just to see."

"We haven't seen Paige yet," Gideon says.

"Why would I care?"

"I know you don't," he replies. "That's why I mentioned it. Expressly because I know how much you don't care."

"Shut up," she says, but not without a small smile.

"Wanna dance?" Gideon says.

"Yes, go dance, go away, both of you."

"I was talking to you," he says. "We can all dance."

For a second, I'm reminded of Iris and Paige way back when, dancing together in front of the literature building. Iris holding back until Paige took her hands, then the both of them jumping around, uninhibited.

Right now she levels Gideon with a look and is met with his easy smile. Then she shifts her gaze to me.

"Come on," I say. "It'll be fun."

Iris sighs, getting to her feet. "Ugh, sure, I guess. If it'll pass the time."

It passes the time quite well. Gideon is a ridiculous dancer, but I would've expected no less.

People, as always, seem to gravitate toward him, so we get a good group going. Gideon twirls Iris around and hip-bumps Noah and busts out all sorts of moves—some successfully, some not so much—and basically doesn't stop until finally a slow song filters on.

Then he looks at me hesitantly. "Want to dance?"

"What have we been doing for the last hour?"

"I meant, like, with me."

"Who have I been dancing with all this time? Did someone get a face transplant with your face?"

He grins. "You know what I'm saying."

I glance around, but the rest of the group has melted away. Even Iris has disappeared.

So I step up to Gideon and clasp my hands loosely behind his neck. I mean to leave some space, but he steps closer, circling his arms around my waist so it's more of a hug than a traditional dance hold.

We sway back and forth. My entire front is warm. Everything is Gideon Prewitt sensory overload, but then I don't think there could even be such a thing. I don't think there could ever be too much of him.

"You never definitively responded to the face transplant thing," I say.

"Do you need me to confirm my identity?"

"Yes. Say something only Gideon Prewitt would say."

"Connect Four is the greatest game ever invented."

"You could've looked that up online."

"Bloomin' Onion," he whispers right in my ear, and it tickles but also sends a spark of electricity through me. I let out a laugh.

He laughs, too, his shoulders rising and falling a bit, and then it's quiet.

Until Gideon murmurs, "Thanks for coming with me tonight." His mouth is still close to my ear. "I really, um." He pulls back the slightest bit, looks at me for a second. "I really like it when we hang out."

"Me too."

"Sometimes . . . around some people, I feel like I have to, like . . . *try*, you know? Like really hard." His hands tighten a bit on my waist. "But with you—when I'm with you, I can just . . . exist. You know what I mean?"

His expression is open, his eyes serious.

I know exactly what he means.

I nod. And stare at the stitching on Gideon's lapel.

He stops swaying, ducks his head to try to look at me. "Claude?"

Someone taps my shoulder. "Claudia, will you take our picture?"

It's Lena, dressed in yet another variation on her patented minidress. She's holding her phone out to me, smiling expectantly.

Mechanically I step away from Gideon and take the phone, snapping a few pictures of her and Sudha and Madison, their arms around one another.

When I look back at Gideon, he's running one hand through his hair, a chagrined sort of smile on his face.

I try to return it, but I'm not sure how convincing it is. "I, uh. I need to find Iris," I say. "I have to ask her about something." I know he'll offer to look with me, so I break away, calling "I'll be back" over my shoulder.

The lawn dividing the gym from the parking lot is perfectly manicured, and the grass is soft and plush beneath my shoes as I cut across it.

I make it to the sidewalk bordering the lot. I don't have my coat, or my phone, but I don't care.

When I'm with you, I can just exist.

It's the same notion as Will Sorenson's, isn't it? Just packaged differently. Someone you exist around. Someone you feel regular about.

I want to deny it, squish it down to nothing, go back inside, throw my arms around Gideon again. But I can't. Or rather, I can, but I won't, because I know the truth—it's over before it's even started.

I just need air. I just need to be alone.

But I'm not. Not for long, anyway. I hear a set of footsteps making their way from the gym.

"Hey, I saw Iris but she disappeared again, you'd think she's—" Gideon pauses when he reaches me. "You okay?" And then, "It's cold, geez," and he's shrugging out of his suit jacket and it's all too much.

"Is this a date?" I say.

He blinks, extending the coat toward me, but I don't take it. "I mean, it's a . . . it's a dance date. Not like a . . . *date* date. But still kind of a date?" There is a hopeful upward inflection at the end of that sentence. "I was actually . . . I sort of wanted to ask you about that."

"About what?"

"Maybe you and me could . . . maybe we could go on a date. A real one. Maybe we could be, like. Dating." There's a small smile on his lips, and he's still holding the coat.

I'm meant to say something. I'm supposed to respond.

I like you, you majestic space prince.

How hard would it be to say that? It's the truth. How hard would it be to close the distance between us? Thread my fingers through his hair, thumb the corners of his jaw, kiss him right.

But.

I'm the kind of person you feel regular about. I know that. And if anyone is going to find me . . . *not* regular . . . it certainly isn't going to be Gideon Prewitt.

And if he thinks he does, it's because I'm amusing, the same way trick birthday candles are amusing. Just in the moment, just situationally. Interesting until they aren't, diverting until they've served their purpose. He likes that he can exist around me—he likes it now—but he doesn't even realize it, that it's the very reason his feelings will wear off later.

I force myself to speak: "It's really . . . flattering. You know. But . . . I just think . . . Maybe it's not such a good idea."

"Why?"

"I just . . . I'm just trying to look out for myself."

"I don't understand."

"No, you wouldn't, would you?" I say, and he frowns, takes a step forward.

"Did I do something wrong?"

"Gideon, it's not . . ." I shake my head. I can't look him in the eyes, so I look up instead. I speak to the velvety sky above, my breath billowing up so that the words appear to puff out of me: "You're great, you're lots of fun, but I just don't think of you that way, okay? I'm not . . . interested . . . in you like that."

250

This is a lie, and some small stupid part of me hopes that Gideon will challenge it.

But he doesn't. It's quiet. Until finally he says, "Oh." And then, softer: "Oh. I thought you were."

I think of Havil the Wise: *The kill, young warrior. It must be clean, it must be swift, it must be complete.* "Yeah. Well. You were wrong."

When I dare to glance at Gideon, he's looking off across the parking lot, the coat now hanging limply at his side.

"Can we still be friends though?" he says, small.

"Of course," I reply. And I want that to be the end of this conversation. I want him to walk away. And maybe he'll turn back at the last moment with a wink and a cheeky grin because he doesn't really like me. Not really. He just thinks he does, and this will cure him of it. He'll head inside and dance the night away with the masses.

But he just looks in my general direction, and when he speaks, it's halting, stilted in a way I've never heard him speak before.

"I'm sorry if . . . like, if I made you—uncomfortable, or anything. I didn't . . . I thought . . ."

"It's okay."

"But we're still friends?"

"Yeah." I nod, too vigorously. I can salvage this. I can make it okay. I can be so chill.

I hold one hand up and say "High five?" like the colossal idiot I am. Gideon just smiles, lopsided, and he's blinking fast.

"I'm just gonna—I think I'll—" And then he nods, like he finished the thought, and walks away, in the opposite direction of the gym.

I lower my hand.

forty-five

I find Iris in the gym, back on the bleachers in the same spot we found her earlier.

"Do you want to go?" I say.

She frowns. "What happened?"

"Can we just go? Please?"

She looks at me for one beat more, and then she stands, tucks her clutch under one arm, and guides me out of the gym.

We go back outside, and I'm halfway crying by the time I realize that Gideon drove me, so I have no way to get home. I'd have to call my parents and try to explain how I rejected my date mid-dance, or Alex, who's not speaking to me, or Zoe, who would have to borrow a car and is still probably not speaking to me.

I look over at Iris, who's now on the phone.

"What are you doing?"

"Calling a ride," she says, before having a brief conversation with whoever's on the other end of the line.

A sleek black sedan whispers up to the curb a few minutes later, and we both get in the back. The driver is not Iris's mom or dad but rather a youngish-looking guy in a suit.

"Tell him your address," she says as we strap in.

"You have a driver?"

"No," she says, but it's in direct contradiction to the person currently sitting in the front seat. I blink at her, and she elaborates. "My parents have a driver. Sometimes."

I give the man my address, and we ride in silence for a few minutes until Iris finally heaves a sigh.

"Do I have to do the whole 'tell me what happened' thing, or can you just tell me what happened?"

"You just did the thing," I say, and sniff.

"Claudia."

I squeeze my eyes shut and tell her what happened in the parking lot with Gideon.

"I'm doing us both a favor," I say when I'm finished. "I'm being responsible. This is better than . . ." Than doing the whole thing. Hanging out and dating and getting attached and feeling feelings and having them be meaningless afterward.

Iris nods. "Yeah."

"Tell me I did the right thing."

"What if I can't?"

"Then *lie*, Iris, that's what friends do," I say, before a sob escapes.

"You did the right thing."

"How do you know?"

She doesn't reply for a moment, and when she does, her voice is even, measured. "Because I know you. And I know . . . you'd do what you thought was the right thing."

"But it feels terrible," I say.

She reaches out and pats my shoulder awkwardly.

I blink through the tears. "What are you doing? What is that?"

She pulls her hand away. "I don't know, I'm bad at this. Do you want a bottle of water?"

"What? Why?"

"I don't know! They keep them in the car! And you're like . . . losing fluids. I said I was bad at this."

I let out a weak laugh.

"Hey, look at that," Iris says, and she almost looks proud. "Maybe I'm better than I thought."

I wipe my eyes on the back of my arm. "Maybe."

It's quiet. Until Iris pulls out her phone. "Some pap pictures of Kenji went up earlier, do you want to see?"

I nod, and she pulls up an impressive array of photos of Kenji in skinny jeans and a slouchy hat, looking disgruntled as he walks into a fro-yo store and then out of a fro-yo store.

"He wore that shirt when the boys were on *The Tonight Show*," Iris says, and taps the photo, zooms in on Kenji's shirt. "It's Gucci. Do you like it?"

I nod. "He looks good in blue."

"Did you ever see the suit he wore to the VMAs last year?"

I shake my head.

"God, you've missed so much. Okay. Brace yourself."

I manage a small smile.

"What?" Iris looks up from the phone.

"Nothing." *I'm glad you're here.* "Show me."

* * *

I get a text about an hour after Iris drops me off. Gideon.

Are you around? Do you want a ride home?

No, I type and then pause before hitting send. *Thanks,* I add, *I'm good.* And then delete that. *I got a ride but thanks anyway!!!* Delete.

I squeeze my eyes shut for a moment. And then type, *Already home,* and hit send.

forty-six

Monday brings the first tech rehearsal.

It's an all-afternoon, into-the-evening affair. A handful of people are called to the shop at the start to pick up specific costume pieces that they want to rehearse with.

Kaitlyn Winthrop needs her skirt, which is a little tougher to move around in than the other fairies' outfits. I help her get it on and then fuss with it a bit.

Gideon has come, too, to get his cloak. I manage to only glance his way when he's spinning around for Del to assess. After she adjusts a few little things and pronounces him finished, she turns to help Aimee with her stuff.

"All done?" Kaitlyn says.

"Um." I turn back to the seam I'm supposed to be fixing, smooth it down, and nod. "You're good to go. Let me know if you need anything else."

"What do you think?" she says, and when I look up, I see she's addressing Gideon, who's come up behind us.

"Ravishing," he replies. "What about me?"

Kaitlyn grins. "You look like a sexy pirate."

"Thank you," Gideon says quite seriously, and then Kaitlyn heads off to talk to Caris. Leaving me and Gideon alone.

Silence. I start sifting through my sewing kit like I'm looking for something.

He picks up a pincushion on the table beside us and then puts it back down. "Hey. So . . . sorry for leaving you hanging the other night. High-five-wise."

Sorry for abandoning you at the dance. "No problem."

Gideon shifts from one foot to the other. Scratches the back of his neck. I almost want to laugh—with him wearing that cloak, it's like I'm having a really awkward moment with some mercenary mage in Battle Quest.

"And I'm sorry," he says after a pause. "You know, if I made things weird. I thought . . ." I glance at him, and he's looking off across the room, his eyebrows pulled down. "I thought about it, and I realized you always . . . I mean, you've always been really nice and friendly, but you've never done anything to—like, encourage me, and I think I was just seeing something there because I wanted something to be there, and I—I'm sorry."

When I speak, it comes out kind of short, kind of gruff, because I don't know how else to control my voice: "It's fine. Don't be sorry."

He nods.

I go back to my kit. I don't know what else to do. Gideon just stands there.

Del finishes with Aimee, and Aimee pauses at the door, waiting for Gideon.

"You should probably get back," I say.

"Yeah. Okay. I . . . I'll see you, I guess."

I nod, then say "See you" tightly. Gideon and Aimee leave.

I drop my sewing. Lower my head into my hands and squeeze my eyes shut.

"Why are you doing this to yourself?" comes Del's voice from the corner.

"Are you ever not listening? Seriously."

She doesn't dignify that with a direct response. "Is this about whatever Lena said to you at Brunati's?"

"No," I say. I hear Del move across the room.

When I open my eyes, she is standing on the other side of the worktable, leaning against it and looking right at me. "Say it again to my face."

I look away.

Del just shakes her head. "I don't understand why you would listen to her."

"It's not about *listening*. It's just . . . I just . . ."

"What?"

He loves something until he doesn't. "If someone says the thing that you're afraid of . . . If someone thinks it, and you think it, too, then it has to be at least a little bit true, right?"

"That's bullshit," Del says.

"Is it, though? It's like . . . someone agreeing with you. It's like validation."

"Maybe you're both wrong. Did you ever think of that?"

I don't reply.

It's not about Lena, not really. It's just easier to never start something than to have to see it end.

* * *

We break for dinner.

Iris comes to the shop, and we split the Pinky's sub I brought. Four point five inches of sandwich apiece. She tells me about tech thus far, which involved a lot of stopping and starting and people forgetting their lines. She says *people* emphatically.

"Lena?" I say.

She shakes her head, a wrinkle between her brows. "Paige."

"Really?"

"She was having trouble."

"Huh."

"I hope everything's okay," Iris says quietly, pulling a piece of shredded lettuce out of her sandwich and frowning at it.

"There's nothing wrong with that lettuce."

"I meant with Paige."

"I know, but you're giving the lettuce a suspicious look."

"What makes you the lettuce expert?"

"Well, I do work at Pinky's."

Iris blinks at me, still frowning. "You work at Pinky's?"

"Yeah . . ."

"Seriously? What else are you hiding? Do you also work for the CIA?"

"I'm not *hiding*, I just . . . it's never come up. I haven't been working much since we've been doing the show anyway."

"Oh."

It's quiet.

"What?" I say.

"Just. I don't know." She looks up, almost hesitant. "I . . . am sorry. For the paper. That we had to do this because we—because

259

I—fucked up the paper. I'm sorry if it, like . . . disrupted your life."

I blink down at the Pinky's wrapper, having already decimated my four-point-five inches of sandwich.

"Yeah, no." I look back up at Iris. "I think I'm kind of glad the show happened. Even with . . ." Everything. Even with everything.

"Me too," Iris says. "A little bit. Maybe."

I smile.

Noah comes by after the dinner break to practice getting the donkey head on and off for his big transformation scene. One of us will need to be backstage during the show to help him with it, so we all run through it a few times.

They're about to start teching this scene, so Del turns to me when we're finished. "Claudia, why don't you go back up with him?"

I glance at Noah, who is fumbling with one of the ears.

"Yeah, sure."

So I get custody of the donkey head, and we head back up together.

As soon as the door to the shop closes behind us, Noah speaks. "Hey, so it's probably none of my business, but . . . did something happen with Gideon?"

"No," I say, starting down the hall toward the stairs.

"Because he's been acting weird since Homecoming."

"I thought he told you everything."

"He does. So it's particularly weird that he hasn't said why he's being weird." We reach the staircase and head up in silence. But Noah stops at the top. "Look, I just . . . I'm just worried about him."

I think of the babies in sailor suits, and *did you ever want a brother too?*

I already have one, remember?

"He asked me out," I say. "I said no. That's all."

Noah blinks. "I thought you guys liked each other."

"That doesn't really matter." I start toward the auditorium.

"What's that supposed to mean?"

I pause as we reach the door to the theater. "He doesn't know how to like something for more than ten minutes," I say. Lena's words on my lips. "He refuses to go to parties because of the cups. He remembers the presents people give him but not the people themselves. That's just . . . it's just how he is, right?"

Noah just shakes his head. "You don't know him at all." He starts through the door but then turns back. "For real. If you think that, then you don't know him at all."

Then he walks away.

forty-seven

Tech runs mostly smooth on Tuesday—they make it all the way through to the end of the show, at least—and Wednesday brings the first dress rehearsal.

Paige comes into the shop for a costume fix after school, before everyone's due in the auditorium for the run-through. Del and Caris are occupied, so it falls to me to help her. I try to chat about the show while I adjust the straps on her top, but she seems distracted.

When I finally give up on conversation, she speaks.

"Are you, um." Paige looks up at the ceiling and then says in a rush, "Are you and Iris dating?" Before I can answer, or even react, she goes on: "I know I'm being unfair, I know we broke up, and I don't have any right to know her business but, like, do you like her, are you guys dating?"

"No," I say.

"But . . . she seems really . . . happy. Around you. And I noticed, at Homecoming . . ."

"What?"

"I noticed that you came with Gideon, but you left with Iris. And then he seemed kind of upset when I saw him later. . . ."

"Does he think I turned him down for Iris?"

"No, but I sort of just . . . figured. Wait, so you did turn him down?"

"No. I mean, yes, I did, but not for Iris. We're not together."

Only because I am actively working on Paige's torso do I note the little breath she releases at that. A small sigh of something that can only be relief.

I have to tell Iris. Iris, who was sitting on the bleachers at Homecoming in that pink dress, several months too late to be wearing it, but wearing it all the same.

Del suddenly appears at my shoulder, batting my hand away. "Not like that. Let me. Look at Josie's hem, will you?"

I nod. Josie is busy admiring herself in the mirror. Her fairy costume is pretty awesome, if I do say so myself. Not that I had any hand in designing it, but I did sew the shirt and collar, and the petticoat that Del constructed looks awesome. But Josie snagged a hem during rehearsal yesterday, so I make her stand still, and I start pinning.

I finish with Josie, and she leaves just as Iris arrives.

She spots Del and Paige, laughing about something, and scowls instantly.

"Hey, come here," I say, but Iris barely gives me a glance. "I have to *tell you something important.*" There is no way to communicate *Paige is still into you* with my eyes, especially not when Paige and Del are standing so close together and Iris can't rip her gaze away from them.

"How's it going, Del?" Iris says loudly.

Del glances up, looking decidedly put off. "Fine, Iris. How are you?"

"I was wondering if you heard from any other design schools yet, or if you had just been rejected from the one so far."

Oh shit.

"What's your problem?" Del says, lips curving into a smile that is zero percent friendly and 100 percent bad news for Iris. "Seriously."

"I don't have a problem," Iris replies.

"Literally everyone who's ever met you would beg to differ."

"Um," I say, awkwardly loud. "Del, will you help me with—"

"I mean, isn't that why things didn't work out between you two?" Del looks between Paige and Iris.

"Hey, how about we not?" Paige says with false brightness.

"Oh, wait, I remember why," Del continues. "It's because you're selfish as fuck. That seemed to be your main problem. Because she wanted you to be *better than you are*."

"Del," Paige says.

Iris just blinks. "What did you say?"

Del doesn't repeat it, but she doesn't have to. We all heard.

For a second, I think Iris might go at Del. Like seriously have a go at her. It would be a bit like a terrier taking on a Great Dane, but I have no doubt that Iris could inflict some damage if she wanted to.

But instead she turns to me, and there's color high in her cheeks. "You told?" she says, and her voice is choked. "You told her?"

I blink. And then it registers. Of course it does. I was the only one who heard Paige say that. The only one besides Iris, that is. "I didn't," I say. "I wouldn't tell, I wouldn't—"

"You're so full of shit," Iris says, and then leaves.

My legs move almost of their own volition, carrying me out into the hall after her. She's moving swiftly away, and I have to jog to catch up.

"I didn't tell, I swear," I say, and there's desperation to it. My heart is beating faster, and it feels like all the blood is rushing up my neck, up and around my head, every nerve ending suddenly alight with panic, with the way that Iris looked at me in there. Like I'm the ultimate betrayer. "Iris." I put a hand on her shoulder to stop her, and she turns, but she wrenches away from me.

"I knew it," she says, and even though she's crying, her words come out quick, clear, harsh: "I knew it from the start but I didn't listen to that voice telling me to not bother with you, because you were nice to me, and I was lonely, and that's on me. But being a lying piece of shit? That's on you, Claudia."

She didn't lay a finger on me, but it hurts like she did, like she laid a punch right to my solar plexus.

"I didn't" is all I can say.

"Go screw yourself," Iris replies, and leaves.

This time I don't follow.

forty-eight

As I return to the shop, Paige bursts through the door.

"I'm sorry," she says, eyes wide and sad. "I'm sorry, I'll talk to her. I'll tell her the truth."

"What truth?"

"That it was me. I told Del."

"This isn't like a broken picture frame—you can't just take the blame for it."

"But I did. I told her. After Iris and I broke up, I . . . talked to Del about it some, and it helped. I'll tell Iris. I will."

I take a deep breath. Then I shake my head. "It's fine."

"No, Claudia—"

"Really. It doesn't matter." That's a lie. "I don't care." And another.

I walk past her and into the shop, grab my bag off one of the worktables and ignore Del, who has paused in front of a dress form with Hippolyta's wedding dress on it. *Worth it, not worth it. Worth it, not worth it.*

"That was mean," I say finally. "And really unnecessary."

Del doesn't reply. Doesn't acknowledge that I've spoken at all. I leave.

I walk around the Grove for fifteen minutes.

It seemed reasonable to storm off, but rationally, I need to be there for rehearsal. I have to do last-minute fixes on the costumes. I have to be on hand to take care of the donkey head.

So I go back. And I suffer through the last-minute fixes and rehearsal, standing backstage to claim the donkey head after Bottom has been officially restored to his original self.

When it's all over—late into the evening—I go home and log into Battle Quest. I start a side quest for a blacksmith in the capital city, journeying out into the Blaze to collect some rare ore from a miner.

It's dark out there in the fields, the middle of the night. At least momentarily.

The Aradanian suns have risen and I've gotten the ore by the time my chat window dings.

>Gideon Prewitt waves at you

Viola is positioned next to a hillside just outside the capital city. I'm all alone, or so it seems, until I toggle my view around and see Gideon Prewitt, now a level-nine notary signore, standing nearby.

>Gideon Prewitt strikes a gentlemanly pose

>Gideon Prewitt twirls

>Gideon Prewitt does the Horsenfeld shuffle

I don't respond. Viola just stands, stoic, and there's no way that Gideon can know that I'm sad, that I feel inside out and upside down, there's no way that he can tell. But the chat window dings again.

>Gideon Prewitt: you okay?

On-screen, avatar Gideon Prewitt walks right up to Viola. And it's so stupid, I'm so stupid, but I wish he was here, I wish it was real. I wish I could bury my face in his neck. I want it so bad my fingers twitch on the controller, straining not to make my stupid game character hug his stupid game character so at least some facsimile of it can exist.

I stay still. Viola stands, motionless.

>Gideon Prewitt: claude?

When my fingers finally spring into action, it's to log off.

I set my computer aside and lie on my bed, and I can't help but think of the first day of preschool.

I knew that school was a place that Julia went off to every day. Alex had started going, too, and I knew that he liked it—the coloring and the block corner and the little round tokens you could exchange for treats on special days.

But I wanted to stay home with my mom, who was still just part-time back then, working evenings after my dad got home from work.

On the first day of preschool, my mom held my hand and walked me into the classroom. She got me situated at a table where a couple of kids were doing puzzles and then hung back a bit while I started in on mine. The puzzle was tricky, but I was getting the hang of it—I almost had it—

Then I turned around and saw that she wasn't there anymore.

I cried and cried and cried when I realized she had left. I cried even as a little girl from one of the other tables came up to me. She was wearing denim shorts and a purple striped T-shirt. Her hair was

arranged in little twists, clasped at the ends by plastic flower barrettes in an array of neon colors. The barrettes clicked against one
another as she moved toward me.

"She's gonna come back," she said as I hiccupped in between
sobs. "Your mama. She'll come back later. Mrs. Parson said."

Her eyes were very solemn. I didn't understand solemnity or concern; I couldn't define the fact that she was looking at me like I was
important. Like I mattered. But it stopped my crying, momentarily.

I didn't know what to say. So I reached out and touched one of
her barrettes.

Her face split into a smile. She reached up and unclipped the
barrette, and before I could react, she grabbed a hunk of my hair
and tried to clip it in. But it was too much, the barrette wouldn't
close. So she just pressed it into my hand instead—a lime-green
daisy clip.

I admired it, the perfect flower shape, and then held it out to her.

"You can keep it," Zoe said. And just like that, we were friends.

I sit up.

And stand and cross over to my dresser, to the jewelry box on
top. I slide open one of the tiny drawers, top left. If the jewelry box
had a heart, this would be it.

I pick up the barrette. Clasp it hard and hold my fist against my
mouth. I know that it will press a daisy shape into my palm, and I
don't even care.

I cry hard.

forty-nine

I'm crossing through the Grove on Thursday before the start of dress rehearsal. The leaves on the trees have thinned—most have fallen in a carpet of yellows and reds and browns—and I see the figures up ahead before I hear them.

It's Gideon and Noah, heads bent in conversation.

It reminds me of the first day of school—coming here with Caris and Robbie. Gideon raising his arms in the air like a referee, calling us all over. Asking everyone about their summer like he actually cared.

It's too late to turn away when they see me. Gideon waves, tentative compared to that first-day-of-school enthusiasm.

I reach into my pocket to clasp the green daisy barrette that I've been carrying around today like a totem. Like it will bring me comfort, or peace of mind, like it will help guard me against Gideon and his cautious smile.

Except the barrette isn't there.

I check my other pocket. I turn them both out. I spin around, in case it slipped out just now.

But the barrette is nowhere on me, nowhere in sight.

I had it in calc this afternoon, I had it at my locker after class, and as I headed over here, I'm certain I did, mostly certain, fairly certain—

"Claudia?"

Leaves crunch as Gideon and Noah head my way.

I'm frantically scanning the ground when they reach me.

"What's wrong?" Gideon says.

"I lost something." I can't keep the panic out of my voice, and it's stupid, I know it is, but—

"What is it?" Noah says, brow furrowed.

"A hair clip. It's green, and it's shaped like a flower—"

The look they both give me says that my reaction is not proportional to the situation. I shake my head. "It's important. I have to find it."

"Then we'll find it," Gideon says. "When did you last have it?"

"Right before I got to the Grove. It's bright green and plastic, it's—" I watch as Gideon starts searching in earnest, but Noah is still giving me that look. "I know it sounds stupid, but I need it."

He nods. "Yeah, okay."

We start retracing my steps back up toward school, but there are so many leaves on the ground, I already know deep down that this is basically a pointless endeavor. But I keep looking anyway.

I pull my phone out of my pocket eventually to use the flashlight. But as soon as I click it on, I see texts from my mom and four missed calls.

I pause, opening the texts first:

Juju's in labor.

I blink.

Going to Indy.

Daddy's coming too.

Will call with more news.

"Claude?"

It's too early.

I read the words again:

Juju's in labor.

"What is it?" Gideon's stopped off to the right of the path, looking my way.

"My sister's having her baby," I say, and Gideon's expression brightens, but I shake my head, my heart pounding. "Too early, it's too early." She's only thirty weeks. I know because my mom has enthusiastically noted it on our kitchen calendar for every month—

JULIA AT SIXTEEN WEEKS!

TWENTY-FOUR WEEKS!!

JUJU AT TWENTY-EIGHT!!!!!

He frowns. "Maybe . . . maybe it's a false alarm?"

I dial my mom.

It's for real.

I'll keep you updated, Mom said on the phone. *I'll tell you as soon as we know something.*

Gideon offers to drive me home. As we're getting into his car, my phone rings. Alex.

"I'm on my way home," I say.

"Okay." A pause. "Good."

We hang up, and all I can think of are the babies at Roosevelt-Hart, the ones that are so tiny they look like nothing more than a bundle of blankets. I didn't know human beings could ever be that small, could ever be so fragile.

It's quiet on the ride until I can't take the quiet anymore.

"My mom made all these hats," I say. "Baby hats."

"Yeah?" Gideon replies.

"Yeah."

I twist my fingers together in my lap, and I try to focus on anything other than my mom picking out the patterns and comparing yarns, rubbing different skeins against the inside of her wrist in the aisle of a craft store to see what was the softest. The last one she finished was yellow with a little orange flap across the forehead like a duck's bill, and when we showed it to her on Skype Julia said it was "fricking adorable, Mom, but seriously, the kid only has one head."

"And it will always be warm," Mom replied.

Out of the corner of my eye I see Gideon glance over at me. And then he looks straight ahead again, but he rests one hand on the console between our seats, palm up. Like an invitation. Like I could take it if I wanted.

I don't hesitate.

And it's quiet again until I realize how tight I'm holding on. I ease up but don't let go. "Sorry."

He shakes his head. "Vic used to hold my hand when she was little, like when she would get shots and stuff? She has this crazy iron grip. When she got her ears pierced in fifth grade, I thought she broke my finger. So I'm used to it. I don't . . . I don't mind."

When we pull up to my house, I have to let go of Gideon's hand. I swallow and look out the window, and that's when I see someone is sitting on our front stoop.

Zoe.

She has her arms wrapped around her knees, her hands pulled into the sleeves of her sweatshirt.

I get out of the car before Gideon's barely even stopped it, cross the lawn, and hug her hard.

She hugs back.

"What are you doing here?"

"Alex texted me."

"Where is he?"

"Inside. It was weird so I thought I'd wait out here."

"Zoe—"

"Is that the space prince?"

I let go of Zoe and turn. Gideon is hovering awkwardly by the car.

I grab Zoe's hand and lead her over. "This is Gideon." I gesture to Zoe. "This is Zoe, she's my best friend."

"Nice to meet you," she says.

"You too," he replies, and then it's quiet.

"Well, I should—" Gideon starts, just as Zoe says:

"You should—"

"Sorry?"

"Stay," Zoe says. "You should stay."

"I . . ." Gideon looks torn. "I have to get back for dress rehearsal."

I clap a hand to my head. "Rehearsal. Fuck. I didn't tell Del—"

"Don't worry. I'll talk to her," Gideon says and then pauses. "I could . . . I could stay, though," he says, looking hesitant. "If you want."

"Don't be ridiculous. You have to do the show."

"I could come back after. I could . . . bring food."

Don't worry about it is what I should say. *We'll be fine.* Instead I nod. "Yes. Yeah. Okay."

"Okay." He nods too. "I'll be back." And then it's silent for a moment.

Until Zoe says "Drive safe" next to me, too loud, and I almost jump.

"Did you forget I was here?" she says as we watch Gideon pull away from the curb. She pokes me. "Don't lie. You did. You totally did. You were lost in the space prince's majestic eyes."

"I was not."

"We should've tried to make him laugh, I want to hear that weird chuckle."

"Zoe, geez." I smile, but it turns into a grimace, and she pulls me into another hug. "I'm scared," I mumble into her shoulder.

"Me too."

"But I'm glad you're here."

Her grip on my back tightens slightly. "Me too."

fifty

"I would've picked you up," Alex says when we get inside.

"Have you heard anything new?" I reply, even though I know he probably hasn't. He shakes his head, and it's quiet for a moment, me and Zoe in the doorway to the living room, Alex on the couch with his phone at his side. If it's good news, my mom might call either of us. But if it's bad news, she'll definitely call him.

He has his computer open on his lap. He inherited Julia's when she finished college. It's seen better days, like mine, but it still runs Battle Quest, and that's what matters. "I think I found it," he says after a moment, eyes dropping to the screen. "The gateway to the Lord of Wizard."

"What?"

"I ran a quest for a druid who gave me a scrying stone. But not the normal kind, like the mages get? I only noticed after I was reading up online—and that map you found in the Blaze? The one I asked for a while back?" I nod. "I put them together, and it lit up this portal in the outer rim. I think . . . I think it might be it. It's not a dungeon we've ever played before, it's not something anyone's mentioned from the last patch."

"Should we go?" Zoe says, her eyes on me. She hasn't looked Alex's way once. I wonder briefly if this is how it's going to be from here on out between the three of us. Stiff and awkward and so unlike it was before.

"I don't know," I say. "Maybe we should wait for Julia."

Alex considers it for a moment. "We'll just go check it out. We can come back with her and Mark when they . . . if they want to play again."

There is nothing else to do but wait for news, to sit and ruminate about baby hats.

So we go.

Zoe and I get our laptops, and then Viola, Korbinian, and Alex's character, Eustace Everfire, are trekking across the Blaze.

I was just here, moving through this very same part of the country, with Iris and Gideon. Seeing Alphoneus Centurion. It seems like ages ago.

We follow Alex's charmed map to the outer rim, and it takes us to a large rock formation. As we get closer, I can see the outline of a door within it, emitting a weak glow.

Korbinian walks right up to it, presses one gloved hand to the door, and attempts to open it. Nothing happens.

"There's an inscription," Zoe says.

I toggle the view so I can see closer.

Traveler, to enter—the cardinal touches, the stallion gambols.

It's quiet for a bit as we think, Viola, Korbinian, and Eustace standing motionless, the small strip of light around the door pulsing faintly.

277

Suddenly Zoe breathes in sharply. On-screen, Korbinian moves, touching a finger to the door—top, bottom, and each side. Korbinian steps back, and four symbols alight on the door, one in each spot that Korbinian touched.

"Cardinal directions," Zoe says. "North, south, east, west."

We wait.

"What about the stallion?" Alex says.

"Gambol means like, to jump around," I say. "To prance." I flash on Iris suddenly: *That was an SAT word.* She and Gideon aren't nearly experienced enough with Battle Quest to make it in a boss battle like the one potentially waiting for us behind this door. But part of me wishes they were here with us too. Gideon would have avatar Gideon Prewitt twirling, jumping around, doing the—

"Horsenfeld shuffle," I say.

"What?"

"Stallion gambol. Do the Horsenfeld shuffle."

I start Viola off dancing. Eustace and Korbinian join in, and suddenly the door glows bright white and swings open to reveal a dark tunnel.

"Yes!"

We head inside. The door slams behind us. It's pitch black.

Suddenly, a booming voice echoes through the tunnel.

>Lord of Wizard: Travelers, are you prepared?

>Lord of Wizard: To battle the Lord of Wizard, to accept your fate?

>Lord of Wizard: Are you prepared to sacrifice your soul to the island forever, should you fail?

"Sorry, what now?" Zoe says.

"Where is he?" On screen, Eustace Everfire lights up an orb that fills the tunnel with faint light. We're alone. But the Lord of Wizard continues to speak.

>Lord of Wizard: Will you meet your end head-on?

"What does that even mean?" I say. Is that why no one's talked about this battle? Because if you fail, you have to start over? I look over at Alex. "He can't actually kill our characters, right?"

"If you die against the Lord of Wizard, you die in real life," Alex murmurs, and Zoe huffs a laugh.

"I'm serious," I say. "What does that mean? Sacrifice our souls to the island?" I've spent too long building up Viola's stats, running her through the different classes, to give her up now.

"Let's find out," Alex says.

>Lord of Wizard: Do you accept?

We all click yes.

It's not long before we're running from an army of the undead.

They started popping up in twos and threes, and at first it was manageable. We'd slay a few and move forward, farther and farther through the winding tunnels.

But soon they come in larger numbers, slowing us down, and then there are too many to reasonably fight off without the risk of dying, so we start to run. The tunnels narrow and widen and narrow again.

Zoe is in the lead. "I think I see a light up ahead." Korbinian quickens, Viola and Eustace right behind, advancing on what appears to be an opening, lit beyond by the dancing orange glow of torchlight. I cast a quick look back and see that the undead hordes trailing us have thickened immensely.

We're almost there—they're gaining on us—we throw ourselves through the opening—

A door swings shut behind us. Torches lining the walls flare brighter, illuminating the single cloaked figure in the middle of the room.

His back is turned to us, but I know it's him.

>Lord of Wizard: Here, travelers, will you meet your doom.

He turns to us, nothing but darkness beneath the hood of his cloak, except for the gleam of a smile.

A number of the undead detach from the walls of the chamber and surround the Lord of Wizard, forming a protective barrier around him. In order to get to him, we'll have to go through them.

There are just three of us—with Julia and Mark, maybe, playing healer and doing combat, too, we might make a dent, but as it is, it's just Zoe healing, Alex tanking, and me doing damage, trying to strike where I can while Alex draws the attention of the undead soldiers.

Finally we break through the horde and get to the Wizard himself. But as we approach him, the Wizard claps his staff against the ground once, twice, three times, and begins to grow.

And grow. And grow.

"Not fair!" Zoe says. "He was normal-sized before!"

>Lord of Wizard: Do you have faith in your abilities, travelers?

>Lord of Wizard: Are you prepared to die by your own sword?

The Wizard brings his staff to the ground again, and a burst of electricity sweeps from its base. We barely jump back in time, and as it is, Korbinian is licked by a tail of lightning, and his health bar drops in half.

Alex and I both launch a series of attacks against the Wizard,

Alex pulling back when he can, trying to draw the Wizard's attention away from us, but the ring of undead soldiers around him has replenished, and they start to attack as well. The Wizard himself seems to be surrounded by a shield—any magic I send his way rebounds off him.

It's quiet among us, just the clicking of our keys as we fight—on-screen, explosions and bursts of lightning and the Lord of Wizard's laugh, rising above it all.

>Lord of Wizard: Are you ready to accept defeat?

"I have an idea," Alex says, and suddenly Eustace Everfire glows purple.

"What are you doing? What is that?"

"A new spell."

Eustace Everfire's health bar begins draining rapidly as he absorbs attacks from the surrounding monsters.

"It's like a switch," Alex says. "You just have to wait to flip it."

"Alex, you're gonna—"

"Keep fighting," he says, and glances over at me. "You got this."

"If you're out, you're out, you might not come back."

"You got this," he says again.

"Zoe, stop him."

"Keep going!" she says. "One more push."

Eustace is absorbing the Wizard's attacks now, his entire body pulsing.

>The Lord of Wizard: BOW BEFORE ME.

Eustace suddenly glows white and lets out one giant surge of magic aimed at the Wizard. The shield falls momentarily.

"Do it," Alex says. "Now!" Eustace falls to the ground in a crumpled heap, the health bar above his head at just above zero.

I don't have a moment to waste. I launch a series of attacks. Zoe heals me, adding to the attack when she can.

Together, we fight, giving it everything we've got. The Lord of Wizard's energy finally, finally drains.

>QUEST COMPLETED.

"Yes!" Alex yells. "Fuck yes!"

"We did it," Zoe says, and it's almost a question. "We did it!"

We cheer. We yell. We jump around.

Until Alex's phone chimes.

Still in labor. Probably a few more hours.

And we all sink back down onto the couch.

fifty-one

We decide to put off exploring the Island of Souls until we can come back and repeat the battle with Julia and Mark. Instead we watch TV. At least, we're all acting like we're watching TV, but to me, it barely registers.

Eventually, there's a knock at the front door.

Gideon is standing on the porch, holding a stack of pizza boxes.

"Sorry," he says when I open the door. "I should've called. Is everything—do you want—"

Yes. The pizzas and also him.

"Come in," I say.

He hesitates. "I brought Iris," he says. "And I usually drive Noah home, so he's here, too. I could, uh, I could just leave the food, or I could drop them off and then come back if you want—"

"Everyone can come in. You and them and the pizzas and you."

His lips quirk, an almost-smile. He waves to the car, and Noah and Iris get out.

Iris has her arms folded, head down. She stops inside the door, even as Noah and Gideon go ahead.

"It's me from before," I hear Gideon say inside. "And this is Noah Edelman. He's one of the best people I know."

"How's your sister?" Iris says, studiously examining the doorframe.

"Still in labor. No news yet."

She nods. "I can . . . call a ride. I just wanted to see if you were okay. If you needed anything. And . . . I wanted to say I'm sorry." She meets my gaze. "I know that you didn't tell Del. Paige talked to me. And even if she hadn't, I know you wouldn't, I know that. I just . . ." She shakes her head. "It's kind of like, my mom, she had this dog when I was little, this really ugly Affenpinscher? She had gotten him before I was born. And he was old, and if you came up behind him and he didn't hear you, he would just snap at you, it didn't matter who it was, he just . . . reacted, and sometimes, I just . . . react. I'm not like you and Paige; when it comes to people, the only thing I'm good at is saying shitty things to them, and I . . . I'm sorry."

She straightens up. "Anyway, I hope your sister's okay, and I hope the baby is okay. Just . . . let me know if there's anything I can do."

She turns to go.

"Wait. Do you want pizza?"

"Like . . . to take with me?"

"Like, to eat here, with us."

Iris blinks. "You forgive me?"

"Of course."

"Just like that?" she says. "It's that easy?"

"Sometimes. Sometimes not."

"But this time?"

"Yeah," I say. "It's that easy."

We spread the pizzas out on the table in the living room, and I go into the kitchen for plates. Gideon and Noah follow me in.

"There are drinks in the fridge," I say, and then stop with one hand on the cabinet door and check my phone again. Nothing.

Noah goes into the fridge, but Gideon just leans against the counter next to me as I start pulling some dishes down from the cabinet.

"I was born six weeks early, you know," he says quietly.

"Really?"

"Yeah," Noah says. "And just look at him." He closes the fridge. "Seriously, look at him." Gideon straightens up and begins doing a model walk across the room and into the hall, swinging his arms, fingers extended, kicking out each foot with his head held high.

"Look at those legs," Noah says. "Look at that bone structure. Look at those eyes, you could get fucking lost in them."

"You need GoogleMaps to find your way out of my eyes," Gideon says, executing an elaborate turn before catwalking back. "Or at least a comparable navigation app."

I smile a little.

We eat and watch TV, and there's not a whole lot of talking in general, but it's . . . nice. It's comforting.

Iris and Gideon fall asleep eventually—Iris in my dad's lounger, Gideon on the floor at her feet. Zoe and Alex are sitting on either side of me on the couch. I get up at one point to show Noah where the bathroom is, and when I come back they're as far apart from each other as the couch will allow, their eyes fixed on the TV as Gideon snores softly.

This isn't what I want. But it's not even about what I want, is it? It's about what they want and how I got in the middle of that.

"I can't with you guys," I say. "I can't do this. Get up." I look pointedly at them both. "Seriously."

"What?" Zoe says.

"You're going to go talk." I grab Alex's arm and pull him up.

"About what?"

"Feelings and stuff," I say, pulling Zoe to her feet too. "All the gushy stuff deep down inside. Don't hold back. Just never tell me about it."

Neither of them move.

"Go upstairs," I prompt. "Don't come back until it's all sorted out."

Finally—finally—they look at each other. Zoe smiles, the slightest bit. Alex nods.

And then they go upstairs.

I sink down on the couch, rest the crook of my elbow over my eyes. The pressure feels good.

Footsteps shuffle back in after a couple minutes.

"Want some more pizza?"

I shake my head, uncovering my eyes and looking up at Noah.

We haven't talked much since our conversation outside the theater at Danforth. Since *you don't know him at all*.

He gestures to the spot next to me. "Can I?"

I nod.

He sits and then stretches out his legs on the coffee table in front of us. For a little while it's quiet, save the TV and Gideon's snores.

"Can I tell you something about me that not a lot of people know?" he says eventually.

I nod.

"When I was eight, I really wanted to be on *America's Got Talent*. Like I had an act and everything."

"What was your act?"

"Tap dancing."

"You can tap dance?"

"No, I'm terrible. My mom took an audition video of me and told me she sent it in, but I'm pretty sure it never saw the light of day, thank God."

I smile a little.

"Do you want to know something else?"

"Sure."

"I have epilepsy." A pause. "I wish I could blame it for my bad tap dancing, but you can have epilepsy and still be a great tap dancer; the two aren't mutually exclusive. I just genuinely sucked at tap dancing."

I look over at him. His eyes are fixed on the ceiling, a small smile on his lips.

"It's not like a secret or anything. It just . . . I don't know, it doesn't come up until it comes up, you know? I should've said something at Triple F—we must've seemed nuts—but that's why Gideon . . ." He shrugs, his smile fading. "That's why. I want to get my license, but my parents won't let me try until I've been seizure-free for six months. And . . . I haven't been. So."

"Oh," I say. It feels insufficient, but I'm not sure what else to say. *I'm sorry* comes to mind, but that doesn't feel right. I get the impression Noah doesn't want me to be sorry.

It's quiet for a moment. And then he goes on.

"Do you remember that party? When he refused to go in because of the cups?"

"Yeah," I say, and my eyes dart over to where Gideon is lying on the floor.

"Don't worry, when he sleeps, he's dead to the world," Noah says, and then: "It wasn't because of the cups. It was because they had a strobe, and he was afraid it would set me off. I don't even . . . they're called photosensitive seizures? I've never even had one triggered by that. But he's so . . . paranoid." He shook his head. "Maybe that's mean. He's cautious. He's annoyingly cautious."

"Why did he lie about the cups, then? Why wouldn't he just say?"

"Because he'd rather look like an asshole than embarrass me in any way. Not that I'd even be embarrassed, but that's just . . . how he is." A pause. "Though that's not to say that every time Gideon looks like an asshole, it's because he thinks he's keeping me from embarrassment. He picks those shirts himself, after all."

"I like the shirts," I say.

"Of course you do."

It's quiet.

"What triggers yours, then? If not lights and stuff."

He shrugs. "Lots of things. If I don't take my meds properly, or if I'm tired, or stressed. Alcohol can do it, too," he adds with a little smile.

I look over at him. "The RumChata Incident?"

He meets my eyes, briefly, and grins. "Yeah. The first and only time we ever drank. Gideon didn't know . . . he didn't know it could cause it. I did. It was Christmas break freshman year and we stole a bottle of RumChata from my parents' cabinet and got hammered in my room. . . . When I woke up, I had the worst grand mal I've ever had. I fell off the bed, hit my head pretty bad on the nightstand." He pushes his hair back from his forehead with one hand, revealing a scar that disappears into his hairline. "It scared Gideon a lot," he says, quieter, letting his hair flop back down. "He's been annoyingly cautious ever since."

"He cares a lot about you," I say.

"I know. That's why I'm telling you. Maybe he changes obsessions every week, you know, maybe he likes lots of different things, but the important stuff . . . the people he cares about . . . he cares *so much*."

A pause. "After the RumChata Incident, when I got back home from the hospital, he came over and we were sitting outside—Ellie, my little sister, she still had this play set, we were sitting on the swings—and he looked at me and he said that he wished it was him." He shakes his head. "I said, you know, it's not gonna change anything, it's not gonna hold me back at all. And he said he knew that, he knew that nothing could, but that he still wished he could do that for me. If we could switch . . . he'd switch in a second, no question. Because . . ."

"Why?"

"Because he loves me," Noah says, and lets out a breath of laughter. "What a dick." A small smile. "Sometimes I wish there were like a combination of a hug and a punch 'cause that's what I would do to him. Like I want to punch-hug him, but also keep anything bad from ever happening to him. Because I . . . Like, that's how I love him, too. If it were him, I'd wish it were me."

I can't imagine loving someone that much, but at the same time, I know exactly how it feels, because that's how I feel about Zoe.

And fuck it, that's how I feel about Iris, too.

"That's why I got upset when you said that stuff about him.

I didn't mean to be a jerk about it. I just . . . I don't like people thinking things about him that aren't true. Not when he's literally the best person I know."

I shake my head. "I was being a jerk."

A colossal jerk.

It's quiet for a while after that. Finally I glance over at Noah again.

"If you could have a superpower, what would it be?"

"Super spit," he replies without a moment's hesitation.

"What—that's not even a thing. Why do you guys think that's a thing?"

He smiles.

fifty-two

We wake up Iris and Gideon eventually. It's late, and a school night, and they've got to be ready for opening night tomorrow.

"I could stay here," Gideon says, all sleep-soft, rubbing his eyes.

"It's okay. Can you drive though?"

"You can't get drunk off pizza."

I smile. "But are you too tired?"

He shakes his head.

They gather their coats and shoes. I thank them for the pizza. They make me promise to text as soon as I hear something. I say I will, even though I know I won't text until the morning.

Noah pauses inside the door. "This was one of the weirder parties I've ever been to," he says, and I manage a laugh.

I watch them go. Iris waves from the backseat as Gideon pulls away from the curb.

I go upstairs and get ready for bed, even though I'm not sure I'll fall asleep. The door to Alex's room is still closed.

I'm climbing into bed when there's a light knock at my door.

"Yeah?"

Zoe sticks her head in.

"Can I sleep over?" she says.

I pause, the covers halfway drawn up. "Sure. I mean. You and Alex can do whatever you want."

She makes a face. "I meant in here."

"Of course."

I find her some pajamas, and then we get in bed and lie awake.

"Did you fix it?" I say.

She looks over at me, nods. "I love him, Claude."

I nod back. "I'm sorry I was a dick."

She turns her gaze to the ceiling. "I should've told you before. I was scared. And not just of how you'd react, but . . . of things being different. Like, if you didn't know, then I could pretend that every-thing could stay the way it is."

It's quiet.

"Do you remember that first night, right when we started vol-unteering?" she says.

"Yeah."

"I always thought that maybe there was something a little wrong with me, because I didn't feel it like you did. I felt sad, obviously, like I felt really sorry for the kids and their families and I wanted to help, but when we had that talk about it, I remember thinking . . . 'Claudia feels it so much more than I do.' You just care so much, you know? And sometimes I feel like I'm cut off from stuff because my first instinct is like, 'okay, how can we fix this, what can we do to make it better.' But your first instinct is just like, 'how must the other person be feeling?' It cuts so close with you."

"I don't think that's a good thing," I murmur.

"No, it is. I think it is. I, like, admire it. And I think . . . You know, maybe we're friends because you're the way you are, and I'm the way I am, and I'm just . . . really fucking scared, Claude, of everything being different." She lets out a breath. "I told myself that I didn't say anything because I was worried about how you'd take it. But really I'm worried about me. About things changing so much and you not being around to feel things for me, you know? Like what am I gonna do then?"

"I'll always be here."

"But you won't. You're gonna go to school, and you're gonna do great. I already know because you have . . . good friends," she says. "You found really good ones."

I did. I got lucky, somehow.

"I meant here for you," I say. "Always."

"Really?"

"How is it even a question?"

"Even if me and Alex break up?"

"Of course."

"Even if we don't?"

"I'm gonna get so drunk at your wedding."

She laughs.

fifty-three

It's late into the night, and I've actually almost drifted off to sleep when I hear footsteps in the hall and someone pushes my bedroom door open.

Alex pads across the room and hands the phone to me, the light glowing blue-white through the darkness. I can't read his expression as I take it.

Zoe's still asleep. I get up and go into the hall.

"Mama?"

"Yeah, honey. I'm here. I'm sorry it's so late. We're all here."

She tells me that Julia delivered the baby. They've taken him to the NICU. He weighs three pounds, nine ounces, and his name is Jack.

I take a deep breath and let it out. And then another—breathing in sweet relief. "That's a good name," I say finally.

"Julia wants to talk to you."

She hands the phone off.

"You're okay? He's okay?" I say instead of hello.

"He's so little, Claude," Julia replies.

"But he's going to be okay?"

"He's on oxygen, but he's breathing okay; they said he doesn't need a ventilator. They put him in an incubator, like he's a . . . like a baby chick in an elementary school class. Do you remember that?"

I do remember that. We got eggs and waited for them to hatch in a plastic incubator with a lamp above it.

"How are you feeling? Are you okay?"

She doesn't speak.

"Julia."

"No," she says finally.

"Did they give you painkillers and stuff?"

"Not that. I feel—guilty." Her voice hitches on the word.

"What? Why?"

"I fucked up my first act as a mom," she says. "I evicted him from my uterus ten weeks early."

"That'll teach him to pay his rent on time."

Julia huffs wetly.

"He's going to grow up big and strong," I say. *Like Gideon.* "If he's anything like you and Mark, he's going to be so annoying."

"Claude," she says, but it's with a hint of a laugh.

"Before you know it, he's going to be twenty-five and you're going to be evicting him from the apartment over your garage because he refuses to get a job and spends all his time on elaborate Claymation re-creations of his favorite scenes from fantasy novels."

"Oh great, that's what you envision for my son?" she says with a laugh—in earnest this time, but it shifts partway through. "My son," she repeats. "My baby," and she's crying again.

"Jujube."

Silence.

"It's all going to be good," I say. "It's going to be so, so good."

She doesn't speak for a while.

"We're gonna come up there tomorrow."

"No, you can't," she says, her voice still hoarse. "Your play, Claude. You've worked so hard."

"I really haven't."

"No, you have to go. You and Alex can drive on Saturday."

"It's fine, really—"

"I had to hear you talk about it all this time. You're not missing that show. One day won't make a difference."

"Maybe he'll be bigger by Saturday."

"Maybe," she says. I'm afraid she'll cry again, so I go on.

"Say bye to Mom. I'll call in the morning."

"Yeah."

"Love you."

"Love you too."

I give Alex his phone back, and we both stand in the dimness of the hallway, quiet between us. And then I step forward and rest my forehead against his shoulder. He pats me on the back, a few bro thumps, before letting his hand rest there for a moment.

"It's okay," he says, and I nod even though I'm not sure what he means, whether it's everything with Julia—*she's okay, the baby's okay*—or the whole thing between us (*I would've picked you up*). Maybe a little of both.

I step back and look at my brother, who really would've picked me up tonight. Who broke up with Zoe even though neither of them wanted to. Who risked death for me to fight the Lord of Wizard, even after everything I said to him.

I want to say I'm sorry. I want to say I know how terrible I was, how selfish. But in this moment all I can get out is, "Do you remember Spooky Tree?"

He looks surprised. "Yeah."

"Thank you for kicking Spooky Tree."

One corner of his mouth lifts up. "Claude, I would kick a thousand Spooky Trees for you."

I nod. "Me too." My throat feels tight. "I mean, maybe not Spooky Tree exactly, but, like, a different, similarly scary tree."

"I might take you up on that one day," he says with a smile.

"Good. I'll be ready."

fifty-four

I text everyone about Jack in the morning.

AUNT CLAUDIA REALNESS, Gideon texts back, almost instantaneously.

I say good-bye to Zoe, talk to my mom again before I go to school, and then the day passes by somehow.

Iris and I grab something to eat after school and take it back to campus before the call for the show. We eat in the hall outside the shop, and she tells me about the final dress rehearsal last night—a few dropped lines, a couple prop mishaps, but mostly okay. I've just seen bits and pieces so far, but I'm excited to see the whole show, even if I have to watch part of it from backstage, on donkey-head duty.

"Noah was great," Iris says. "He's so freaking funny. And Gideon . . ."

"What?"

"I don't know, he's really good, too." She pulls on the straw in her drink, lifting it up and down a few times so it makes that obnoxious squeaking sound.

"Please don't do that," I say, just as she says:

"Are we ever going to talk about it?"

"What?"

"The whole Homecoming debacle."

"Are we calling it a debacle?"

"I call 'em like I see 'em."

I don't speak.

"Why'd you really turn him down? You're obviously obsessed with each other."

"We are not ob—look, okay. I just. It won't work out. I want it to, but I just know that it won't."

"Why?"

"Because." The truth: "Because I'm the kind of person you feel regular about."

Iris just looks at me. "How can you say that?"

And when I don't respond, she says it again: "How can you say that? Seriously. Because some dickbag said it to you one time? Look at me. Look at my face, Claudia, and, like, listen closely to the words that are coming from it, okay?"

I look at Iris's face.

"You have a best friend and siblings who love you. Gideon looks at you like you fucking hung the moon, and I—you have—" It doesn't make sense, but Iris's voice catches at that, her eyes shine all of a sudden. "I give a shit about you, too, you know. We all do. And so to say that . . . it's like you're saying we're wrong. Do you think we're all wrong? All of us? To care about you like that? To . . . value you, the way we do?"

I blink. The way she says "value" makes it sounds strikingly interchangeable with "love."

"No," I say. "Not . . . not when you put it like that."

"Okay," she says fiercely, and then nods. "Okay. So. If you don't want to date Gideon because you don't like him, then obviously don't date him. But if you're not with him because you think, like, you're not *worthy of love* or some bullshit like that, then reevaluate the situation with that in mind, okay?"

I nod.

"Good." She looks away, fussing with her straw again.

"Don't think that just because you said a bunch of nice stuff about me, I won't poke you for making that sound," I say when I can speak again.

"I would expect nothing less," Iris replies.

The door to the studio opens then, and Del comes out into the hall.

"You're here," she says.

"I am."

"Everyone okay?"

I nod.

"Good," she says. "We've got work to do."

fifty-five

The costumes have all been moved upstairs to the dressing rooms, so that's where Caris, Del, and I end up, running around and making sure everyone has everything they need. A junior named Alyssa Peters does makeup for the fairies; apparently she and Del worked together on creating distinct "looks" for each of them.

I'm helping Kaitlyn tie up the ribbons on her top—it's sort of a deconstructed corset—while Iris is having her makeup done. I look up in the mirror as Alyssa applies a thick glitter under Iris's eyes, running down onto her cheeks. Iris sticks her tongue out at me when she notices me looking.

Del comes by when Alyssa is finishing with Iris.

"Kaitlyn's next," she tells Alyssa as Iris gets up out of the chair. "What's with your hair?" she says to Iris.

We've made a number of different hairpieces for the fairies. Mostly old jewelry—pins and brooches and parts of necklaces—attached to bobby pins and barrettes, but also random things attached to them as well, like plastic figures and Matchbox cars, halves of old compacts and fake flowers.

"What?" Iris says, touching her hair. She's got one clip in, a gold-painted plastic army man attached.

"Iris. Seriously?"

"You said our hair was self-guided."

Del gestures to the open chair next to Kaitlyn's. "Sit."

Iris sits, and Del begins threading ribbons through her hair and putting assorted clips in here and there. When she's finished, Iris considers herself in the mirror.

"It looks nice," she says finally. "Everything . . . looks good."

Del gives a curt nod. "Thank you."

Then she heads off to assist elsewhere.

"You look really pretty," I say.

"Keep it in your pants," Iris replies, but I catch her smile in the mirror as she turns away.

"Hey!" Lena catches me when I step out of the dressing room. She's all done up as Helena, who looks positively bookish compared to Lena's usual out-of-school look.

Lena's holding her script, and for a second I panic—she's got her lines down, she has to have them by now—but before I can say anything, she flips the script open and points to it emphatically.

"I figured it out," she says, eyes bright.

"Figured what out?"

"The whole Demetrius thing. Remember when we talked about it? How it's messed up that he's still under a spell at the end? Well, I thought about it, and I was listening to Aimee and Gideon doing their scene yesterday, and I figured it out."

"What?"

"They're *different* spells. The one Oberon places on Titania, he says, *the next thing then she, waking, looks upon . . . she shall pursue it with the soul of love.* Then Puck charms Lysander, and it's kind of like that, he says"—she flips through her script, finds the spot—"*When thou wak'st, let love forbid sleep his seat on thy eyelid.* You explained that one to Aimee, remember?"

I nod.

"But Oberon charms Demetrius." She flips through the script again and then starts to read: "*Flower of this purple dye, hit with Cupid's archery, sink in apple of his eye, when his love he doth espy, let her shine as gloriously as the Venus of the sky. When thou wak'st, if she be by, beg of her for remedy.*" She looks at me expectantly. "Different spells, right?" she says when I don't speak. "The ones for Titania and Lysander are like, love whatever thing you happen to look at next. It could be legit anything. Lysander could've fallen in love with a . . . soda can or something, and it would have been fucking hilarious. But the one for Demetrius is specific—*when his love he doth espy.* When he sees the person he *already loves.* He loves Helena for real, he's just . . . forgotten it. He even says it at the end . . . his feelings for Hermia, you know, just . . . melted away. With the spell, Oberon just . . . brought out what he already felt for her. Reminded him of it." She looks up at me. "Did I figure it out? Did I do Shakespeare right?"

"I mean . . . yeah." I never thought of it like that. "That's good."

She beams at me. "You're a really good tutor."

"No, that was . . . all you."

"I know, right? But still." Before I can react, she throws her arms around me in a crushing hug. "This is gonna be so fun!" And then she's off.

Iris appears at my side. "What was that about?"

"Lena gets Shakespeare," I say.

Before Iris can reply, Sudha emerges from one of the smaller dressing rooms for the leads. When she spots us, she heads over, a look of concern on her face. "Hey, so, no big deal, but Paige is kind of freaking out a little—"

"What?" Iris says.

"And she won't talk to anyone, but maybe . . . maybe she'd talk to you."

We find Paige in the dressing room, sitting slumped in a chair, full Titania outfit on. Her hair is flowing down her back, shot through with gold and silver ribbons. Several strands of pearls have been twisted together into a circlet atop her head.

She looks up when we enter, eyes red, hands knotted in her lap. "I can't do it," she says miserably when she sees Iris. "I can't."

I don't know what to say, but Iris just crosses over and kneels in front of Paige's chair. "You can," she says calmly.

"I can't," Paige repeats.

"But you have to. Literally everyone is counting on you."

This is not the tactic I would've employed. I probably would've gone with something more like "you're going to do great!" or "don't worry, you've got this!" But Iris just rests her hands on Paige's knees.

"Look at me. Look."

Paige looks up, blinking glittery eyelids. Her mascara is still holding, even as tears stream down her face. Alyssa Peters really is a makeup wizard.

"I know it seems scary," Iris says calmly. "And I know that Claudia has just been waiting for the chance for you to screw up so she can throw on a tutu and go out there and make out with Gideon in front of Mr. Palmer and everyone's parents and Jesus."

"I don't—" I start, but Paige just gives a watery laugh, and Iris goes on.

"But she can't do what you can do. Nobody can. So we all need you to go out there and do it. You are . . . so good at this. You're . . . fucking . . . incandescent up there. Okay? And you know me, you know I won't lie to make someone feel better. So you know this is the absolute truth."

Paige nods. And then reaches to cup Iris's face, pulls her in, and kisses her.

I grin.

"I'm sorry," Paige says, pulling away a fraction of an inch. "For what I said when we broke up. I'm sorry."

Iris shakes her head. "You were right."

"No."

"You were. I'm selfish, and I need to be better. I do. And I want to be better. I want to be someone that you could love."

"You are someone that I love."

"But I want to be someone worthy of that," Iris says, and there's a fierceness to it that pricks unexpected tears in my eyes.

"You are," Paige says so softly, and then kisses her again.

I turn toward the mirrors and pick up a tube of lipstick on the counter just to have something to do.

"You are very unnecessary right now, Claudia," Iris says when they break apart again.

I smile. "I'll just be outside."

fifty-six

Paige goes on.

I watch parts of the show that are broadcast on TV in the green-room and sneak backstage to watch other parts from the wings. I wait with the donkey head and manage to get it on Noah in record time before his big reveal.

It's raucous backstage at intermission. Crowded and hectic and wonderful.

I linger in the wings for the start of the second half.

The lights go up on Gideon onstage, wondering what creature it is that Titania has fallen in love with. And then Aimee runs on and declares, *"My mistress with a monster is in love!"* and the show is back in action.

Someone steps up next to me. It's Iris. She smiles. Grabs my hand, leans her head against my shoulder. We stand like that and watch the show.

It's chaos backstage after the curtain call, but chaos of the best sort. Everyone's hugging and congratulating and celebrating. I spot Gideon cutting through the crowd, heading toward me.

"You were so good," I say when he reaches me. "Really, really good."

His cheeks are flushed, like he's been exercising, which I guess he kind of has—running around with Aimee, wreaking magical havoc all evening. "I have something for you," he says. "And also thank you. And also I have something for you. Wait here. Or in the hall? No, wait here, I'll be right back."

And he takes off.

I congratulate a few people, and Caris comes and gives me a hug, and then Gideon returns.

"Maybe out here?" he says, and then promptly turns and heads away, out the side door and into the hallway, which is deserted.

He turns to me when we get out there. He looks in disarray, his necklaces askew, his hair wild.

"Here," he says, and extends a hand toward me.

Resting on his palm is the lime-green daisy barrette.

I don't take it. I'm frozen on the spot. Frozen at the sight of Gideon Prewitt, space prince, standing in front of me, looking bright and disheveled and tentatively proud.

"It was so crazy before the show, I didn't get to see you, and I didn't want to—like, in front of everyone, but we went looking through the Grove, we found it—Noah found it, I'm sorry, I can't lie. He said I should say I found it but really it was him, and it seemed . . ." He falters, his hand still extended. "Seemed important to you, and . . . I mean, this is it, right?"

This is it.

I nod. Take the barrette and put it in my pocket. And then I take his hand, rest it against my cheek, and turn my head to press my lips against his palm.

He just stares.

"What are you doing?" he says.

I loosen my grip, embarrassed suddenly. "Is it—do you not want—"

"No, I want," he says quickly, moving closer. "I want."

Me too is what I should say. *Me too, ME TOO,* but words don't come out, I just look up at Gideon's face, at the smile blooming there, with his unfathomable dimples and his eyes that you need Google-Maps to find your way out of, warm and bright and shining.

You were so silly, denying yourself this, I think. *You were so foolish. Thank God you know better now.*

His smile dims momentarily. "But I thought . . . you said that you didn't . . ."

I shake my head.

"I do."

His brow wrinkles the slightest bit, the softest concern. "Are you sure?"

"Yes." And I fight the urge to sway even closer, because I want him to see my face, I want him to know, for certain, when I say this: "Before, I was just . . . I didn't mean what I said at Homecoming. I'm so sorry. That I said it. That I let you think that. I was just scared."

"Of what?"

"I guess, just . . ." I shake my head. "Sometimes it's hard to know if something's for real? It's hard to believe it, even if you want it to be real. Even if you want it so badly. Sometimes it seems . . . safer, you know. Not to risk it."

He nods, and I'm not sure if he understands, I'm not sure I'm making any sense at all, but he looks at me and there's barely any space between us now. "So you do . . . like me like that?"

"Yes."

"So if I kissed you . . ."

"Yes."

One corner of his mouth ticks up, the dimple reappearing. "I should probably . . . do that, then."

"Or we could keep talking about it."

He grins full-out now, and then we kiss.

Just once, soft and light. His lips part just the slightest bit, and when we break apart, he lets out a breath. I think for a second he's going to say something, but then he brings one hand to my waist and kisses me again, fuller, deeper, longer. I thread my fingers through his hair, and I can hear a faint buzzing from inside the auditorium, the muted sounds of many voices talking at once, but I can't hardly remember what they're all doing there, can't hardly think of anything but this.

Awesome sells it short. Any positive adjective I can possibly think of is not good enough, not potent enough, not worthy to describe it. It's just . . . something else.

When we finally separate again, I rest my forehead against Gideon's.

"You know what?"

"Hm?" He sounds a little dazed.

"That had everything on my must-have list," I say, and then drop down to a whisper: "Luxury. Affordable. Industry standard."

Gideon lets out an unholy snort, and I dissolve into giggles. I bury my face in the crook of his neck, and we both laugh, holding each other tight.

fifty-seven

"Thanks for coming to the show," I say. It's late, and Zoe and I are in bed. My back is resting against the headboard, my knees pulled up to my chest. I feel wide-awake, like I just got a hundred hours' sleep.

"I wouldn't have missed it. A-plus costumes. Stupendous. And the show was good, too, I guess." She cuddles Mr. English closer and then looks up at me. "But before we get into the whos and whats of the fancy school theater scene, I need to know what it was like to kiss the space prince. I need . . . a full-length analysis."

I consider it for a moment. I could consider it for a lot of moments, if left unchecked. Not just the kiss in the hall outside the auditorium, but the ones in the parking lot afterward and at the cast party and on the street outside after the cast party. Gideon with his cheeks flushed and his eyes bright, close enough that he was blurry, saying *I like you, you know. Like so much, so much, so much*—each one punctuated by a kiss to a different place.

"Like going into an instance," I say. "Like . . . existing apart from everything else."

Zoe just looks at me for a second and then gets out of bed and begins circling the room.

"What?"

"That was so sappy, I have to walk it off."

"It's not *sappy*, you asked me to—you said I should—"

She's hopping around now, flapping her hands. "Walking it off."

I throw an arm over my eyes and laugh. "Sorry. Yeah. It's silly. But—"

"It's also sweet," she says, crawling back on the bed. "Really sweet, Claude."

It's quiet for a bit, both of us just thinking. Until I finally turn back to Zoe and say, "I have to tell you something."

"Oh shit. Are you and Gideon running away into the woods to get married? Because I just saw a play about the dangers of that."

I grin. "No."

"What is it then?"

"I really like TION. Like, I kind of love them."

Zoe smiles. "I sort of got that impression."

"Like, not even a little bit ironically. I genuinely love them. If one of them needed a kidney and I was a match, I would genuinely give them my kidney."

"Would you give me a kidney?"

"I'd give you both kidneys."

She wraps an arm around me. Rests her head against mine for a moment.

Tomorrow, we're going to see Julia and Mark, and I'll meet Jack for the first time. The nurse will tell us that *the tallest oaks were once the smallest acorns*, and Julia will smile at her but make a face at me when the nurse leaves. *My son the acorn*, she'll say, and laugh and wipe her eyes.

The show will go on again that night and be every bit as wonderful. And I'll call Gideon when it's over and talk to him long after everyone has fallen asleep, the phone growing warm against my ear. As we say good night, I will want to say *I love you*. I won't say it. But just the thought of it will keep me awake long after. The best kind of awake, the purest caffeine pumping through your veins, where you never want to stop feeling what you're feeling, can't bear the thought of interrupting it, even with sleep.

But right now, it's me and Zoe.

"Okay," she says. "I know you have pictures of TION somewhere. Walk me through it. Give me a crash course."

I smile, reaching for my phone. "Let's start from the beginning."

acknowledgments

Sincerest thanks to Kate Farrell and Bridget Smith, my editor and agent dream team, without whom this book would not exist. Thank you to the creative and dedicated people at Macmillan/Henry Holt, in particular Brittany Pearlman, *the* Ravenclaw you want for your publicity; Rachel Murray, who never fails to brighten my inbox; and the Fierce Reads team (wizards, all of them). Thank you to Liz Dresner for another amazing cover design, with special thanks to Maricor/Maricar for the beautiful work of art.

As always, thanks to Mama, Papa, Hannie, and Cap-Cap. To Rachel and Shawn, for Battle Quest, Viola Constantinople, and late-night boss battle discussions. To Becky, Sara, and Wintaye—the "both kidneys" friends of my childhood/teens/beyond. To Rochelle, the best beta reader, whose opinion I treasure in writing and science and life alike. To Danting, for naming the Huangs, and Andrew, for taking us climbing. To Jing, for the very thoughtful business name, and for putting up with me in lab. To Pei-Ciao and Jiyoon, for all the love and support (and snacks!). To Lakshmi, for being an incredible friend, and lending your last name! To Eshaani, who I love to chat music with. To Sean (TunafishTiger), for recalling the Lord of Wizard at just the right moment. To Lauren James, for delightful correspondence and the best fic recs. To Leigh Bardugo, who is as wise as she is kind, and as kind as she is talented (and she's really flipping talented).

Thank you to all the book bloggers, booktubers, and enthusiastic readers out there reading and reviewing and posting and tweeting and being generally awesome. Thank you to librarians and booksellers, for championing books and doing all that you do.

Finally, this one goes out to anyone who has ever loved a band, or a band member, with their whole heart.